Death

at

Coombe Farm

Phillip Strang

BOOKS BY PHILLIP STRANG

DCI Isaac Cook Series

MURDER IS A TRICKY BUSINESS

MURDER HOUSE

MURDER IS ONLY A NUMBER

MURDER IN LITTLE VENICE

MURDER IS THE ONLY OPTION

MURDER IN NOTTING HILL

MURDER WITHOUT REASON

DI Keith Tremayne Series

DEATH UNHOLY

DEATH AND THE ASSASSIN'S BLADE

DEATH AND THE LUCKY MAN

DEATH AT COOMBE FARM

Steve Case Series

HOSTAGE OF ISLAM

THE HABERMAN VIRUS

PRELUDE TO WAR

Standalone Books

MALIKA'S REVENGE

Copyright Page

Cover Design by Phillip Strang

ISBN: 9781980254300

Dedication

For Elli and Tais who both had the perseverance to make me sit down and write.

Chapter 1

If it hadn't been for the circumstances, Detective Inspector Keith Tremayne would have said the view was outstanding. Up high, overlooking the farmhouse in the valley below, the panoramic vista of Salisbury Plain stretching out beyond. The only problem was that near where he stood with his sergeant, Clare Yarwood, there was a body, and it wasn't a pleasant sight.

'What happened?' Tremayne asked. He was a cantankerous man, he knew that, and he wasn't in a good mood on account of the biting wind and the squelching mud underfoot.

'I found him when I came up here to check on the livestock,' the farmhand said.

'At what time?' Tremayne moved away from the body, attempting to find somewhere drier. The condition of the track up to the site was so bad that the vehicle sent to transport the dead man to the mortuary could not make it up. Even Tremayne and Clare had had to hang onto a tractor to get up the slope, and now the weather looked as if it were about to worsen.

Tremayne had never been keen on farms, and especially horses, although Clare loved them. Tremayne assumed she wouldn't be so fond of the one that trampled Claude Selwood to death.

'Just after five this morning,' the farmhand said. 'I always get up here early. It's not something you expect to see, and Mr Selwood, he wasn't in the best of health. God knows what he was doing trying to ride Napoleon. That horse hated Mr Selwood, always has.' Tremayne assumed Napoleon was the horse in the next field.

'Any reason?'

'It's not as if he treated the horse bad, no worse than some of the others, but Napoleon, he remembers.'

Tremayne had heard of elephants remembering, but a horse? It didn't ring true with him, but he wasn't about to dispute the matter with the farmhand, a man who looked as if he was too old for early-morning starts.

'What can you tell us about Mr Selwood?' Clare asked. Tremayne could see the fresh air suited her, but then she was a lot younger than him. The two had been together for over two years now; one, a gnarled and cynical man approaching retirement, although delaying it for as long as he could; the other, still in her late twenties, pushing thirty and definitely looking for a man in her life.

Tremayne knew he had fared better in the marriage stakes, although his record wasn't enviable. His wife had left him years before due to his irregular working hours, his love of policing, but now she was back in his house, and if not on a daily basis, at least for a few days every couple of weeks.

Clare's former fiancé had turned out bad, not that she had known at the time. He was dead now, having saved her from certain death when her life had been threatened. Even now, Tremayne could see she missed the man, and her subsequent attempts at romance had, until now, been disasters. She'd admit it to Tremayne, although he wasn't sure he always wanted to hear, but then, the two of them had a shared history: their closeness to death over one year before in a wooded area not far from where they were now.

'Mr Selwood, he was a hard man,' the farmhand said. 'I'd been with him for over forty years, and I'd got used to him.'

'What do you mean?'

'I knew what he wanted; I did it before he asked.'

Clare could see the farmhand had the reserved manner of a man who knew his place. 'How was he with anyone else?'

'Everyone calls me Old Ted.'

'Okay, Old Ted. How was Mr Selwood with everyone else?'

'He was a right bastard, begging the lady's indulgence for using bad language.'

'That's not bad,' Clare said, 'and thanks for your politeness.'

'Not that I know much about horses,' Tremayne said, 'but Napoleon, he seems harmless.'

'With me, he is,' Old Ted said, 'but we understand each other.'

'How?'

'I talk to him; he talks to me.'

'What do you mean?'

'Napoleon, he's smart. I take him something to eat, and occasionally I'll give him a brush down. With me, he stands there and does nothing.'

'With Mr Selwood?'

'If he went near him, he'd likely rear up, even in his stable, and that's small enough. He hurt himself once doing that. I had to send for the vet, and he charged Mr Selwood plenty.'

'What was Mr Selwood's reaction?'

'He was angry with the bill. I remember he and the vet nearly came to blows.'

'Are you saying that Mr Selwood was a violent man?'

'Not with me,' Old Ted said. Tremayne could see that the man had difficulty answering direct questions.

'With other people?' Clare asked.

'Nobody liked him. He was always shouting and cursing, even threatened the vicar one Sunday.'

'What for?'

'The vicar gave a sermon he didn't like.'

'Isn't that up to the vicar?'

'Not around here.'

Tremayne had seen it before. Salisbury, the largest city in the area, was cosmopolitan and modern, but in some of the nearby villages, the old-fashioned concept of the lord of the manor remained. Selwood, judging from what Old Ted had said, had occupied that position.

***

A typical village, a not so typical death; that was how Tremayne saw it. Clare, even after all that had happened since she arrived in Salisbury a few years earlier, still maintained an air of optimism, a belief in the goodness of man. Tremayne, older and wiser than her, did not. In some ways, she could understand, but before Salisbury and the police force, she'd led a sheltered life in her parents' hotel in Norfolk, and she couldn't remember any murders there.

But in Salisbury, a city steeped in history, not far from Stonehenge, not too distant from where the British Army trundled their tanks across Salisbury Plain and practised their war games, there seemed to be a surfeit of deaths, and none ever seemed to be straightforward. After all, it wasn't usual for a horse to trample someone to death. An angry horse could throw the rider, even rear up at his approach before mounting, but to stay and walk over the man when he was down on the ground was unusual, but then the village of Coombe was strange in itself. Set off the main road from Salisbury to Warminster, another market town, it had an air of benevolence, yet, at the farm, the mood was distinctly chilly.

Jim Hughes, the crime scene examiner, was almost as cynical as Clare's DI. He was much younger than Tremayne, more Clare's age. 'It's perishing cold up here,' he said on arrival at the murder scene.

Hughes looked around, clapping his hands in an attempt to keep warm. 'Is that the horse down there?' he asked.

'That's Napoleon,' Old Ted said. 'He doesn't look much, but he's got a temper.'

Clare looked at Old Ted and could see that the man was stooped, with a profound limp. He was a man of few words, and if he knew more, he wouldn't speak, having learnt not to become involved unless it was necessary. Tremayne would have said the man wasn't too bright.

Down below, the farmhouse looked more inviting. 'We should go and interview the family,' Clare said.

'Good idea,' Tremayne said. He turned to Hughes. 'We'll be down below. If you need any help, just call.'

'I've got a couple of CSIs coming up here. They've organised themselves another tractor with a trailer to haul up the gear.'

'Once you've got any information, let me know. For now, I'm off with Yarwood to interview the grieving family,' Tremayne said.

'There'll not be much grieving down there,' Old Ted said.

'Why's that?'

'There wasn't much love in Mr Selwood's family.'

To Clare, Old Ted was a dull man, devoid of any highs or lows. A man dies, he shows no emotion. No doubt, if good fortune came his way, he'd act the same way, maintain the same routine. There'd be no offering of a round of drinks at the pub, no flashy car, no trips overseas. For him, it would be up at five in the morning to feed the animals, and then to occupy himself until his work was done.

'Not much of a life up here,' Tremayne said, as he and Clare walked down the muddy track towards the farmhouse.

'It's picturesque,' Clare said.

'Just like on a postcard, but it's not for me. Old Ted, what did you make of him?'

'He gave us the facts.'

'And that's all. Yarwood, this farm is full of intrigue and plenty of skeletons. Old Ted, he may pretend not to know, but he does. He just doesn't want to be involved, can't say I blame him. How much do you reckon this farm is worth?'

'I've no idea. It must be a lot.'

'I'd reckon over ten million pounds, and it all belonged to the dead man.'

'Is his death suspicious?'

'A horse killing a man, but why and how?'

'I used to ride horses as a child,' Clare said.

'Have you ever heard of a horse trampling a man to death?'

'Never.'

'That's why it's not accidental. It's murder, I know it is, and in that farmhouse, we'll find some of the answers.'

***

Five people were in the farmhouse, a listed building, dating back to the seventeenth century. Clare liked it, Tremayne was ambivalent.

'Don't come in here until you've removed your muddy shoes,' a woman in her late sixties shouted as they entered. 'I've just cleaned the floor after the others.'

The kitchen was large with a bare wooden table in the middle. On top of it, some pheasants ready for plucking.

'DI Tremayne, and this is Sergeant Yarwood,' Tremayne said.

'I'm Marge, Marge Selwood,' the woman said. 'Sorry about the shoes, but with this weather, it's hard to keep the house clean.'

'It's a lovely house,' Clare said.

'We like it, at least we did until that fool husband of mine went and rode that damn horse.'

'Are you saying he shouldn't have?'

'Claude was pig-headed, always doing what he shouldn't.'

'I'm sorry about your loss,' Tremayne said.

'Claude, a loss? I don't think so. The man wasn't likeable, have you been told?'

'It's been implied.'

'Old Ted?'

'He mentioned it.'

'Don't listen to him too much. He's here every day. We've told him to take it easy, but he's a simple soul, harmless.'

'He's still employed?'

'Not him. He draws his pension, but each day he's here helping out. If he wants to do something, it's not for me to stop him.'

'What can you tell us about your husband?' Clare asked.

'They're in the other room, the loving family. You'd better meet them first. Tea?'

'That'll be fine.'

Tremayne and Clare were ushered through to the living room; it was impressive. On the walls, paintings, on the floor, a fitted carpet. A blazing wood fire heated the room.

'Why the police?' one of the seated men asked.

'Remember your manners,' Marge Selwood said.

'Mother, I'm old enough not to need to.'

Clare studied the man, judged him to be between thirty-five and forty-five years of age. He was wearing a pair of jeans, a check shirt. His hair was long and straggly, shoulder length. Sitting alongside him, an attractive woman wearing designer clothes. She had her arm in his.

'I'm Gordon, the eldest son, and this is Cathy,' the man said.

'Can't wait, can you?' Marge Selwood said bitterly. 'Can't wait to get me out of here, throw me on the street, you and your tart.'

Tremayne looked over at Clare. She knew what he was thinking.

'Mother, we don't go airing our dirty linen in front of the police, and certainly not today. Your husband, our father, has just died, and you're worried about your fortune and besides, it's not yours, it's mine and Cathy's.'

'That tart you picked up. Over my dead body.'

'Sorry about this,' Gordon Selwood said, his bad manners changed for the better. 'We're a warring family, not the only ones in the area, but I suppose you're not interested in them.'

'Not unless someone else has died in mysterious circumstances.'

'Is it mysterious?' Cathy said. She was blonde, maybe late twenties.

'You see, she's more interested in herself than worrying about me,' Marge Selwood said.

'If you weren't such a bitch!' Cathy said. Clare looked at the young woman and her man. The woman was attractive and slim, even beautiful, whereas Gordon was not. The man carried a noticeable paunch, alcohol-induced if the man's ruddy complexion was any indication.

In another corner of the room, two others sat. One was dressed in a suit; the other wasn't.

'And you are?' Tremayne asked. He was drinking his tea, heavy on the sugar, as he addressed the remaining two.

'I'm Nicholas,' the suit said. 'This is my brother, William.'

Clare, having already taken a dislike to the older brother and his female friend, thought they were decent men compared to Gordon. Tremayne, she knew, had told her enough times that it was unwise to make instant judgements. A suit does not make a man, and uncouth and uncaring does not make a criminal.

Tremayne's phone rang. He answered it. 'Are you sure?'

'Yes, I'm sure,' Hughes said. 'There's foul play.'

'A full report as soon as possible.'

'I know, tonight. You're a slave-driver, you know that?'

'A man needs a slave,' Tremayne said. Clare, who was sitting close enough to Tremayne to hear both sides of the conversation, gave a smile. She knew the relationship that Hughes had with Tremayne, the same as she had with the detective inspector. A man who didn't accept people readily, but once you were proven, the man would support and mentor you against all others, but never expect him to show it, and certainly don't expect him to be condescending. The best way with Tremayne was to answer him back with a degree of sarcasm.

The phone call ended, and Tremayne refocussed on those in the room.

'Nicholas Selwood, can you give us a brief profile of yourself?' Tremayne said.

'Okay. I'm the second son, twenty-nine years of age. I was born in this house, although I now live in Salisbury. I work for a firm of accountants.'

'Not a farmer?'

'Not for me. I did my fair share when I was younger, but I preferred city life to the country.'

'He's done well,' Marge Selwood said.

'Thanks, Mum,' Nicholas said.

'William Selwood,' Tremayne said.

'I'm the youngest, twenty-seven years of age. I'm just finishing a degree in agriculture and advanced farm management.'

'Then you'll come back here?'

'Not if Gordon's going to take over.'

'He's not taking over,' Marge said. 'I'll make sure it stays in my control.'

'Not a chance. I'll take you all the way to the High Court in London,' Gordon, the eldest son, said.

'You're a mongrel. My own son and his tart. Both of them want me out on the street, begging,' the mother said turning to Tremayne and Clare.

'They're the police. What are you doing?'

'They need to know in case I end up dead, like your father.'

'Mother, don't talk rubbish. Nobody's throwing you out on the street, but someone's got to take control of this place. Our father was driving it into the ground, and you know it.'

'William would have been back here within six months, and he'd have sorted it out.'

'Are you joking?' Gordon said. 'He's full of academic theory, that's all. When did he last get his hands dirty?'

'And when did you, Gordon?' William said. 'Unless it was to paw Cathy.'

'You bastard, I've a good mind to…'

'Sit down and shut up. Our father's dead and you just want to cause trouble.'

'I've got a copy of his will. It's mine, all mine,' Gordon said.

'He wrote that ten years ago,' his mother said. 'It's no longer valid. Back then, I agreed when he gave it to you, but now, you'd destroy this place.

'No longer valid? Where's its replacement?'

'He was going to sign it this week, you know that. You all know that.'

'Mrs Selwood, what would the new will have said?' Tremayne asked.

'I would have inherited the farm in totality, with the provision, that in the event of my death, the farm would pass to my three sons. Gordon would receive a one-off payment to not become involved, Nicholas would be entrusted with a fifty per cent share to deal with the financial management, and William would run the farm, another fifty per cent share.'

'Would that have been acceptable?'

'To Nicholas and William, not to Gordon.'

'I'm the eldest son, it belongs to me.'

'And you'll destroy three hundred and fifty years' worth of effort,' Marge Selwood said furiously.

'I'll bring it into the twenty-first century.'

'Rubbish. You intend to sell it. You've already been checking out its value.'

'Is it valuable?' Tremayne turned towards Nicholas Selwood, assuming him to be the most knowledgeable on such matters.

'The market's buoyant. This place is worth plenty, and there are buyers in the area.'

Tremayne stood up in front of the fire. 'The phone call I had previously was from Jim Hughes, our crime scene examiner. He's still with Mr Selwood.'

'And?' Gordon Selwood asked.

'He's also checked out the horse. What he believes happened is that the horse reared and threw the rider on to the ground, one of his hands was still holding the reins, and he was dragged under the horse.' Tremayne paused to allow the others to focus on what he had just said. 'Was Mr Selwood in full control of all his faculties?'

'My husband was suffering from dementia. It was still mild, and not easily noticed, but he was forgetful.'

'Forgetful enough to check his riding gear?'

'I suppose so, but what's to check?'

'I don't know, but we know that his hand became entwined in the reins.'

'If it did, so what?'

'We don't know, but we intend to carry out further tests. Mr Selwood was, we believe, on the ground. The horse should have moved away.'

'Why didn't it?' William Selwood asked.

'Because someone was firing pellets at it from an air rifle. If the horse moved one way, then another pellet would force it to move in another direction. It would have taken an excellent shot, but Claude Selwood falling off the horse wasn't an accident, he had been hit by pellets as well.' Tremayne paused and scrutinised each of them in turn. 'This is murder, and someone, possibly in this room, is responsible.'

Mrs Selwood collapsed to the floor. Clare and Cathy rushed over to help her. Marge Selwood accepted Clare's help, pushed Cathy away.

'Now what?' Gordon asked.

'Our crime scene team will continue their investigation. Afterwards, please make yourselves available for further discussion and interviews. Also, we'll need copies of fingerprints, as well as a complete check of this house, and any weapons that may be here or nearby.'

'But why?' Claude Selwood's widow said.

'You know why,' Gordon said. 'Somebody didn't agree with our father's plans.'

'You didn't,' Tremayne said.

'Maybe, I didn't, but my father changing his will while he had dementia? They'd throw it out in court.'

'I'll fight you all the way to protect this family,' his mother said.

Clare observed the Selwood family, thankful that *her* parents were boringly normal. They'd argue, like any married couple, but there was never any dispute over inheritance, no issues about the division of assets.

But in this farmhouse, a war was about to break out.

Chapter 2

Back at Bemerton Road Police Station, the inevitable visit of Superintendent Moulton. 'Another one, Tremayne,' he said.

'A warring family, and enough money at stake to make them all potential suspects,' Tremayne replied.

'Never the easy ones for you, is it?'

'We'll deal with it.'

'I know that, and besides, I'm not after your retirement this month. Maybe after you wrap up this case,' Moulton said. Clare could see the uneasy truce between the two men.

Clare settled down at her desk, paperwork to do. Tremayne opened his laptop after Moulton had left, took a cursory look at his emails, opened up the reporting template and closed it again. Jim Hughes walked into the office holding a mug of coffee. 'The horse trod on his throat, crushed his windpipe,' he said.

'Could he have survived?'

'The horse was spooked. He could have trodden anywhere, even missed the man.'

'Shooting at the man and his horse is not rational, even if it was only a warning.'

'Pathology will conduct an autopsy. Maybe they'll come up with something else.'

'Claude Selwood's health?'

'A little overweight, but I'd say he was fit.'

Clare came into the office. 'We've got an unknown,' Tremayne said.

'What is it?' Clare said.

'According to Hughes, the man's death may have been accidental.'

'That's not conclusive. If he hadn't died, then whoever was shooting the pellets could have taken him out with a bullet.

There's no shortage of weapons up at the farmhouse,' Hughes said.

'There were some single-shot rifles at the farmhouse,' Clare said.

'No doubt every farm in the area would have one or two.'

'Did you check those at the house?'

'We checked the serial numbers, the ammunition, nothing more.'

'Had they been used recently?'

'That wasn't our concern. We were looking for the weapon that shot the pellets,' Hughes said.

'Any luck there?'

'The pellets are in Forensics. Matching them with a gun will be difficult. We've taken all the pellet guns we could find at the farmhouse for testing, not certain we'll find much. Whoever fired the shots would have been wearing gloves on account of the weather.'

Jim Hughes left Tremayne's office. Clare took his seat. 'It's still murder until proved otherwise,' Tremayne said.

'Judging by the animosity in the Selwoods' house, it's not the last one.'

'Check out the family, give me a breakdown on each of them. I didn't like Gordon Selwood, but that doesn't make him a murderer, and Selwood's widow, what's with her? It's not often you see that intensity of feuding between mother and son.'

'Isn't it?' There's a lot of money at stake.'

'Not with my wife and me,' Tremayne said. 'Mind you, we barely had two pennies to rub together. How about you, Yarwood? Would you be tempted?'

'My parents have more than two pennies, but no. There's a pub in the village where the Selwoods live. It may be a good idea to have a pub lunch there, see what the mood is, what people think of the family.'

'Yarwood, you'll make detective inspector yet.'

***

'Claude Selwood, you'll not find many around here who'll be sad at his passing,' the publican at the Coachman's pub said.

'Why's that?' Tremayne asked as he drank his pint of beer and enjoyed his steak, well done, as usual. More like burnt, to Clare, who was eating a salad and drinking a glass of white wine.

'Are they titled?' Clare asked.

'There was a lord in the past, ended up dead for treason, and then another one who ingratiated himself to the next king and reclaimed the fortune. Nowadays, there's no title, although Claude used to come in here sometimes expecting us to bow and scrape. I'll give the man his due; he certainly made a success out of that farm. Some swear he had made a pact with the devil. Each and every year, his cattle would win prizes at the agricultural shows in the area, and his crops would always command premium prices.'

'The devil?' Clare said.

'I'm just talking. We had some in another village who believed in ancient gods. Did you ever get over there?' the publican, a short, jolly man, said. Tremayne realised he was the typical publican, ready with a story while the patron continued to drink and spend money.

'We both were,' Tremayne said.

'Nasty business. Around here they can be superstitious: no walking under a ladder, seven years bad luck if you break a mirror, but that's it.'

'What else can you tell us about the Selwoods?'

'Marge, his wife. She's not a bad sort, didn't come from around here. She can be aloof, but she means well.'

'The sons?'

'Gordon, he's a layabout, only wants to spend the money. Nicholas, a quiet lad, sensitive, and then there's William.'

'What about William?'

'Polite, well-intentioned. You'll not hear a bad word about him around here. The only ones the village had problems with were Claude and Gordon.'

'Were Claude and Gordon close?'

'After a few pints maybe, but otherwise, Claude thought Gordon wasn't fit to take over from him, but he's the hereditary male. I heard that Claude was thinking of isolating his son, giving it to the other children.'

'To his wife?'

'That's the same thing. She's close with Nicholas and William, remote with Gordon. Strange when a family can be so dysfunctional that a mother does not like her son?'

'I suppose it is,' Tremayne said. 'Old Ted, what can you tell us about him?'

'He's lived here since he was Baby Ted. I doubt if he's been further than two miles from this village for the last seven years since his wife died.'

'Suspicious?'

'Ted's wife, no way. She was a small woman, almost as round as she was tall. Always a cheery disposition. One day she's out on the street talking to a group of women, the next minute she keels over, heart attack. A big turnout at the church that day. After that, Old Ted's been in his own world. I'll give Claude Selwood his due; he did make sure the man kept his cottage, rent-free until his death. I don't know what will happen now.'

'Old Ted kept working for them.'

'Not really, but if there's something needs doing, he'll be there. His family and the Selwood go back generations. Old Ted reckons it's over three hundred years, but that may be him thinking it did. Anyway, he's always been around here, popular too. He rarely comes in here, but when he does, my wife always gives him a free lunch.'

'Generous.'

'Not really. Every week or so, there are two dozen eggs on our back doorstep from him.'

'Coming back to the Selwoods,' Tremayne said. 'What about this feud between mother and son; have you heard about it?'

'Gordon, he likes to drink a few too many sometimes. He starts talking. We all know his plans. Once he's got control, he'll sell it to the highest bidder, and he'll take off for God knows where with his latest floozy.'

'He was with a Cathy up at the house.'

'She's been around for a while. I heard that she married him.'

'She has. What do you know about her?'

'She turned up about six months ago and moved in. I can't see her being serious about Gordon. Apart from his claim to the money, he's not got much going for him. He's certainly not a farmer, not much of anything really. When he was young, he was a hooligan, graffitiing around the place, attempting to seduce the local girls.'

'Any luck?'

'Back then, son of the biggest landowner in the district? He wasn't a bad-looking teen, so I've been told, the sort the girls go for. There was one, the daughter of the doctor, she disappeared and never came back. Her father left soon after.'

'Any reason?'

'It was believed she was pregnant with Gordon's child, but nothing more was heard. If she were, the child would be sixteen, maybe seventeen now. No doubt a claim to the property through its father, if its proven.'

'It's a long bow to stretch, that one. The others would have a stronger claim than the illegitimate child of the eldest son.'

'Maybe, maybe not. The farm has passed male heir to male heir, the son of the previous for generations.'

'Could the right of an unknown child take precedence over the other sons?'

'I don't know,' the publican said. 'Around here, the old ways still apply, but the law may say otherwise. It's just a thought.'

***

Clare had found the village of Coombe to be attractive; Tremayne enjoyed its pub. Neither of the two officers felt the need to linger. Claude Selwood's death by the horse could not have been guaranteed, although there was no doubt about the intent of hurting the horse and the man. The question was, who had fired the shots. 'It could have been someone young,' Tremayne said to Clare on the drive back to Salisbury. She was driving as usual, not that she minded.

'According to Jim Hughes, the pellets had hit the horse and Selwood, and both were moving around. It would have taken a good shot.'

'They're a strange bunch.'

'There's a lot of money at stake,' Clare said. 'His widow showed no emotion. That's illogical, even if she despised the man.'

'It can't be much fun, the wife of the eldest son and the matriarch under the same roof.'

'It could be a lot of fun, especially for Gordon.'

'You think he's a man who enjoys watching the fireworks?'

'I'm sure he does. He doesn't seem to be interested in much else. He's the most likely culprit at the present moment. Maybe a warning to the father not to change his will in favour of the mother.'

'We never understood what Gordon did for a living. It's clear he has money, judging by the wife and the car outside.'

'They live in the house; it's big enough for the warring factions to keep apart.'

'It still doesn't explain what the eldest son does with his time. He's not a stupid man, and he had the most to lose if his inheritance was placed in doubt.'

'He said he would fight a new will in the courts.'

'That costs money, and if it's all tied up in the farm, and his mother has control, he'll not stand a chance.'

Tremayne leant back in the passenger seat to mull over the case. Clare looked across, knowing that before they arrived at the police station, he would have dropped off for a few minutes. She knew that she was fond of the man, even if his penchant for gambling on three-legged horses, and his predilection for pints of beer and cigarettes, were not to her taste.

Her relationship with her parents, especially her mother, was loving, yet formal. With Tremayne, she could let down her guard, occasionally get angry, even answer him back when he was talking nonsense or heading down the wrong track with his analysis. With her mother, it was a case of remembering your place and doing the right thing. Clare was old enough to be independent, yet her mother treated her as a child, and there was always a man of her age invited to dinner whenever Clare went home: her mother's matchmaking.

'It's time to get over Harry,' her mother would say. 'You need to get yourself married, have a few children and to forget this foolishness about being a police officer, and spending all your time with that old man.'

Clare wanted to say that the old man, as her mother disparagingly referred to Tremayne, was important to her, professionally and personally. It had been he who had snapped her out of the melancholy after her fiancé's death, not her mother, who would only talk about moving on. But moving on wasn't easy, Clare knew that; her mother would never understand. She had not been there when the man that she loved had been snatched from her and thrust up into the branches of a tree. She had not heard the last gasps as he had died.

It had been long enough since his death, and Clare knew she should have forgotten him, but she hadn't. She was confident she never would, not totally, but she also knew that her biological clock was ticking and she wanted children, but with a man she loved.

Back at the station, Tremayne retreated to his office, Clare to her desk. She switched on the laptop and entered the name of Claude Selwood into the search engine.

Chapter 3

A family that should have been united in grief, but wasn't, sat around the table in the kitchen of the farmhouse.

'Does she have to be here?' Marge Selwood said. She was looking over at Cathy, Gordon's wife.

'If you want me to be here,' Gordon said. His other brothers were sitting upright; he was lounging back attempting to project his seniority.

Gordon, everyone knew, was a man who had spent too much money and time on women and fast cars, not enough as a farmer. The despair of his father in his later years, the bane of his mother's existence.

'Is our father's death suspicious?' Nicholas Selwood said. He was at the head of the table, his mother at the other end.

'His actions, as well as those of our mother, have created tensions,' Gordon said.

'What do you mean?' Marge Selwood said.

'This attempt to alienate me made no sense.'

'The farm must survive, so must the name of Selwood. You would have wasted the inheritance.'

'That's a lie, and you know it,' Gordon said.

'It's not,' his mother said. 'When have you contributed to this family? When have you put in a good day's work on the farm?'

'When I was younger, I did my fair share. You live in the house, the same as our father did. When was the last time the two of you ever went further than the local pub? All that money wasting away, and why do we have employees? They can do the work; we can issue the orders.'

'This is a working farm; it needs a manager. Your father, even though his health was ailing, maintained that position.'

'I'd prefer to do something else.

'Tell us, Gordon. What is it that you'd prefer to do, and we've heard you and Cathy enough times in this house, so don't say screwing.'

'How dare you insult my wife.'

'Your wife? She's here for the money, what else?'

'I happen to love Gordon,' Cathy said.

'What were you before you latched on to my son? A stripper in a club in London?'

'I was a professional woman.'

'Professional, my foot. You were a tart, selling yourself to whoever would pay. It may be best if you ditch Gordon and take up with Nicholas or William. They'll be running this farm, not Gordon, although he intended to sell it. How much for? Ten, fifteen million pounds.'

It had always been the same, Marge knew that. She had married Claude out of love, and back then, he had been the eldest son of the owner of Coombe Farm and moderately wealthy.

It was just before Gordon was born that they had moved into the main house. It had been Claude who had taken the farm and had built it up, even acquiring additional land when it became available in the district. Back then, and up until the first signs of Claude's forgetfulness, later diagnosed as early-stage dementia, the man had run the farm with a firm hand, upsetting a few, gaining the begrudging admiration of others, and now the man had been killed.

Marge Selwood had seen it some months earlier. His decisions for the farm were not as good as before. Sure, every day he was out there, rain or shine, dispensing orders, advising the farm hands, but the edge wasn't there. There was hesitancy in the man, and deliberating, when, in the past, his decision making had been immediate and not open to dispute. One of the farm hands had even answered him back once, and Claude had not reacted with his usual invective.

She knew that decisions needed to be made. The farm wasn't just there to generate money, it was what made the

Selwood family. A land bequeathed by a grateful king in the distant past, it represented heritage and stability, something the village of Coombe needed.

It had been a fateful decision, Marge knew, when she had decided that her eldest son, Gordon, wasn't capable of running the farm, and especially after he had arrived at the house that Saturday night six months before, a woman on his arm.

'This is Cathy. We were married last week.'

And that was it, Marge remembered. The woman had given her a hug, thanked her for letting them stay in the house until they found somewhere else, but never did, and then the veiled threats to have her out of the house once her husband died.

Marge had summed up the blonde woman with the slender figure and the pumped-up breasts for what she was, even hired a private investigator to check her out.

Two weeks later, and with her bank balance two thousand pounds lighter, the investigator came back with his report.

Cathy Franks, born in…

Marge skipped the first page, went straight for the second, and there it was: Cathy Franks, part-time model and professional escort.

Marge knew her son, an easily duped man, had married a woman who sold herself. There had been an argument that night between the prostitute and her mother-in-law.

'You're just a common tart, hawking your wares on a street corner.'

'I'm better than that. I'm educated, a qualified lawyer if you must know, but life's tough when you look like me, and the men in the office and the courts treat you inappropriately. I was there as a lawyer, they just saw me as a quick lay.'

'So, what did you do?'

'I made them pay for what they assumed they could get for free.'

'A tart, nothing more, nothing less.'

'I was a businesswoman. I had the commodity, they had the money.'

'And that's how you met Gordon?'

'He treated me well. He looked past the persona, saw the inner me.'

'Next, you'll be telling me it was love at first sight.'

'And what if it was?'

'I don't believe it. You saw an easy touch, money in the bank. You've got your eye on the bigger picture. Once my husband is dead, you'll be there with Gordon throwing me out on the street, taking all the money, and then you'll be off.'

'Better to be what I am, than a frustrated old woman.'

Marge had wanted to hit the woman that day. She never knew why she did not, and now with Claude dead, and the will still not signed, it was all going to Gordon and his whore. She knew she could not allow the situation to continue.

***

Jim Hughes' report stated that Claude Selwood's death was accidental, although the pellets shot at the horse and the man were contributing factors. If the man's hand had not been caught in the reins, then in all probability he would have only suffered minor injuries, instead of his trachea being crushed by the horse's foot.

It wasn't the result that Tremayne wanted to see, but he realised that Hughes was correct. Pellets from an air rifle would not kill a man, nor would a horse under normal circumstances, not even Napoleon, the horse that did not like Selwood.

As expected, the lull in the Homicide Department's workload meant the appearance of Superintendent Moulton attempting to pension off his most senior inspector. It had, however, been a weak attempt, as the superintendent enjoyed his encounters with the straight-talking DI.

Some in the police station, Moulton knew, were subservient, always attempting to ingratiate, but not Tremayne. The man, he knew, would never try to butter him up, and would still give straight answers to straight questions.

'We've not heard the last of the Selwood family,' Tremayne said.

'It's not murder,' was Moulton's reply. The man was sitting down in Tremayne's office.

'It doesn't make sense. It's just after five in the morning, the weather's lousy, and it was almost impossible to get up to where the man died, and yet, there is someone else up there with an air rifle, and not only that, someone skilled.'

'Any other tracks up there?'

'None. There was a herd of cattle, and their tracks were clear enough.'

'What was it? A warning?'

'Probably, but why? We're aware of the animosity within the family, and we know Selwood wasn't liked by a lot of people, but firing pellets seems to be the act of a fool.'

'And that fool has killed someone.'

'Not only that. He's opened up a can of worms. They buried Claude Selwood at the weekend, a big turnout according to the publican in the village.'

'You've kept in touch?'

'I have. This is not over yet. The stakes are too high, and there are anger and jealousy in that family.'

'The eldest son?'

'He's taken control. The mother attempted to wrest control, but she couldn't.'

'Where is she now?'

'She's licking her wounds, taken a room above the pub.'

'And that's it?'

'I know it's not. It's a case of wait and see.'

'If there's no murder, then you and Yarwood have nothing to do.'

'Give us a fortnight on this. Something's going to happen, and I want us to be ready.'

'Tremayne, will you ever leave?' Moulton said.

'Not me, sir.'

'That's what I thought. Try and get an idea who the shooter is, and what the mother is doing.'

'That's what I intend to do,' Tremayne said.

***

Marge Selwood, a woman who wasn't short of money, regardless of her protestations about being thrown out on the street, was in a benign mood. Tremayne and Clare had made the trip out to Coombe to see her. The village was only small, no more than one hundred and fifty inhabitants, and the majority of the cottages that lined the main street were old, with thatched roofs. Clare had looked at a house that needed rethatching when she was looking to buy a place in the Salisbury area, eventually settling on a more modern cottage in Stratford sub Castle, not more than ten minutes from the police station.

The pub in Coombe, once the centre of activity, along with the church, had lost its impact due to the advent of motorised transport and the internet. The publican had confided to Tremayne on a previous visit that he was thinking of leaving, and there would probably be no takers for the licence.

In one corner of the pub, secluded from the other patrons, Marge Selwood sat. In her hand, a glass of sherry. Tremayne ordered a pint of beer for him, a glass of wine for Clare.

'One's enough for me,' Marge Selwood said when Tremayne offered.

Clare could see the anguish on the woman's face.

'Mrs Selwood, thanks for meeting us,' Tremayne said.

'A refugee in my own country,' the reply.

'We understand your son has exerted control of the farm.'

'He and that woman.'

'Cathy?'

'That's her. I checked her out, you know.'

'What did you find out?'

'She only wants Gordon for his money.'

'Your son has left you homeless?'

'I've got money, but I'm not going far. Here I'm near to Claude and my house.'

'Claude?' Clare said.

'He's in the churchyard. I go up there every day to talk to him.'

'What are your plans?'

'I've no idea. I may take a cottage in the village, or I'll see if my lawyer can do anything.'

'Is that likely?'

'I don't think so, but my other two sons, they'll do what they can.'

'Will your eldest son sell the farm and the house?'

'Either that, or he'll carve up the land, keep the house for himself and his woman.'

'You intended to let Nicholas and William run the farm?'

'They would have done a good job, even better than Claude.'

'You could go and stay with them.'

'Here is where I belong; here is where I'll stay.'

'Why was the original will in favour of your son, and not you?'

'It's always been that way. Tradition mainly, and I agreed initially when Gordon was younger, but then, he left home, got in with the wrong crowd. And now, he's got a tart, and he has no interest in the land. As long as he's got her, then he doesn't want anything else. The family name means nothing to him.'

'Mrs Selwood,' Clare said, 'we have been told of a local girl that your son was involved with when he was in his teens.'

'Rose Fletcher. I suppose that was bound to come out one day.'

'Did she have a child?'

'Yes, although I've no idea where the mother and the child are now. The Fletchers left the village, and they've never been back.'

'Why did the horse your husband was riding not like him?' Tremayne asked.

'I don't know, nobody knows. Claude was firm with the animal, not afraid to take the whip to him, sometimes too much.'

'Enough for the horse to remember?'

'Not really. Napoleon's a thoroughbred, not a nag, and he could be temperamental. Some of the others wouldn't ride him.'

'Old Ted said he was fine with him.'

'Old Ted never rode him. It's one thing to give the animal a carrot and a brush down; it's another to ride him fast across the fields.'

'Did Gordon ever ride the horse?'

'He's a natural, the best in the family. Gordon showed such promise when he was younger, but then bastardy runs in the family. Unfortunately, it was passed on to him.'

'Bastardy?' Clare said.

'Not what you're thinking. Our family goes back nearly four hundred years. In that time, there's been a few that have been illegitimate, a few that were first cousins, not so unusual back then. Every so often, the black sheep turns up.'

'And Gordon is the black sheep?'

'He's the one who'll lose the fortune. It'll be for another generation to reclaim it.'

Tremayne could see a proud woman unwilling to be daunted by her circumstances. A room above the pub, a cottage in the village, wasn't likely to be a substitute for the magnificence of the farmhouse, but the woman, he knew, would take it in her stride. He had to admire her resilience in the face of adversity.

Clare wasn't so sure about the woman. For some reason she did not trust her, as if she was capable of more, even isolating her son from the farm and his wife. And if Cathy had a dubious past, it did not automatically make her bad. An earlier murder case, the trophy wife of a wealthy man had turned out to be the most honourable amongst a group of others who oozed respectability. Clare would reserve judgement on Cathy until she met her again.

Chapter 4

Bemerton Road Police Station on an overcast day wasn't Tremayne's idea of fun. He was a man conditioned to be out and about in the field. However, the investigation had come to a standstill.

He looked at his sergeant through the open door of his office. He could see her typing away on her laptop. He looked at his, saw only disinterest and boredom. What he needed was a cigarette, and in line with the regulations, he was relegated to the outside of the building.

'Come on, Yarwood. I need a break,' he said.

'You're not going to breathe that smoke over me again, are you?'

'Don't go all official on me. We need to free ourselves from this office. I'm still unsure about Claude Selwood's death.'

'You know it's an accident.'

'It's too convenient. We know the Selwood family was in turmoil, the father was not making good decisions, and the son is there with his tongue hanging out, his woman in tow.'

'At that time of the morning when Selwood died, everyone had an alibi.'

'I know that. William Selwood is at his college, verifiable. Nicholas is shacked up with his girlfriend, and there's no reason to doubt her. And we know where the others were.'

'Are you certain the pellets were shot by one of the family?'

'Who else would have benefited?'

'What if the man was unstable, attempting to sell the farm. There would be a lot of people who depend on the Selwood family in the village, even if they didn't like Claude Selwood.'

The two police officers walked out of the police station and around to the designated area. Apart from them, two others were there, cigarettes in their mouths. One was on his phone, the other was attempting to blow smoke rings.

Tremayne seemed oblivious to the surroundings; Clare could only shiver. 'Come on, Yarwood, a little bit of rain is good for the soul.'

'Good for yours, not mine.'

'I can't prolong this case for much longer. Moulton's holding off for the present, but you know him.'

'You know him better than me. You two are like Laurel and Hardy whenever I see you together.'

'And which one is the fat one? And be careful how you answer.'

'I've no intention of answering.'

'Okay, back to something serious. If Rose Fletcher had a child, a son, would he be the next to inherit after Nicholas and William?'

'According to Marge Selwood, the child of Gordon would take precedence over Nicholas and William.'

'If she's intent on claiming the farm back, an unwanted inheritor is the last thing she needs.'

'Or maybe it isn't. Marge Selwood could well be playing a smart game. She's staying close to the house and the farm for a reason.'

'The village and the farm have been her life for a long time. I can understand her reluctance to move away,' Clare said.

'Okay, I'll give her the benefit of the doubt, but this unknown child, male or female?'

'We are assuming male. If it were female, then Nicholas would inherit in case of Gordon's death.'

'It appears that the forces are in play to ensure that Gordon and his wife don't have long enough to change the wallpaper.'

'Are you certain they'll be another death?'

'The Selwood family have a history stretching back centuries, and there would have been skulduggery and murder over the years. Marge Selwood will not let this go, nor will Gordon and his brothers. There's a battle going on that we don't know about, a battle that will have casualties.'

'Cathy Selwood?'

'You need to meet her, see what she knows, check how far she's willing to go to maintain her husband's claim.'

'And if she genuinely loves her husband,' Clare said.

'Relevant?'

'I believe so. She's being portrayed as the scarlet woman, but is she?' We know what she was once, but that doesn't make her a bad person, and someone still took shots at Claude Selwood.'

***

Cathy Selwood, it was known, had a penchant for spending money, and her visits into Salisbury to check out new furniture for the house that she and Gordon now occupied made her easy to find. Clare, still decorating her cottage, although not with the budget of the other woman, intentionally ran into her in the store that both women enjoyed. 'Mrs Selwood,' Clare said.

'I'm not casing the joint,' Cathy said.

'I never thought you were.'

'Gordon's mother, she can hate. The first time I walked into that house, she was straight onto me.'

'Have you got ten minutes for a chat?'

'A police grilling?'

'Nothing as dramatic as that.'

'Why the interest?'

'Let's say we're concerned. Your father-in-law dies under mysterious circumstances, your mother-in-law has set herself up in the village, and two younger brothers are champing at the bit, believing they are what is right for the Selwood family.'

'You're reading too much into it, but I could do with a break.'

The two women left the store and walked down Fisherton Street. They entered a small café and ordered; Cathy insisting on paying.

'Gordon, he's not a bad person,' Cathy said. 'Sure, he's not interested in the farm, but not everyone is cut out for it.'

'Do you love your husband, Mrs Selwood?'

'Yes, I do. That's a little impertinent, asking such personal questions. I thought we were here for a chat.'

'And we are. Excuse me, but we've seen these situations before: old family, steeped in history. The conflict between the family members doesn't abate; it's constant.'

'I'm not sure I understand.'

'Your background?' Clare asked.

'Middle class, north of England.'

'The average family.'

'If you say so. My parents are still alive and living together, and as for an inheritance, a half share in a former council house is hardly worth fighting over.'

'Marge Selwood checked you out. Did you know?'

'I knew. She's a vindictive woman, a person who'll do anything to protect the Selwood name, not that it's that worthy.'

'What do you mean?'

'They have a historical record of the family stretching back from before the land was bequeathed to them. It doesn't gloss over the rogues and villains.'

'Anything that would be of interest to us?'

'One was hanged for treason, but that goes back nearly three hundred years.'

'And your family history?'

'Four hundred years of peasant stock, but I've never checked, never needed to. What someone did in the past makes no difference to my life. My fortune is dependent on what I do, not who slept with whom in the past,' Cathy said.

'Is that in the Selwoods' historical record?'

'There was a female ancestor, two hundred and fifty years ago, who was the mistress of the King. I've looked on the internet, but I can't find any reference to it.'

'It may not be true,' Clare said. She was sitting back, realising that the two women had been chatting for more than ten minutes, more like thirty.

'It probably is, but it's not important.'

'According to Marge Selwood, you have a dubious background.'

'We all have skeletons, even you,' Cathy said. 'Mine is that I went through a rough patch in my life.'

'And you sold yourself?'

'Yes. Gordon knows, so does his family, and no doubt, everyone in the village of Coombe. I'm neither proud of my past, nor ashamed. It's a fact, and I'll not deny it. It doesn't define me.'

'You seem to be a more balanced person than your husband, more driven.'

'Gordon is a bit of a waster, but he means well.'

'Marge Selwood believes you're with him for his money.'

'She can believe what she wants. If Gordon's father had not died, we'd have still been living with that insufferable woman.'

'Is she insufferable, or is she just the grieving widow?'

'Check on her background,' Cathy said. 'Find out where she came from. It's easy for the pot to call the kettle black.'

'Do you know something?'

'I recognise a fraud when I see one. Her posh accent, her pretence at nobility, none of it's true, I'm sure of it.'

'Have you mentioned this to Gordon?'

'Not him. He lost all respect for his mother years back.'

'Why?'

'You know about Rose Fletcher?'

'We do, but we don't know where she is, and what happened to the child.'

'Marge does. I found a piece of paper in a drawer in the house. Rose Fletcher's name was on it.'

'Does Gordon know?'

'Probably not. Marge has been using a private investigator to keep tabs on the woman.'

'And the child?'

'He still lives with the mother. Supposedly, they've had no contact with the Selwoods for years. Apart from that, I don't know anything more.'

'You realise that if Gordon died, then the child of Gordon and Rose could possibly inherit the house and the farm.'

'Gordon knows that.'

'Which means that Marge does as well. Why are you telling me this?'

'I've nothing to hide. I want to stay with Gordon. He's a decent person who treats me well.'

'And the money?'

'It's important, I'll not deny it, but if it comes with all the baggage, I'm not sure it's worth the cost.'

'The cost?'

'I've read the family history, brother against brother, father against brother. It's all there, and nothing has changed.'

'Nicholas Selwood?' Clare asked.

'Ambitious, bright, probably not honest.'

'Why do you say that?'

'He's a man who weighs up the pros and cons, the percentages. He'll play his game tactically.'

'And William?'

'Young, energetic. He would make a great addition to the farm.'

'But Gordon wants to sell it.'

'He has this idea of cruising the world, staying at the best places.'

'And you?'

'I'd rather stay here and have children.'

'That's not how Marge Selwood portrays you.'

'I've seen through her; I've seen the black heart. No doubt, she's seen through me, and my heart is pure. I want nothing more than what I have now.'

'And the sale of the farm?'

'I'll convince Gordon to stay. He's malleable, at least to me.'

***

In a housing estate in Salisbury, a studious youth of sixteen read through the essay that he was to present the next day at Bishop Wordsworth's Grammar School. He was oblivious to the events in Coombe, not that he would have cared.

'Dinner's ready,' a voice from downstairs. Always obedient, even though he was of an age to be rebellious, the youth left his work and walked down the stairs.

'How's the essay?' a woman in her mid-thirties said. Rose Goode, the surname a result of a failed marriage in her mid-twenties, when she had needed love and Crispin had required a father.

It was unusual for such a bond to exist between mother and son, but it did. Rose, her parents no longer alive, having died young. Her mother, she knew, from shame after they had found out their virginal daughter was pregnant. Payment made by the father's family to conceal the fact and to pay for Rose's confinement at a private hospital in London where discretion was assured.

'The essay's fine, but I'll be late home tomorrow. There's a rehearsal for the school choir. I'm trying to get a solo.'

'You'll make it, I know you will.'

As Rose sat there looking at her son, she reflected back to when he had been conceived, something she had not done for many years, not until she had read that the Selwoods' patriarch had died in a horse-riding accident. She remembered the anguish of her parents, the sobbing of her mother, her unwillingness to talk to her only daughter for days afterwards, the slap across the face from her father.

She knew she should not have made love to Gordon Selwood, but he was young, as she was, and fate had thrown them together. It had only been a short-lived romance, mainly harmless, until that one night when he had got hold of some alcohol, and the two of them were sitting behind an old stone wall around the back of the churchyard.

Up until then, it had been heavy petting, not going the whole way, but with the alcohol and the starlit sky and Gordon, she had relented. It had been neither romantic nor agreeable. All in all, she had to register it as not unpleasurable, but not as it was portrayed in books. There were no moments of abandonment, no melding of two bodies. It was just sex, and it was over in a couple of minutes. And after that, the meetings with Gordon, the inevitable sex at the end, the reluctant admission that it had all been a disappointment, and then, the missed period, and then, having to tell her parents.

Rose knew little of the agreement that had been struck between her father and Gordon's father, other than there had been a hastily arranged marriage ceremony at a registry office in Southampton, a city to the south of Salisbury, and then, after the birth, a divorce. Neither she nor Gordon had spoken to each other during the marriage and in the years subsequent. She had seen him on several occasions in the city, but he had not recognised her.

Back in their teens, she had been young and slim, but now, she had a disposition to put on weight, and her once flowing dark hair was blonde and short.

The last time she had seen him, he was no longer the athletic teenager. She had made no attempt to contact him, not even after the death of his father, although Gordon was now the owner of the farm, and her son, Crispin was his heir.

Rose looked over at her son, a young man without vices, a young man to be proud of, yet within him were the Selwood genes, genes that were tarnished. She knew that she needed to tell her son the truth as to who he was, but not today. Today, he had an exam, and he'd be home late. Tomorrow, she thought, but the idea did not appeal. He was hers, and hers alone. She did not want to share him, and certainly not with a Selwood.

Chapter 5

Old Ted walked up the track at Coombe farm, the same as he did every day, rain or shine. It was early, and it was still dark. He looked at the view when he reached the top. Down below, the farmhouse, and further on, the village of Coombe. He knew the Gordon Selwood and his wife were sleeping peacefully in the house below, Gordon's mother in the pub. He remembered when she had first arrived in the village, a slim, upright woman. The locals had been suspicious, an outsider, but with time they had accepted her.

He did not trust Gordon, the eldest son, although he could admire Nicholas and William. To him, they represented stability, the need to maintain the traditions, even if William would want to change how the farm operated.

Where Claude Selwood had died was no longer muddy. He walked over to the site, knowing that Napoleon was in the stable down below, and he was still being ridden by others, including Cathy. Old Ted did not know what to make of her. He had heard the scurrilous comments of her mother-in-law; who hadn't if they frequented the local pub or walked around the village, but to him, she was an attractive woman who loved the animals, especially Napoleon. If he did not get time to spend with the horse, she'd be out there with him.

They had spoken on more than one occasion; he, the farmhand, she, the wife of the farm's owner, and there had been no doffing of the cap, no calling her Mrs Selwood. She had been adamant that her name was Cathy.

Old Ted had respected Claude Selwood, did not like his wife, but with Cathy, he found a kindred spirit, a person who loved the area and the farm. Gordon was contemplating selling the place, it was local gossip, but his wife had confided in him that they were going nowhere. And William, the youngest, would take over the management of the farm, Nicholas would deal with the money side, and her husband could do whatever he liked, and if that included involvement in the farm, so much the better. If he did not, it did not matter, as she would take up his mantle.

Old Ted liked Cathy Selwood immensely, he knew that. Over in the distance, not more than one hundred yards, he could see cattle grazing. He sauntered over to them revelling in the serenity, only to be disturbed by the sound of a motorbike in the distance.

As he approached the animals, the sound of gunfire. Old Ted collapsed. From behind him, a person approached. Once alongside the man on the ground, the person who had fired the first shot aimed the rifle at the head of Old Ted and squeezed the trigger. The only witnesses, a herd of cattle that initially moved away, but soon resumed their chewing of the grass.

***

It was mid-morning when the call came through, and Tremayne wasn't well. Too many beers the night before, and he had a throbbing headache as well as a stomach that was feeling unduly sensitive.

Clare had no sympathy when she picked him up from his home. Her previous day had consisted of cleaning her cottage and then sitting with a book while her cats sat nearby.

'We'll be busy now,' Tremayne said as Clare drove. This time Tremayne wasn't checking out his form guide, he was attempting to catch up on his sleep.

Clare had been briefed by the village policeman as to what they were going to find at the scene. For once, the weather was improved, although it was still cold. As they drove into the farm, there was the presence of Gordon Selwood. 'We've got a Land Rover that will get us up there. The track's dried out in the last few days, and there's not a lot of mud.'

'The same place?' Tremayne asked. Clare could see that his condition had improved. He still looked like a bag of potatoes to her with his rumpled clothes, his shirt hanging out. For once he wasn't wearing a tie.

'It was Cathy who found him. She was riding up there.'

'Napoleon?'

'She gets on well with the animal, not like my father.'

'Where is your wife?'

'She's in the house. She's upset over the man's death.'

'Aren't you upset,' Clare asked. 'After all, the man had been here from before you were born.'

'I'm sorry to see the man go, yes. He was a good worker, never knew when to stop, and now, he's dead. But he was lonely with his wife gone. All he really wanted was to be with her.'

'The crime scene investigators?' Tremayne said, looking at Clare.

'They're on their way.'

'Any way up apart from the track?' Clare said.

'There have been no vehicles,' Selwood said. 'There's a couple of dogs that'll bark like crazy if anyone they didn't know went up there.'

'Very well. Let's go.'

At the top of the hill, the Land Rover parked at some distance from the body. The three of them walked over towards it taking a circuitous route in case there was evidence that they may disturb. On the ground, Old Ted, a local uniform standing nearby.

'The cause of death?' Tremayne asked.

'He's been shot twice, once close up, the other at a distance. A .22, I'd say, judging by the wound,' the uniform said.

Clare looked at the body, remembered an old man who talked slowly and said very little. 'Whoever did this would have had to be a marksman,' she said.

'If the rifle had telescopic sights, and the shooter had a steady hand, it wouldn't need too much skill.'

'Could you have executed the shot, Mr Selwood?' Tremayne said. Clare had noticed him taking deep breaths of the fresh air. He was almost back to normal now, even having tucked in his shirt.

'I had nothing against the man.'

'That's not an accusation, just an observation. Could a woman have made the shot?'

'Not Cathy. She can't stand weapons of any sort.'

'I wasn't levelling an accusation against your wife, either. Mr Selwood, this is a murder enquiry. We need to ask questions, questions that may seem irrelevant, accusatory.'

'Understood.'

'I'll ask again. Could a woman have shot Old Ted?'

'Yes. Some of the women in the village are better shots than the men: steadier hand, keener eyesight.'

Clare realised that Tremayne was thinking of Marge Selwood. The woman was devious, and Old Ted knew of the family skeletons.

Clare asked the question. 'Your mother. Was she a good shot?'

'Yes, but…'

'There are no buts,' Tremayne said. 'Only facts.'

Clare realised that Tremayne did not like Gordon Selwood and that he had cut the man off short.

Another vehicle reached the area. 'Touch and go getting up here,' Jim Hughes, the crime scene examiner, said on his arrival. 'You've got your murder,' he said to Tremayne.

'He was known as Old Ted, although his name is Edward Garrett.'

'How old was the man?'

'He was in his seventies, that's all I know. They'll be records at the house,' Selwood said.

'Fine, that'll do for now,' Hughes said. 'I see you've been careful in approaching the body. It's not necessary for you to stay around, just give us a shoe print, so we can exclude yours from the investigation.'

'We've not found where the shot was fired from,' Tremayne said.

'Leave it to us. What time do you reckon the man was killed?'

'He normally came up here between five to six in the morning, the same routine every day.'

'And the body was discovered at ten?'

'Yes.'

'Did anyone hear the gunshot?'

'It's probable, but the occasional gunshot, someone shooting at a fox, or a pheasant, wouldn't be unusual,' Gordon Selwood said. 'Most times, you'll find the people in the area will just ignore it.'

The four had pulled back from the body, and Jim Hughes' team of crime scene investigators were erecting a crime scene tent over the body.

'How long?' Tremayne said.

'Before I start?'

'You know the routine.'

'You pester me till I give you something. Then you go away.'

'That's it.'

'I'll phone you when I know something,' Hughes said.

'We should go to the house,' Clare said. She wanted to see if Cathy Selwood could be the murderer.

Gordon Selwood drove down the track and up to the house. On entering, hot chocolate for everyone. 'I could see you coming. It's cold up there,' Cathy said.

'How are you?' Clare asked.

'I'm fine. Just a little shocked to see Old Ted lying there. I thought he had just collapsed, heart attack, but it wasn't. I walked over to him, and that's when I saw the blood. Is it murder?'

'There's no question,' Tremayne said. 'Is there any reason that anyone would want him dead?'

'Not that we know of,' Gordon said. 'He would know more about this family than anyone else. It's hardly a reason for his death, is it?'

'Why not? Maybe he knew something about your right of inheritance.'

Clare turned to Cathy. 'Let's go and see the horse.'

***

'What's the truth?' Clare said once the two women were in the stable. 'This farm. Is it up for sale or not?'

'I thought you were going to ask me about Old Ted.'

'You didn't kill him, but you may know who did. Your husband?'

'He was in bed when I left, and he'd been there all night.'

'You're certain?'

'What are you trying to do, divide and conquer? You've left Gordon with Inspector Tremayne. Are you going to compare notes later?'

'Probably, but that's not the reason we're here with Napoleon.'

'What is it, then?'

The two women were standing with Napoleon, brushing him down. 'I love horses,' Clare said. 'I had one when I was younger.'

'You can ride Napoleon anytime you want.'

'Once this case is resolved, I'll take you up on that.'

'Anyway, what is it you want?'

'Gordon's mother has been bad-mouthing you in the village.'

'We've spoken about this before.'

'How do you feel about it?'

'Did you check on my history? What did it say?'

'That you have been employed as a stripper, and then, as a professional escort.'

'Marge is only telling the truth. I was a whore, no need to pretend.'

'Did Old Ted know?'

'He judged the person, not the rumours, true in my case.'

'Are you saying that you didn't hate what your husband's mother was saying?'

'What would be achieved by my calling her out?'

'Nothing, but it would be the normal reaction of most people.'

'I'm not most people. I've been in that gutter; I've dealt with the abuse and the men who mistreated me. I'm not going back there. The anger in me is gone.'

'And Gordon?'

'It's not the greatest love-match, I'll grant you that, but with him, I'm safe.'

'No intention of moving on?'

'None. I wanted him to make peace with his mother. I told him so, and I want to stay here.'

'I can understand you wanting to stay. This place is magnificent.'

'You need to find a man for yourself,' Cathy said.

'I had one.'

'And?'

'He died. It's a long story. It's not something I want to talk about.'

'Everyone knows in the village.'

'They will never know the whole story, only what they read in the newspapers, on the internet.'

'It's still hard to take?'

'Yes, but we came here to talk about Old Ted's death, your position here, your suspicions.'

'Marge was a good shot, although I don't believe she killed Old Ted.'

'Why?'

'What for? The man minded his own business, never said anything about the family.'

'You were friendly. Did you try to find out anything?'

'I just wanted to know if his evaluation of the family was the same as mine.'

'And did you?'

'With Old Ted, not a chance. The man was always non-committal. He was, I believe, totally loyal to the family. It would be a tragedy if one of them killed him.'

'It would be. Any ideas who?'

'Not me. Apart from Marge, everyone else is placid.'

'Would you let her back in the house?'

'Not now, too much has been said, but there are other places on the farm she could live. Old Ted's cottage, it's not big, but it's charming. I'm sure Gordon would fix it up for her, but never in the big house. It was hers for too long; she would interfere, and we need the opportunity to live our lives, to bring up our children.'

'Children?'

'I'm pregnant, or at least, I think I am.'

'No horse riding?'

'Maybe you could take Napoleon for a ride when I have to stop?'

'Maybe,' Clare said. She did like the horse, and to have come out at the weekend, or on a balmy summer's night when it didn't get dark until after ten in the evening would be idyllic.

Chapter 6

Inside the house, Tremayne continued with Gordon Selwood. 'What are your thoughts on Old Ted's death?'

'I'm sorry to see him killed,' Selwood replied.

'Who could have killed him?'

'I've no idea. Maybe it was nothing to do with this family?'

'The man had no interest outside of serving the Selwoods. It's something to do with this house and this farm. Old Ted knew something, and he was likely to tell someone what it was.'

'Not Old Ted. He'd never be disloyal to us.'

'Then why was he killed? You know something.'

'If you're trying to get me to say something, you're wasting your time. My mother's upset, causing trouble, but Cathy and I are fine. She wants to stay here; I'm willing to go along with her.'

'You're aware of your wife's background?'

'Is it relevant?'

'It could be. What if she has skeletons, people from her past?'

'My mother had her checked out, you know that. I saw the report, not that it changed my mind.'

'What do you mean?'

'I was in love with Cathy. Her past belonged back there. I wasn't about to be judgemental.'

'Most people are.'

'Most people are hypocrites, looking for the worst in others. Cathy had a bad period in her life; she did things she's not proud of. We never speak about it, although my damn fool mother is telling everyone around the village.'

'Have you told her to stop?'

'My mother is a one-woman juggernaut. Once she's got a bee in her bonnet or a cause, she'll pursue it to the bitter end.'

'And your wife is the cause?'

'I'm running a close second. The black sheep of the family, the generational throwback. I've heard it all and more.'

'Does it upset you?'

'It's water off a duck's back.'

'Did you fire those pellets at your father?'

'Is it a crime?'

'Yes.'

'Then no, I did not. I could have, but I didn't. My father was a tyrant, a self-satisfying sanctimonious bastard. He had no trouble to get out his belt to us when we were children.'

'And towards your mother?'

'She went to bed with the occasional black eye.'

'This has not been mentioned before.'

'There's no need to hang out our dirty linen in public.'

'But it's a murder enquiry.'

'My father's death was not.'

'Old Ted would have known all this.'

'No doubt he did, but he never mentioned it to anyone.'

A knock on the back door of the house. Selwood opened the door. 'DI Tremayne, is he here?' Jim Hughes said.

'Come in, wipe your feet.'

'What is it?' Tremayne asked.

'We'll need to take all the rifles in the house, Mr Selwood.'

'You checked them before.'

'Only the types and the serial numbers. This time we'll need to check to see if they've been fired recently and whether the bullets match with the gun.'

'Anyone apart from your mother who could shoot?'

'We could all shoot. William is a good shot, so is Nicholas.'

Outside the house, Tremayne and Hughes spoke. 'Any possibility that the pellets and the bullets were fired by the same person?' Tremayne said.

'It's possible, probably not verifiable. We know where the latest shooter was when the first shot was taken.'

'Where was that?'

'There's an old wooden shed up there. You must have seen it.'

'I have.'

'The person was propped up there; we found some footprints.'

'Identification possible?'

'Most of them belonged to Old Ted. He kept some farm equipment in there, fence mending tools, some fencing. We'll not be able to get a positive ID from there. We never ascertained where the pellets were fired from due to the lousy weather and the mud. It could have been from the old shed. Don't place too much credence on it being the same shooter.'

'Claude Selwood wasn't liked, whereas Old Ted was liked by everyone. This investigation is illogical.'

'When were your cases anything other?'

The two men walked over to the stables. They could see Clare and Cathy Selwood talking. 'Leave them to it,' Tremayne said. 'Yarwood will find out more in there than in an interview room at Bemerton Road.'

'She's a good police officer,' Hughes said.

'Don't you ever tell her, but, yes, she is.'

'Any romances since Harry Holchester's death?'

'None that matter.'

'A woman her age, on her own. It's not natural.'

'Maybe it isn't, but there it is.'

'It's a beautiful place here,' Hughes said as they walked around to the front of the house. Before them a manicured lawn, a fountain in the middle. To one side of the house, a large garage for the various vehicles, Gordon Selwood's Jaguar concealed under a sheet. The other vehicles, two Land Rovers, a Toyota for Cathy, and an old tractor were there as well.

'I could live in a place like this,' Hughes said.

'A lot of work, and now Selwood is not selling it.'

'You had him down as a possible suspect before.'

'He's the one who's gained the most from all this, but why Old Ted? What did he know?'

'Don't look at me.'

'Any chance of identifying someone? It's still someone in the family, I'm sure of it.'

'Always the same, isn't it? These people have got it made, yet they get involved in petty squabbles, instead of living a life of plenty.'

***

It was six in the evening before the three, Tremayne, Clare, and Jim Hughes, were ready to leave the farm. 'Fancy a pint?' Tremayne said.

'Why not?' Hughes said.

'I would have thought you'd have had enough after last night,' Clare said.

'Don't go on, Yarwood. You're not my mother.'

'If I were, I would have disowned you by now.'

Hughes smiled at the banter between the two officers. Others may have seen it as close to impertinence on Clare's side, abuse on Tremayne's, but Hughes knew that it came with affection from both of them.

'You can keep to orange juice if you like, and besides, the local pub after a murder is a good place to find out more.'

'I'll have a glass of wine, and one of their pub meals,' Clare said. She took out her phone and called her next-door neighbours to feed her cats.

Inside the pub, it was busier than usual. A momentary hush came over the place as the three police officers entered. For thirty seconds, they were the focus of all the eyes in the place as they went and claimed their seats in one corner of the bar. In another corner, Marge Selwood. Tremayne went to the bar to place their orders; Clare went over and sat next to the woman.

'It's sad,' Clare said.

'It's not unexpected.'

'What do you mean?'

'Old Ted, not so old when I first came here, was a man who saw plenty, said little. He'd have the dirt on half of the people in this village.'

'They seem to be law-abiding.'

'Most are, but some, those who've come down from London to buy their holiday cottages, they get up to some monkey business.'

'Such as?'

'Parties, carryings-on.'

'Drugs, women?'

'Old Ted would have known.'

'So would you, Mrs Selwood. There's not much that goes on around here, that you don't know about.'

'I suppose that's true, but I've kept it to myself.'

'So had Old Ted and now he's been murdered. Could it be you next?'

'It's always possible.'

'So why have they not dealt with you before, if, as you say, there are secrets that some would have preferred to stay hidden.'

'It depends on the secret. There are the affairs, even wife-swapping a few years back, but I don't know anything more than that. Not a lot anyway, and I don't think anyone would kill me for what I know.'

'Do you think Old Ted knew something more?'

'It's possible. We didn't talk about it. Rarely talked to each other, if the truth is known.'

'Why?'

'No reason really. We were civil, but that was all.'

'Have you spoken to your son since you left?'

'We speak. Our relationship was always strained.'

'But why? He seems a decent man, even if he's not interested in the farm or much anything else.'

'The mother-son bond never existed. We sent him away to boarding school from the age of seven, and he'd only come home for long weekends and holidays.'

'Why?'

'That was what landowners did then. Nicholas and William went to the local school until they were eleven, and then Bishop Wordsworth's Grammar School after that. With them, I'm fine; with Gordon, it's impossible.'

'He's not thrown you on the street, but you're telling everyone he's the villain, you're the victim.'

'Maybe I was angry.'

Clare sipped her wine, Marge Selwood, her vodka. The meal that Tremayne had ordered for Clare was delivered to her. Clare looked over at Tremayne, could see that he and Hughes were speaking to some of the locals.

'Tremayne, he seems to be a decent man,' Marge said.

'Don't let him hear you say that.'

'Why?'

'He likes to portray himself as gruff and difficult, and sometimes he feigns ignorance, but not much gets past him. He'll solve Old Ted's murder.'

'Is this going to be the last one?'

'What do you know that I don't?' Clare said.

'His death could well stir up a hornet's nest. There are people here with secrets, and maybe they've nothing to do with killing Old Ted, but it could make them nervous.'

'We've seen it before, all too often.'

'I know of your history, Avon Hill,' Marge said.

'Painful memories. It's best if you don't go there. What's your background?'

'You've checked me out?'

'To some extent, but I'd like to hear it from you.'

'There's not much to say. My father was an army officer, and we spent a lot of time overseas, more of an empire back then. One of his last commissions was at Bulford, the army camp not far from here. I met Claude at a dance in Salisbury when I was twenty-two, and he was twenty-three.'

Clare knew she had not been told the full story; Cathy Selwood had suspected it in part, and subsequent checks by the police had proved that at the age of eighteen, expelled from school for disruptive behaviour and improper conduct, Marge had left the family home and had spent time in London. Up there, the records showed clearly that she had vacillated between working in a shop, on her feet all day, or flat on her back at night; the latter being the more profitable. Marge Selwood was a fraud, a woman who professed her virtuous credentials to the local ladies at the church and to the landed gentry in the area.

With no more to say for the present, Clare left the woman and went back to where Tremayne was indicating that he was ready to go.

'Anything interesting?' Tremayne asked.

'She lied about her past.'

'Not something to be proud of, is it?'

'She must know we would find out.'

'She's probably been living a lie for so long, she doesn't even remember what she was, and besides, who are we to judge. Cathy Selwood was open about her past.'

'Old Ted must have known.'

'He would have, but he kept it to himself. No reason to see her secret as a motive.'

'On the face of it, no, but we'll keep it as a possibility.'

***

Clare arrived home at ten in the evening to find her next-door neighbour sitting in her kitchen. 'It's one of your cats,' he said.

'Boris?'

'I'm sorry, but he died. We were here with him, my wife and I. It wasn't long ago, and we knew you were on the way.'

Clare sat down and cried; in her arms, the cat wrapped in a blanket.

'You should bury him in the garden. Would you like me to dig a hole for you?'

'Yes, please.' Clare sat there with the cat; it had been getting progressively older for some months, its rear legs struggling to support it, and now it was gone. She was pleased it had passed away at home, instead of her having to take it to the vet, and yet, she was very sad.

She thought back to Old Ted, realising that she had felt sorrow at seeing the dead man, but not the sadness she felt for an animal that clawed at her furniture and left its fur everywhere. Old Ted was not the first body she had seen that had died needlessly, although she had seen worse, even her fiancé.

She wondered if she was becoming inured to death and violence, as Tremayne was, as Jim Hughes appeared to be. She was sure she was, and she did not like it.

Outside in the garden, the neighbour, a man older than Tremayne, older than Old Ted, dug a hole for Clare. She carried the animal out of the cottage and lovingly placed it in the hole, the blanket still wrapped around its lifeless body. The other cat, younger and more agile, was nowhere to be seen. A few words were said, the neighbour shovelled soil over the hole, Clare patting the ground until it was firm. She then placed a flat rock on the grave and went back inside.

Even though she had already drunk two glasses of wine, she opened a bottle.

'Do you want me to stay with you, or do you want to come and stay at our place?'

'No thanks,' Clare said. 'I'll be fine.'

She then went up to her bed, a glass of wine in her hand. Upstairs on her bed, the other cat, the one who usually lay down at the end of the bed, was lying on the pillow.

Clare turned on the television, a depressing movie. She turned it off and put the glass of wine, still untouched, on the table at the side of the bed and switched off the light.

It had been a long day, culminating in more sadness. Within five minutes, she was fast asleep.

Chapter 7

'Now look here, Gordon,' Nicholas Selwood, the older of the two younger brothers, said at the farmhouse. 'Our mother is staying in that pub, while you're up here lording it up, and what about your wife?'

'What about Cathy?'

'This is our mother's house, not hers, and there she is redecorating the place.'

'And doing a good job, don't you agree?'

'That's not the point. Our mother looked after this house for forty years, and you kick her out.'

'For one thing, she wasn't kicked out. Cathy and our mother cannot be in the same house, it's fireworks when they're together.'

'We know that, but our mother? How could you?'

'Decisions needed to be made. We're staying, not selling. You two will have free run of the place, and our mother has a cottage if she wants it.'

'A farmhand's cottage? What is that compared to this house?'

'It's the only compromise, and you know it.'

'If we run the farm, where do we live?'

'Nicholas, you're the financial manager. You don't need to be here all the time. You can even keep your accountancy firm in Salisbury. We can always build a place for William. There's no shortage of land.'

The two younger sons could see the hand of Cathy. Gordon, they knew was a weak man, susceptible to a pretty face and a good story. His life had consisted of very little, and now he was acting decisive and resolute, whereas his past history would have indicated that he would have taken the money and run.

Nicholas and William, both still relatively young, had come up with a proposal that would allow them to pool their financial resources with their mother's and to buy Gordon out, but now there was a fly in the ointment: Cathy.

It grated, they both knew, as they sat there and listened to their brother. The farm was big enough for them and their mother, as well as their wives and children in the future, and Old Ted's farm cottage, if modernised and extended, was excellent accommodation, although they did not intend to let that be known at this time.

Down in the pub, Marge Selwood waited for an update, hopeful that the result would be positive, aware that it probably would not. She had known what Cathy Selwood was from the start, an opportunist who had latched on to a weak man. Wasn't that what she had done with Claude. He had been picked by her as a suitable subject, been made strong, almost too strong for even her to handle.

In London and in her early twenties, she could see there was no future in the life she had been leading. Always a smart woman, she had checked out where she wanted to go and who she wanted to ensnare. Salisbury seemed the best place for her, having lived in the area as a young woman.

She remembered a young man she had met when she was fourteen; they corresponded by mail for a few months afterwards; he, the son of a wealthy landowner, she, the daughter of an army officer. He stayed in the area; her father was posted overseas.

She had phoned up her first love purely on the off-chance after eight years, found that he wasn't involved with anyone else. They met that weekend in London, made love, became engaged and married within two months. Since then she had never looked at another man, and now, that man's son, the child she had carried for nine months, was denying her the farm and the house that were hers.

After two hours, the two sons who remained loyal to her entered the pub. Nicholas ordered a beer, William, a whisky.

'She's controlling him,' Nicholas said as he sat down next to his mother.

Marge felt neither dismay nor disappointment, only a realisation that it was up to her to address the situation. 'I thought you were wasting your time. Did you offer him our proposal?'

'Not then. It's Cathy who holds sway. He will do what she tells him.'

Marge knew that she had taken Claude, a weak and dilatory person and transformed him into an aggressive and dynamic man. She could see Cathy was doing the same with Gordon.

She admired the woman, even if she hated her. If her sons could not deal with the situation, then it was up to her. Nicholas was a professional man who would abide by the law, but it would require unlawful activities to succeed, and, as for William, he was still young and idealistic. If she needed to act, she needed to do it alone and unhindered.

'Leave it with me. I'll talk to Gordon,' Marge said.

'Cathy?'

'She will not last long.'

'What do you mean?'

'Gordon is weak, I'm not. It may take some time, but I'll be focussed on the end game.'

'In this pub?' Nicholas asked.

'Not for me. I will make peace with Gordon and his wife. I will take up his offer of the farm cottage.'

'Have you sold out?' William asked.

'You're my son. What do you think?'

'Be careful, Mum. You know what can happen.'

'Nothing can happen unless I wish it.'

'And the offer to Gordon?'

'There will be no mention of it for the time being. At the appropriate time, it will be offered again.'

***

The mood in the village of Coombe was calm. Claude Selwood had not been well regarded, although his business acumen had been sound. Apart from Old Ted, another fifteen worked at the Selwoods' house and farm. The initial concern over Claude's death had abated once it was clear that Cathy Selwood would be taking control, the village collectively discounting Gordon as the weaker of the two.

Marge Selwood was regarded as capable, as were her youngest sons, and it had been hoped she would have taken control, but it had not come about, and then there was the death of Old Ted. His murder still concerned people, but not as much as it should have. There were some in the village who had taken to ensuring their windows and doors were closed at night.

Tremayne and Clare took the opportunity to check out the area. So far, they had only visited the pub and the farm. 'It's a pretty place,' Clare said as they walked around. On one corner, a local store, a telephone box outside, as well as a post box.

The pub stood proudly in the centre of the village, just across the road from the church and the graveyard. Tremayne and Clare walked around the graves, finding Claude Selwood's with no difficulty; it was the only one with a headstone that wasn't old. Clare read the engraving, Tremayne casually looked and moved away.

'Not interested?' Clare said.

'He's dead and buried. He'll not help in solving Old Ted's murder.'

'It's related, though.'

'Probably.'

'And there's no way to prove it?'

'How? We've no idea who fired the pellet gun.'

As they stood there, the local vicar came over. 'Claude Selwood, a hard man,' the Reverend Walston said.

Clare could see an athletic man in his forties with a pleasant face. She hadn't expected to be excited on meeting the vicar, but she was.

'He gave you some trouble, so we're told,' Tremayne said.

'He'd be here every Sunday, the same as Marge.'

'Religious?'

'Marge may have been, but I don't think Claude was.'

'Why did he come?'

'His family had held sway for centuries around here. He saw it as his duty. He was not a man you ever really knew.'

'In what way?' Clare said.

'With some people, he was strict; with others, he was kind and generous.'

'Why is that strange?'

'If you had met him you would understand.'

'We only saw him after he died.'

The three of them had moved away from the grave. It seemed almost sacrilegious, Clare thought, to talk ill of the dead while standing next to the man's grave.

'He wanted to interfere as if he regarded this village as his.'

'Was it?'

'In the past, and it's not as if the Selwoods were titled. There's an earl, supposedly an ancestor, buried in the church, but he died back in the seventeenth century.'

'I thought titles were hereditary?' Clare said.

Apparently not,' the Reverend Walston said.

'He's a bit old for you, Yarwood,' Tremayne said as the two of them walked away from the church.

'A bit religious, as well.'

'He was making eyes at you; you liked the look of him.'

'Don't go matchmaking, guv. I can always find someone.'

'You've been moping around for too long. Sorry about your cat, but it's not a substitute. You need a man in your bed.'

'A little too familiar, don't you think?'

'With you? Hell, Yarwood, I've listened to your failed dates, their attempts at seduction. I reckon I've earned the right to make a comment. If the vicar's your cup of tea, religious or not, grab him.'

'We've got a murder case to investigate. Maybe once this is over.'

'There's no time like the present. The man's not suspected of being involved.'

'Why not? It could be anyone in the Selwood family or on the periphery. The vicar had been controlled by Claude. What's to say that he did not fire the shots at Selwood, enough to frighten the man.'

'It's a long bow you're stretching there. I think you should have a drink. In fact, I think I should as well,' Tremayne said.

'For once I agree.'

***

Marge Selwood did not want to stay in the pub. A single room, as good as it was, was no substitute for the splendour she had enjoyed before. It had been she who had taken the main house at Coombe Farm and renovated it to her standards. It had even been featured in a magazine on one occasion.

She would not let her eldest son, Gordon, suffer, but his wife was another matter. She needed to make peace.

'I'm willing to accept your offer,' she said to Gordon and Cathy Selwood in the front room of the main house.

'That's great,' Cathy said, who came over and gave her mother-in-law a hug.

Marge reciprocated through gritted teeth. 'We'll be neighbours,' she said. 'I'd like that. It's time for me to move on, and this house is too big for me.'

'That's what we thought. Sorry about the unpleasantness,' Gordon said.

Marge looked over at her son, realising that not even Cathy could mould the man into another Claude.

'I'll organise a firm to come and start work on the cottage,' Marge said.

'That's fine,' Cathy said. 'Just send the invoices here.'

Marge looked over at the woman and outwardly smiled. Inwardly, she seethed.

'Will you stay for dinner?' Gordon said.

'I'd love to,' Marge said. She had to admit the house looked good and that Cathy, a friend under other circumstances, was a capable administrator, and someone who would ensure the legacy of the Selwoods, but it was her bloodline that she intended to run the place, not the bloodline of a woman who had sold herself. Marge knew that she had given herself to other men out of necessity; Cathy had apparently enjoyed the experience.

Gordon sat back in his chair and looked at the two women in his life. He was pleased they were friends. Cathy Selwood was under no illusion as to the reality. One day, she knew, there would be problems, but for tonight, she would enjoy the magnanimity.

Chapter 8

Crispin Goode, a joy to his mother, was in a good mood as he walked to school. Not only was it close to the end of the term, but his exam results were, as expected, excellent. He saw the law as his vocation, and he had set his sights on entry into Oxford University when the time was right.

He knew his mother was a woman who liked everything in its place, even his room. He preferred that she would leave his bedroom the way he wanted it, chaotic, but every night, there were the clothes in the drawers or on hangers, the papers and magazines neatly stacked. He had spoken to her enough times about it, but he knew she would not change.

Sometimes, he wondered about his father, but it wasn't often. His mother's only comment: 'It was a long time ago. One day, I might tell you, but not until you're old enough to make the right decisions, to forgive me.'

'What's to forgive?' Crispin said.

As he was about to cross the road to his school, Bishop Wordsworth's Grammar, a friend shouted out. 'Come on Crispin. You're late.'

Crispin, noting a lull in the traffic, walked across the road, even though no further than twenty yards away there was a marked crossing.

As he crossed the first lane, a car could be seen coming in the opposite direction. Crispin could see it. 'It's going fast,' the friend said.

'Don't worry. It'll slow down,' Crispin's reply. He continued to cross, raising his hand in acknowledgement of the driver slowing.

'It's not slowing,' the friend said again.

Crispin was hit full on and thrown over the bonnet of the car, landing heavily on the road. He was unconscious, and his friend was desperate. Another pupil phoned emergency services, an ambulance was on the scene within five minutes, a police officer within eight.

At the hospital, Crispin was rushed into emergency; his condition deemed as critical. At the accident scene, the officer took a statement from the friend and two other pupils who had been witnesses.

'The car was slowing down, and then it sped up. The person's foot must have slipped off the brake and back onto the accelerator,' the friend said.

'Did you get a number plate?'

'It was a Toyota Camry, that's all I know. Blue in colour.'

Rose Goode arrived at the hospital to find her son in a stable condition. 'He's lucky,' the doctor said. 'Two cracked ribs and a severe concussion.'

'When can he come home?'

'He'll need a few days in here for observation. He'll be out of service for a few weeks, and he'll be sore.'

'He had hoped to go on a trip to Europe in a week's time.'

'Not this time, he won't.'

***

It took two days for Marge Selwood to organise a local handyman to come to Old Ted's former cottage and to clear the kitchen, one of the bedrooms, and the sitting room. After that, a professional cleaning company from Salisbury had gone through the house in infinite detail until it was liveable. The handyman and one other had painted the main areas, an interior decorating firm had been in, and had fitted the renovated rooms with items of suitable quality. The exercise had cost plenty. Marge sent the invoices straight up to the main house. The rest of the cottage would take another four weeks to complete. By then, Marge hoped to be back in the main house.

On the fourth day in the cottage, Nicholas and William Selwood came to visit. 'It's looking good, Mum,' Nicholas said.

'I used to like this cottage when I first came to the village,' Marge said.

'And now?'

'It could burn to the ground for all I care.'

'Don't go destroying our inheritance,' William said. 'And when you're back in the main house, I'd be happy to live here.'

'It's yours.'

'Has Gordon been here?'

'Cathy has. She brought me a potted plant as a housewarming present.'

'Where is it now?'

'In with the rubbish.'

'The hatred remains,' Nicholas said.

'She's a capable woman, more than I can say for Gordon.'

'She'll make a success of the farm, you know that.'

'It is ours, and I intend to get it back.'

***

Six in the morning and Clare was at Bemerton Road Police Station. It was still dark outside, an excellent time to catch up on the paperwork. She knew that Tremayne wouldn't be in until later, a visit to the dentist was long overdue for him. He had admitted to her there wasn't much he was afraid of, apart from someone drilling into his teeth. 'When I was young, we had this dentist; he didn't believe in injections or gas. He'd be straight in there with his drill, and I'd be climbing up the wall,' he had said.

Clare had to tell him that times had moved on, and his fear was irrational. But, she knew that Tremayne was a man set in his ways, and he'd endure the dentist and be back in the office later that morning.

As Clare typed on her laptop, a woman who had been brought into Homicide by another officer, spoke. 'Someone's made an attempt on my son's life.' Clare looked up at the woman. She could see a conservatively-dressed woman in her thirties.

'Please take a seat,' Clare said. She saved her work on the laptop and focussed on the woman.

'My name is Rose Goode.'

'Rose Fletcher?'

'You've heard of me?'

'We're aware that you were involved with Gordon Selwood in your youth.'

'My parents were ashamed of what I'd done. We moved away from the area.'

'You had a child?'

'My son, Crispin. He's a pupil at Bishop Wordsworth's Grammar School.'

'Where is your son?'

'He's in hospital, a hit and run near the school.'

'Serious injuries?'

'Broken bones, a concussion, but he'll survive.'

Clare went and made the two of them a cup of tea.

'And you believe it was an attempt on his life?'

'I know it was.'

'How? From our knowledge, your whereabouts were unknown.'

'I thought they were.'

'Is there a Mr Goode?'

'For a while, but he's gone now.'

'Gone?'

'We separated a few years back.'

'I'm sorry to hear that.'

'He's not important, my son is.'

'Certain facts need clarifying,' Clare said. 'Is your son the legitimate child of Gordon Selwood?'

'I've a marriage certificate, my parents insisted on that from the Selwoods.'

'Why?'

'My parents, dated ideas. They didn't want their daughter giving birth to a bastard.'

'You were young, yet you kept the baby.'

'The plan was to have it adopted, but once it was born, my parents immediately fell in love with it, and I brought it up with their help.'

'Your parents, where are they now?'

'They are no longer alive.'

'Who else apart from your parents knew you were living in Salisbury?'

'Nobody that I know of. I've never had any contact with Gordon since before Crispin was born. The last time was at the marriage in a registry office. The divorce was dealt with by my parents.'

'I need to meet your son,' Clare said. It was still early; she phoned Tremayne. 'You'll need to cancel your dentist's appointment. There's been a development,' she said.

'Another murder?' Tremayne said.

'Rose Fletcher. She's here with me at Bemerton Road.'

'Give me thirty minutes.'

'My senior. He'll be here soon.'

'And what about my son? He doesn't know who his father is.'

'How old is he?'

'He's sixteen now.'

'He deserves to know the truth.'

'I've told him that I would tell him when the time was right, and Gordon is hardly a good role model. Crispin, he's a good student, a son to be proud of. I didn't want him associating with his father until he was older.'

'He'll need to know. Let me come back to the accident. You believe it was attempted murder, but nobody knew you and your son were in Salisbury.'

'Someone did.'

'Were you close to Gordon?'

'We were childhood friends, adolescent teens. We could hardly avoid each other in Coombe, small as it was. It was just the two of us in that churchyard, a bottle of wine between us. Plenty of dreams for the future. You know how it is when you're young.'

Clare did, having gone through the silly and sexually active stage in her teens, only to slow down on meeting Harry Holchester, and now, to have stopped.

'Have you been to Coombe since?'

'Never. I know it's not far, but I've never felt the need, not after that night when I told my parents. I remember my mother's reaction, my father's anger towards me. He hit me and hard, and then, he's storming up to Coombe Farm, me in tow.'

'What about the other sons, do they know?'

'It was only Gordon's parents in the house that day.'

Tremayne walked into the office. He introduced himself to Rose Goode and sat down. 'Mrs Goode, you're aware of our interest in you?'

'I know that Gordon's father has died, and a man has been murdered.'

'Did you know Old Ted?'

'Probably by sight, but I can't remember him.'

'Old Ted would have known the whole story,' Clare said.

'Yarwood's right,' Tremayne said looking at Rose Goode.

'Do you believe that it was attempted murder, my son's car accident?'

'We think it's a possibility. The best defence is if you and Crispin are visible, and the connection is made to the family.'

'I never wanted to.'

'That's as maybe, but the circumstances make this inevitable. Assuming that the farm is inherited by the eldest son, then Crispin can lay claim on it if Gordon dies.'

'Believe me, neither of us wants it.'

Chapter 9

Events in Coombe returned to normal within a short period of time. Old Ted's body was released from Pathology, and he had been buried in the local churchyard alongside his wife. For once, the weather had been pleasant. All of the Selwood family attended, an uneasy truce declared.

Tremayne and Clare watched from outside, observed the easy banter between Marge and Cathy Selwood, the discussions between the three sons. From up the road and hidden under a hat and sunglasses, Rose Goode.

The woman had said she had not been to Coombe since that night when she had told her parents she was pregnant, but there she was. Clare was sure she had lied that time at Bemerton Road.

Clare had met Crispin, initially as a police officer interested in the accident, subsequently as a member of Homicide, when he had understood the implications of what his mother had told him.

The young man's protestations that he wasn't interested in the fact that he was the legitimate son of a wealthy man did not ring true with Clare. Crispin Goode, sixteen, almost the age to learn to drive, ready to take out the local girls, and the best his mother could offer was a ten-year-old car, whereas his father could give him something worthwhile.

Clare thought the young man to be polite and well brought up, no doubt better than if his father had been involved, but he was still a young man with a young man's dreams and ambitions. She knew that at some stage he would confront Gordon Selwood. It was another complication of the enquiry into the death of Old Ted. The gun used in the shooting had not been found, and the motive for his death was unclear.

Tremayne waited outside the churchyard for the mourners to file out. He wanted to sense the mood; whether any were genuinely sad, or whether there was a pretence. Old Ted had been known by everyone in the village, and no one had a word against him, although no one spoke of him in endearing terms.

Clare took the opportunity to slip away from where she was and to walk up the street to where Rose Goode was hiding. After five minutes she caught up with her. 'First time here?' Clare said.

'I read the notices in the paper. I felt the need to come,' Rose said.

'You've been here before, haven't you?'

'I've driven through on a couple of occasions.'

'You denied that in the police station.'

'I can't help being interested in my past, and when Gordon's father died, I felt the need to see the place again.'

'And what did you think?'

'Nothing's changed, except everyone looks older.'

'Did anyone recognise you?'

'A young girl of fifteen then, a woman in her thirties? It's possible, but I kept a low profile, wore a wig and sunglasses.'

'Did you talk to anyone?'

'I bought a drink in the pub, but no one knew who I was.'

'And Crispin? What about him? Doesn't he deserve the right to meet his father?'

'Never. The Selwoods paid their blood money. My parents took it.'

'Did the Selwoods pressure your parents to keep the child? It was, after all, a Selwood.'

'I wouldn't know. I was not involved. I stayed with my parents for three years, and then, one day, I'm on my own, just Crispin and myself.'

'It must have been difficult.'

'It was, but my parents supported me. Believe me, with a child, you soon grow up. I even managed to get an education, and I've supported us ever since.'

'Mr Goode?'

'I've told you. We were together for some years, but then we divorced. He wasn't a bad man, and he did look after Crispin.'

'Where is he now?'

'He went to London. The last I heard, he had married again.'

'No regrets?'

'Over him, no.'

'Gordon?'

'Some. He was an attractive young man back then. He doesn't look so good now.'

'Marge Selwood?'

'A hard woman. She came into the place where I work. I spoke to her, but she didn't recognise me.'

'Are you sure?'

'With her, who can ever be sure. I'm certain she did not. My voice has changed, and I don't look anything like I did back in the village.'

Clare was suspicious, although, she realised it would only be natural for the woman to be curious. Hadn't she, after the death of her fiancé, revisited old haunts, old friends, when she had gone back to live with her parents in Norfolk for a few months. Until, in sheer despair, she had driven back to Salisbury and reported for duty with Detective Inpsector Keith Tremayne, the one rock in a sea of pebbles that offered comfort without consoling, without telling her to get on with her life. He had just kept her busy, and she knew that she was the better for it.

Tremayne, Clare could see, was down the road talking to Gordon Selwood and his wife. 'What do you feel when you see him down there?' Clare asked.

'Who's the woman?'

'That's his wife.'

'I thought it was. What's she like?'

'She's a pleasant woman. Why do you ask?' Clare did not want to say too much, knowing that Rose's presence in the village had elevated her status from the mother of an injured man to a possible murder suspect.

'Just curious. If I'd stayed married to him, then that would be me.'

'Maybe it would, but life is not predictable, is it?'

'If I hadn't drunk that wine, then I wouldn't have Crispin.'

'Do you regret that?'

'He's the one constant in my life. Without him, I'd be nobody.'

'He'll leave one day.'

'That's fine, as long as he remembers me. My mother barely said a word to me after that night, and my father, he was always cold.'

Rose Goode opened the door of her car and left. Down the road, the mourners were moving across to the pub. Clare walked down to join them.

In the pub, the publican pulling beers, serving up snacks. There was no one from Old Ted's family, only the Selwoods, and a smattering of villagers.

'No one really knew him,' the publican said. 'He was a man who kept his distance, although when his wife died, there must have been close to a hundred in that church. I made plenty of money that day.'

Over on the far side of the room, Gordon Selwood raised himself up on a chair. 'Ladies and gentlemen, Old Ted was a part of our community for many years, and a faithful employee and family friend of the Selwoods. He will be sorely missed. I propose a toast to the memory of Old Ted.'

A rousing cheer of Old Ted's name, a clinking of glasses, a downing of the drinks. Clare held a glass of wine, Tremayne had a pint of beer. 'Not a bad send-off,' he said.

'You saw who I was speaking to?' Clare said.

'I did.'

'How about the others?'

'Gordon Selwood pretended not to look, but I could see his eyeballs trying to angle in the direction.'

'Do you think he recognised her?'

'Maybe, but who knows. His mother never misses a trick.'

'The son's accident?'

'It's too coincidental. Outside of the school, clear road signs everywhere, and then the car doesn't stop. To me, it's attempted murder,' Tremayne said.

'That's what I reckon, but the mother, she's not the innocent she makes herself out to be. And she's devoted to the son. You harm him, you've made an enemy for life.'

'Enjoy tonight. Tomorrow, we're going to turn up the heat.'

'What do you mean?'

'We're going to confront Gordon with the possibility that his son has been discovered. We'll make sure Cathy is there as well. We'll look for their reactions when they realise that the heir presumptive is waiting in the wings.'

***

Tremayne woke early the next morning. He looked at the clock on his bedside table. It was seven in the morning, and his head throbbed. He pulled himself up from the bed, only to realise he had fallen asleep with his clothes still on. It wasn't the first time he had done so, but each time he regretted it. He, a serving police officer, and he had got drunk on duty. The phone was ringing; he picked it up.

'There's been another death,' Clare said. Tremayne remembered vaguely that she had driven him home, mentioned something about the Goode woman.

'Who?'

'Cathy Selwood.'

'Give me twenty minutes. Pick me up at my house.'

Tremayne went into the bathroom, turned on the shower, dispensing with his clothes on the floor. He looked in the bathroom mirror, did not like what he saw. Under the water, the sobering-up process, and then the realisation that his tooth hurt, the one that he had been going to the dentist for, and not only did it hurt, it also ached, and it was excruciating.

He sat down on the edge of the bed and took a painkiller. This time he knew a tablet was not going to do the trick. He phoned Clare.

'Yarwood, it's my tooth. I can't go with you. You're on your own on this one.'

'I'll see you later,' Clare said.

Tremayne phoned the dentist, even though it was early. 'It's an emergency. I've got another murder, and I need to be out there.'

'Ten minutes,' the dentist's reply.

***

Clare phoned Jim Hughes, woke him up. He would have his team ready to go within the hour. Out at the scene, the local uniform was securing the area.

Clare drove out on her own to Coombe, Tremayne having phoned her to say that he needed three fillings, a tooth removed, and to give him two hours.

'Tremayne, you're an optimist,' the dentist said when he heard Tremayne on the phone. 'You'll not be going anywhere today, except to your bed.'

'Do what you must, but Yarwood needs help, and it's a murder. I must be there.'

'Very well. I'll give you an injection.'

Tremayne looked around him at the dentist's surgery. He did not like the look of it; he did not like the look of the needle. He said no more, his mouth opened wide for the man to do his job.

Out at Coombe, Clare drove straight up to the Selwoods' house. Inside, in the kitchen, a local uniform, and Gordon and Marge Selwood.

'Nicholas and William are coming up,' Marge said.

'Why Cathy?' Gordon said. Clare could see that the man was not handling the situation well.

Outside of the house, Clare asked the uniform for an update.

'According to the husband, his wife goes for a walk every morning before daylight. She had left at six in the morning as usual; he didn't expect her back for at least an hour.'

'I received a phone call at six forty-five,' Clare said.

'Mr Selwood, he phoned me; I phoned you. He wouldn't have gone looking for her, but there was the sound of a gunshot.'

'They're all sensitive around here after Old Ted had been shot,' Clare said.

'Mr Selwood leaves the house and follows the route his wife always takes. He found her no more than one hundred and fifty yards from the house. She'd been shot. He knew where I lived, so he ran fast to my place and banged on the door. That's when I phoned you.'

'You'd not seen the body?'

'Not then, but I have now. Cathy Selwood is dead, a clear shot to the head.'

'The same as Old Ted?'

'The crime scene investigators can confirm, but I'd say it was. No idea why they would have killed her. She was a popular woman around here.'

Jim Hughes and his CSIs arrived within forty minutes. Clare stayed with them for another fifteen, before returning to the house. Inside, Gordon and Marge Selwood had been joined by the younger brothers. There was a pot of tea on the table; Clare helped herself to a cup. The Reverend Walston was there. To Clare, he still looked as attractive as he had the previous time they had met, but now, he was consoling the family, offering quotes from the bible.

Clare found that she did not like him as much on their meeting for the second time. Tremayne phoned. He was recuperating from the dentist's surgery.

'If you must come here, get someone else to drive,' Clare said.

'I've got a police car organised. They're picking me up in sixty minutes.'

'That long to get there?'

'The dentist, he's a tyrant. He's insisted, and besides, he's right. I feel awful, but at least the pain's subsiding.'

'And the drill?'

'I didn't feel a thing.'

'Paranoia, the domain of an old man.'

'Watch it, Yarwood. I've still got some bite left in me.'

'Just testing to see if you're up to coming back to work.'

'I'll be there, and don't muck up the investigation. I'm there for support; you're running the show today.'

'You've taught me well. I'll not let you down.'

After her conversation with Tremayne, Clare turned to the Selwood family. She could see William texting on his phone, Nicholas pretending to care. Only two people seemed genuinely upset, although Clare realised that she would have made the third if she wasn't focussed on the investigation.

'Is it the same person as Old Ted?' Marge Selwood said. Clare could see that she was sitting close to Gordon, patting his knee.

'We can't be certain, but all indications are that it is probably the same person. Our crime scene investigators will confirm in due course.'

'Why Cathy?' Gordon continued to repeat.

'Why Old Ted?' Clare said. 'If it's the same person, then the two of them must have known something of importance. Something that is integral to this family.'

'There is nothing hidden in this family,' Marge, the matriarch, said.

Clare knew there was, but did not comment. 'Mr Selwood, I've been briefed by Constable Andrews. You found your wife?'

'I did, and then I ran down to his house.'

'We know when your wife was killed. The issue is why? What did she know that you all probably know as well?'

'There's nothing,' Marge said. 'There had been some disagreement amongst us after my husband died, but now we have resolved those differences.'

Clare knew they had not.

'I've got some appointments today,' Nicholas said. 'When can I go?'

His mother looked over at him, gave him a look. He sat down without uttering another word. Clare noticed the interaction, the ability of the mother to control the man. In another corner, the youngest son continued to play with his phone. Marge, Clare thought, knowing the woman and some of her history, was play-acting and was probably overjoyed that the usurper was gone. Gordon looked to be genuinely sad at the turn of events, but it was clear that the mother was there to fill the void. Clare knew it would not be long before Marge Selwood was back in the main house and in control. Gordon was a weak personality, putty in the hands of strong-willed women.

A knock at the door, and in walked Tremayne. He looked awful, although Clare wasn't going to offer a comment. 'My apologies, I've just been to the dentist, severe pain.'

Tremayne realised that discussing his dental problems was a dumb way to enter into the house of a bereaved family. He took a seat and left it to Clare.

A text from Jim Hughes. Clare left and went outside to talk to him. 'It's the same calibre,' he said. 'We've also found where the shot was fired from.'

'Same weapon?'

'It's probable, but we'll need Pathology to remove the bullet and Forensics to confirm.'

'Any idea as to who?'

'Nothing confirmed. The floor of the place where the shooter stood is covered in straw. We'll not find much of use there. The family?'

'The husband seems upset.'

'The others?'

'Who knows what they're thinking.'

Chapter 10

Forensics confirmed that the same weapon had fired the shots at Old Ted and Cathy Selwood. Not that it helped, as the gun had not been found at Coombe Farm. All their weapons were licensed, and they had full records of who they had sold them to, who they had bought them from.

Tremayne improved immeasurably once he and Clare were back at the police station. As Tremayne walked in, there was Superintendent Moulton. At the sight of the man, Clare noticed that Tremayne lifted his shoulders and wished Moulton a good day.

'Bit of a strain back there,' Clare commented once they were back in Homicide. Some of the other sergeants in Bemerton Road found the interaction between Clare and her DI disturbing. Some of them were struggling with a senior who saw them as only secondary, whereas to Tremayne, she was his equal, even if she was not as experienced. With Tremayne still looking the worse for wear, Clare took control in the office. She knew the man would not take time off work, and she understood why. Not only was Moulton looking for her DI's retirement, but Tremayne wasn't a man to ease up when the going got tough, and the soreness in his mouth after the injections had worn off was not pleasant, coupled with his not being able to smoke for a couple of days.

Clare went and made Tremayne a cup of tea, heavy on the sugar for him. 'I'm not an invalid, you know,' the only thanks she was likely to receive.

'Make your own tomorrow. See how you feel then.'

'Okay, Yarwood, what have we got?'

'Apart from one detective inspector feeling sorry for himself, not much.'

'Apart from him,' Tremayne said. He always enjoyed the bantering with his sergeant, a woman young enough to be his daughter. His former wife had teased him relentlessly about the old police inspector and his attractive sergeant when she had first met her, but the women had hit it off straight away.

'Sherlock Holmes had a crusty doctor for an assistant, you've got Clare,' his former wife had said.

'She's a good police officer,' Tremayne had offered in his defence, but it wasn't necessary, he knew that. He had two women in his life who cared about him, two up on what it had been for many years.

'We know the same weapon killed the two people, and then, there's Claude Selwood's accident which resulted in his death.'

'It doesn't necessarily point to just the one person.'

'But who gained from their deaths?'

'No one, at least not legally. Marge Selwood has benefited to some extent that she's back in the main house, and she's back to mothering the family.'

'A strong enough reason to kill Cathy Selwood?'

'She's a driven woman.'

'So was Cathy Selwood.'

'A battle of the Titans, is that it?'

'Why not? Mind you, it doesn't explain the death of Old Ted.'

Tremayne knew the situation in Coombe was raw and the murders could well continue, and then, there was the issue of a new owner of the farm and the house, if Gordon Selwood died. The two police officers got back into Clare's car and drove to Coombe.

The main house was empty apart from Marge Selwood. 'They've taken Gordon down the pub.'

'Nicholas and William?'

'Yes. There was no point him moping around here.'

'Have you moved back in?'

'I have for Gordon.'

'Mrs Selwood, Gordon was married once before, there was a child. Do you know where they are?' Clare said.

'It's been a long time. Claude agreed to Gordon marrying the girl. Nicholas and William don't know the full story.'

'What do they know?'

'Not a lot, only that Gordon made a local girl pregnant.'

'They must have known the girl.'

'Not really. Gordon was older, and William was just approaching puberty. Nicholas was starting to be interested in women, a few posters on his bedroom wall, but that was it.'

'Do you know where this woman is now?'

'She was talking to Sergeant Yarwood at Old Ted's funeral. I could see them up the road.'

'You recognised her?' Clare said.

'There's a mysterious woman in conversation with a police officer, keeping a watch on us going and coming. Who else could it be? Where did you find her?'

'We didn't find her, she found us. Someone tried to kill Gordon's son. Was it you, Mrs Selwood?'

'How dare you! I love Gordon. Why would I do such a thing?'

'Because you love Nicholas and William more. If Gordon dies, who inherits this place?'

'The eldest son, Nicholas.'

'But he's not the eldest son of the eldest son, is he? If Gordon and Rose Fletcher were legally married at the time of the child's birth and the child were male, then he would inherit. Is this how it works?'

'That is what Claude's last will and testament said.'

'And you did not manage to change it in time, did you?'

'Gordon's not cut out for the farmer's life. His bitch wife would have run the place, but Nicholas and William are the best people to look after the family's inheritance. If Gordon changes his will, then the son is excluded.'

'But if he dies before, then Rose Fletcher's son takes control.'

'Do you have a copy of Gordon's will?' Clare asked.

'No.'

'Does Gordon?'

'Probably not, but he's hardly likely to leave anything to a child he's never met,' Marge said.

'Then without a will, the law will probably decree that the child of Gordon and Rose is entitled to inherit, and you know this.'

'I know it, but Gordon wasn't listening to me, not with Cathy around.'

'You have the best motive for her murder.'

Clare looked over at Tremayne; she could see that the man should be convalescing, not out in the field. Without anyone else, it was for her to look after him.

'It was in that damn churchyard where he made her pregnant.'

'Cathy?'

'No, Rose,' Marge Selwood said. Clare was pleased. The woman was becoming rattled. Tremayne lifted his head, looked at Clare. She could see that he wanted her to keep up the pressure.

'Mrs Selwood, Rose Fletcher has been living not far from here for many years, and you're telling me you never knew,' Clare said. 'I put it to you that you not only knew her whereabouts, but you were also keeping a watch, assuming that one day, her son would cause trouble.'

'Those are scurrilous accusations.'

'They are not scurrilous. Mrs Selwood, you run this house as if it was your own fiefdom with your children as lackeys to do your bidding. Nicholas and William are your favourites, don't deny it. And they do what they're told. With them, you're safe, even if Nicholas has the title to this house and the farm.'

'This is slanderous. I'll sue.'

'For what? This is a police investigation, and there has just been a murder, the second in as many weeks, and the guilty party is you. Maybe you didn't pull the trigger, but Nicholas and William could have. Should we take them to the police station and interview them? They're not up to your deviousness; they'll break, and then the whole sorry saga of what you've been doing will become clear.'

'Please leave my house.'

'Are you willing to confess to the murder of Old Ted and Cathy Selwood? Can you offer anything in your defence?'

'I did not kill them. Yes, okay. I did know that Rose Fletcher, although she calls herself Rose Goode, is not far from here, and that her son is bright, no doubt a credit to his mother, but he is the spawn of two teenagers in a churchyard. The child has no right to this place.'

'Yet, the children of someone who prostituted herself is?'

'That was a long time ago. It's something I regret.'

'Do your children know of your dubious past?'

'No, and that's how I want it to stay. I have served this family, this community, all of my adult life, and Claude had no reason to complain.'

'Is Gordon Selwood the child of Claude Selwood? The dates of your marriage and his birth are very close.'

'He is. I was pregnant when we married.'

'Back of the churchyard, the same as Gordon and Rose, is that it? Mrs Selwood, you're not handling yourself very well here.'

Clare looked over at Tremayne. The man was looking better, enjoying the spectacle of the two women. He knew that his sergeant had the woman on the ropes. He was waiting for the knockout blow.

'I admit to what I'd done in the past, it is not something that I'm proud of.'

'Please don't give us that nonsense. You're a woman who does not regret. To you, sleeping with men for money did not concern you, although it probably did Cathy. She was a good woman, better than you. You wanted her dead, the same as you wanted Old Ted, although we don't know why he had to die, or maybe he knew that Gordon wasn't your son. Had he found out something that you had not? If Gordon is not the legitimate son, then Nicholas may well have a stronger claim. You could have argued the case in court, maybe even won, but now, you're going to jail for murder. How do you plead, Mrs Selwood?'

Tremayne knew he could not have done it better.

Marge Selwood sat down at the kitchen table. She placed her face in her hands. 'Gordon is Claude's son, and I did not kill Old Ted, nor Cathy, and yes, she was a capable woman. I did not fire pellets at Claude. I may be many things, but I'm not a murderer. You will need to look elsewhere for an answer.'

'Thank you, Mrs Selwood. We will be back,' Clare said.

Tremayne and Clare walked out of the door and towards Clare's car. 'You were tough in there,' Tremayne said.

'Not as tough as I intend to be with you. I'm taking you home and putting you to bed. I don't want to see you in the office until tomorrow morning.'

'Who's in charge, you or me?' Tremayne said half-heartedly. He had seen the mettle of his sergeant, and he had been impressed.

'You're not fit for duty; you're being stood down.'

'I'm in your hands, Sergeant. What about Marge Selwood?'

'She's felt the heat. We need to keep a watch on her from now on.'

'Murderer?'

'You can think about that in your bed,' Clare said.

Chapter 11

Clare looked around the office at Bemerton Road, realising that without Tremayne it was a dreary place. She had liked Cathy Selwood, and now the woman was dead. It was unlikely that it was either Rose Goode or her son who were responsible, Clare thought. He was still too young and had only just been released from the hospital. And Rose Goode had no history of involvement with the family for many years; in fact, she had gone out of her way to keep her distance from them.

As Superintendent Moulton came down the corridor, no doubt delighted to hear that Tremayne was starting to show his age and had taken a day off, Clare took off in the other direction.

Too late. 'Sergeant Yarwood,' Moulton shouted.

Clare stopped, turned to face Tremayne's nemesis. 'What's this I hear about Tremayne?'

'He had a tooth out, a few fillings. He's just a bit sore.'

'Who's in charge of Homicide?'

'I'm in constant communication with DI Tremayne. He'll be here in the morning.'

'If you're covering for him.'

'I'm not, sir. He came with me out to the murder scene. I took him home to convalesce.'

'Very well. If he's here tomorrow, then no more will be said. Otherwise, I'll need an independent check of his general health.'

'He's as fit as you and me, sir.'

'Sergeant Yarwood, I know a good story when I hear one. Tremayne's feeling the years, and you know it.'

'He's good for a few years more.'

'When are you ready for a promotion?'

'Anytime, sir.'

'Right. I'll look into it. Someone needs to take over Homicide when Tremayne finally retires.'

'Thank you for your confidence, sir.'

'I recognise ability. Tremayne's taught you well.'

Clare left the station, feeling pleased with herself. She was on a roll; she needed to keep it up. She found Rose Goode at the house she shared with her son. The woman was pleased to see her.

'Crispin's a lot better. He should be back to school within a few days.' Rose said.

'Marge Selwood recognised you out at Coombe.'

'When?'

'That time you were with me.'

'At that distance? Or did she assume that I'd be there?'

'I'm not sure, but she knew about you and Crispin.'

'About us being here?'

'Yes. She's admitted that much.'

'She's not been near us, although we're here in Salisbury. It's not that big a place, I suppose she could have seen me around.'

'It's probably the same with her. And Crispin wasn't important back then, only a minor, but now, he's sixteen and smart. He's a threat, so are you.'

'Do you think it was her who tried to kill Crispin?'

'The police are treating it as a hit and run. It's only DI Tremayne and myself who are speculating that it may have been attempted murder.'

'It was,' Rose said. 'I know it was.'

'How?'

'When Crispin was young, no more than four, he nearly died after someone gave him a sweet.'

'You've not mentioned this before.'

'I only just remembered it. At the time, I thought it was a faulty batch, imported probably. It happens from time to time, but now with Crispin hit by a car, it seems possible.'

Clare could see that suspicion lurked everywhere. All the key players were nervous, seeing conspiracy and mayhem when there was probably none. Tremayne had been on the phone three times since she had left him wrapped up in bed. He had attempted a few wisecracks about him not being a child.

She had even made him hot soup to keep him nourished. With him not phoning for the last hour, it indicated that he had fallen asleep. She knew he'd be in the office the next day; no point in telling him about her conversation with Superintendent Moulton.

'It was a long time ago, as you say. A sweet that makes a child sick is hardly likely to be a murder attempt,' Clare said.

'I heard about Gordon's wife. It was on the news.'

'I've been there, seen her.'

'Gordon?'

'He's the only one upset.'

'We were always friends, even when we were children. I used to go up to his house a lot.'

'His parents?'

'They were always friendly. I used to like his father, even though he was a stern man.'

'That's been said. His wife?'

'She was more standoffish, but I was only young, the same age as Gordon, so I didn't take much notice.'

'Was there a romance?'

'Not then, we were too young, but we used to pretend that one day we would get married.'

'And then you did.'

'It wasn't the way we intended. When I got pregnant, we weren't dating, at least not seriously. He was taking out other girls. I was with other boys.'

'Any risk that Crispin is not his child?'

'None. No doubt Gordon was sleeping with the other girls, but I was still a virgin. Gordon can lay claim to that. Crispin is his, no question.'

'And after you gave birth to Crispin?'

'I was young, full of energy, but I had a child. There were a few men, purely flings, until I met Derek. He had no issues with Crispin, treated him well. We were married for eight years, and then he left. Nothing more to say. He keeps in contact, sends a card at Christmas, but apart from that, nothing.'

'Do you have a boyfriend now?'

'Not now. Once Crispin is finished with school, and then at university, maybe.'

'You've driven through Coombe on several occasions. Has it ever been more than that?'

'Not really. I may have driven past my old house, the churchyard, Gordon's place.'

'And stopped to have a look.'

'Maybe, but no one ever saw me.'

'It may not be important, but the car that hit Crispin is. We've checked the CCTV cameras in the city centre, but nothing that helps, and his friend who was standing there couldn't tell us much.'

Clare left the mother and went to speak with Crispin. He was sat in front of a computer monitor playing a game. 'Your mother says you're on the mend,' Clare said.

'Another few days and I'll be back at school.'

'We've not found the car that hit you.'

'It could have just been an accident.'

'It's always possible.'

'Mum's told me about my father if that's what you want to talk about.'

'I never asked her if she had. How do you feel about it?'

'I don't feel very much. I'd like to meet him at some stage, but not now. Mum doesn't want me to. I'll respect her wishes.'

'You understand the significance?'

'It's on the internet. I've checked. And now my father's wife has died.'

'Murdered. That's why you need to be careful.'

'But why me? I never knew about them before.'

'They knew about you. You confuse them, and someone in that family is irrational. We can never know what will happen next.'

'I'll be careful.'

Clare knew that Crispin Goode's idea of careful was not hers. He was a young man, anxious to make his mark. She knew he'd be fishing around Coombe within the week, regardless of what was said. It had been important for Crispin to know his birthright, although it made his situation more precarious.

Clare left the Goode's house and drove back to the police station, diverting to Tremayne's house. The man was awake and looking for updates. She found him downstairs, a blanket around him, the television on the sports channel. 'There's no hope for you, guv,' Clare said.

'I'm feeling better. I thought I might place some bets on the horses.'

'You lose enough when you're well. You could have given it a break for the day and stayed in bed.'

'Don't go on, Yarwood. A cup of tea would be nice.'

Clare could see that Tremayne enjoyed being fussed over. 'Anything to eat?'

'I could manage some chicken.'

'Just this once. Is there any in the fridge?'

'I doubt it. There's a shop down the road, takeaway.'

'If I'm feeding you, then you'll eat healthily. I'll go and buy some chicken breast and prepare it here. You must give Jean hell when she comes to stay.'

'With Jean, she has me cleaning the house.'

'It's looking better for her influence.'

Clare left the house. She returned in fifteen minutes and prepared Tremayne a meal. In that time, he had lost money on his latest sure-fire winning horse.

'What are the updates?' Tremayne asked as he ate the first homemade meal that he had eaten in a couple of weeks.

'Superintendent Moulton waylaid me, enquired after your health.'

'Did he have his latest retirement package in his pocket?'

'Not this time.'

'What else?'

'Rose Goode suspected that someone tried to poison the young Crispin when he was four.'

'Is it likely?'

'I don't think so. Just bear it in mind for future reference, and Mr Goode, Derek, he's divorced from Rose, but they keep in infrequent contact. No reason to suspect him.'

'Why not?'

'He didn't know about Crispin's father, and Rose wouldn't have told him.'

'Assumptions, Yarwood. Never make firm decisions unless they're backed up by fact. Agreed that this time you're probably right, and seeing that Rose and Derek Goode are no longer together, then it seems unlikely. We may need to interview the man at some stage.'

'Any more?'

'Rose Goode and Gordon Selwood were childhood friends, and she was a frequent visitor at the Selwood house.'

'A romance?'

'Not as children, although they were close. Later on, he's playing the field, so is she, but the friendship remained. It was Gordon that fathered the child, she made that clear, as she had not slept with any other man.'

Clare left the house after one hour, making sure to wash the dirty dishes first. Tremayne was still sitting in his chair watching the television. She thought he looked lost, the most inactive she had ever seen him.

***

For once, the weather was pleasant, even though it was five in the afternoon. Gordon Selwood, no longer able to tolerate his mother rearranging the main house, left by the back door and walked up the track to the top of the hill. He knew he had loved Cathy, had forgiven her for her past, but she was gone, and he was sad, sadder than he had been for a long time. With her, he felt complete, but now, it was his mother back in his life, and he did not want her. She had been in Old Ted's cottage. She could have stayed there, and have left the house to him.

He wanted to cry, but could not, consumed with the hatred he felt for his mother. His father had been strict, but with him, he could stand his own, even if that meant fearsome arguments, but then the old man had started to become forgetful, vague even. Gordon had seen that the spirit had gone out of the man, a hollow shell, and now, he, the eldest son was allowing his mother to reassert her stewardship of the Selwoods' household.

He stopped halfway up the track and looked around him. Cathy had loved the place, although he had not. He had promised her that he would not sell the farm and she would take over the day-to-day management, even bringing in Nicholas and William as necessary, although he knew they were his mother's stooges. He took one further look around him and walked back down the track.

He entered the main house. 'Mother, I want you out. This is Cathy's house. I want it left the way she liked it.'

'You're an ungrateful bastard. I've come over here to look after you, and this is what you say to me.'

'You don't understand. I loved Cathy.'

'She was a whore, only wanting to take you away from me.'

'She was my wife, and someone's killed her. I want you out of here now. The cottage is still there.'

'That's only fit for a farmhand, not for me, the wife of Claude Selwood, the person who drove him onto being somebody, the same as I was going to do for you.'

'I'm thirty-three. I don't need someone to hold my hand to cross the road. I need a woman to love me. A woman that I had.'

'You're upset,' Marge said. 'It's only natural. It's come as a shock to you, to all of us. It'll be better in the morning. Let's talk then.'

'There's nothing to talk about. I want you out of this house in the next ten minutes, and don't ever come back.'

Sensing her son's determination, the family matriarch left and walked towards the cottage. If she had been honest with herself, she would have said that it was more than adequate for her, but her power base lay in the other house. She opened the door to the cottage and made a phone call to her other sons. She knew they'd come. They loved her, even if Gordon did not.

Was it true what the policewoman had said? Marge thought as she sat in the cottage. Nicholas and William were definitely Claude's sons, their similarity to their father, undeniable, their mannerisms, similar to hers.

Gordon, she realised, was taller than anyone else. He was susceptible to putting on weight, whereas no one else in the family was, and his hair colour was fairer than the others. Was he Claude's son? She needed to know, and she needed to know quickly.

Chapter 12

Crispin Goode realised his life had taken a turn for the better. He made a phone call, a man answered. He slammed down the phone regretting that he had gone against the advice of his mother, excited that he had heard his father speak.

'Did you phone someone?' his mother asked.

'Just to a friend, that's all. He wasn't home,' Crispin said. It was the first time that he had openly lied to his mother. He knew it had been necessary.

Clare, after a long day, although exhilarated that she had been running Homicide without Tremayne, sat in the living room of her cottage. Her only remaining cat sat nearby licking itself. It was just the two of them, and she knew it wasn't satisfactory. She had been on a few dates with a couple of officers at Bemerton Road, but they had not worked out. One of the officers, a good-looking man with a loud voice, had only wanted to get her into his bed; she declined. The other, more sensitive, had been the perfect gentlemen, but she had felt no passion.

Apart from that, she had not slept with a man for over two years, and she was nearly thirty. She had said many times in the intervening period after the death of Harry Holchester, that enough was enough. The man was long dead, although emotionally she knew she still loved him, even though he had been a murderer. Not for the first time, she held a handkerchief to her eyes. The cat, sensing that its mistress was sad, came closer.

After five minutes, Clare snapped out of the inertia and phoned Tremayne. She knew he'd be awake.

'I'm having a pint,' he said. 'Come and join me.'

'Where are you?'

'The Pembroke Arms.'

'I'll be there in twenty minutes,' Clare said. She had seen enough sadness for one day, and sitting at home alone feeling sorry for herself wasn't going to help.

At the pub, Tremayne was sitting at the bar. 'I'm going easy,' he said.

'You're looking better.'

'It's you're looking after me that's done the trick.'

'Don't expect it every day.'

'I won't, and besides Jean's coming at the weekend.'

'We may be busy.'

'She'll understand. It'll give her a chance to tidy the house.'

'That sounds like male chauvinism to me?'

'Not from me, it isn't. She likes to fuss around the house, the same as you.'

'I don't like it, but when it's necessary, I will. If you want to live in chaos, that's up to you. I like everything to be tidy, and in its place.'

'Okay, you've said your piece. A glass of wine.'

'Yes, please.'

The two police officers sat there comfortable in each other's company. Whenever she was with him, she felt content. To her, he was the warm blanket, the comforter a child looks for.

***

William Selwood finished his last lecture of the day. The lecturer had been dry and dull, and he had had trouble staying awake, and now, there was a five-thousand-word report to present on what the man had been droning on about. It did not concern him as the subject matter was interesting, even if the man was not.

That weekend, five hours to research, five hours to write, and five hours to edit. It was how he had approached the degree course, compartmentalising each day, each subject. He was on schedule to complete, although the deaths at the family home were making it difficult, and now his mother was becoming demanding.

He knew she was difficult, but then she always had his best interests at heart. It had been she who had convinced his father that his absence from the farm for a few years would reap the rewards in the end, and she was right. He could see what was wrong with the farm, having used it as the reference for most of his time at university.

Sure, every year, the farm had won the best of breed for their cattle, the best barley crop, but he knew it could be improved. With further mechanisation, a comprehensive software farm management programme, he could see at least an eight per cent improvement, as well as a reduction in permanent and casual staff.

He was eager to start, but the death of his father, and then Old Ted, and now Gordon's wife, was jeopardising his return to Coombe Farm. He had known of the antagonism between his father and mother, the despair over Gordon, but he had learnt to ignore it, but now it was impacting, and his mother was looking for him to drive over and visit her in her cottage.

He imagined that there had been problems at the main house. Before having to deal with his mother, he phoned Gordon. 'What's up?'

'Nothing's changed. Cathy is with the pathologist, and I'm here on my own.'

'Mother?'

'I've sent her back to the cottage.'

'But why? I thought there was a truce.'

'Not with our mother. You may be tied to her apron strings, but I'm not.'

'That's not fair. She's done right by us.'

'By you and Nicholas. Look how she treated Cathy and now she's dead. Our mother pretends to care, but she does not. I know that, and it's about time you and Nicholas wised up.'

'Maybe she was against Cathy, but she's still our mother. She deserves respect.'

'She's got respect in her cottage. She's got a place to live, no issues with money. What more does she want? And besides, our father gave this place to me.'

'And who's going to run it?'

'You and Nicholas. I just want a suitable return.'

'And you keep the asset.'

'Why not?'

'I may as well get a job on another farm.'

'You won't. You're full of this family heritage nonsense, the same as our mother. You'll be here, the same as Nicholas, hoping that I have an accident, maybe even helping it to occur. I've not eliminated any of you from Cathy's death. If ever I prove that any of you are involved, then…'

'Then what? Kill us the way you did Old Ted. What did he know?' What skeletons do you have buried? And what about our father? Did you kill him?'

'Watch your mouth. This is my place, and I can throw you out anytime I like.'

William, a mild, even-tempered youth, realised that he was finding an inner-strength. He had to thank Gordon for that. He ended the phone call and walked to his car. If his mother needed help, he'd be there for her.

***

Tremayne was in the office early the next morning. He had appreciated Yarwood coming over and cooking him a meal, although he would not be thanking her profusely; that was how their relationship worked, a good deal of sarcasm, a denigration of the other's importance.

'What's the agenda today?' Tremayne said. He was looking better, even though he had ended up in the pub the night of his convalescing.

'More of the same. We've not found who fired the weapons, unlikely to in the office. The vicar should have a finger on the pulse of the village.'

'You know he fancies you.'

'Maybe he does, but I'm not religious, you know that.'

'What does it matter. You're a woman, he's a man.'

'At least your eyesight is fine,' Clare said.

The two officers left the office, Clare driving. She had phoned ahead; the Reverend Walston would be waiting for them in the church.

Inside the church, they found the vicar arranging the prayer books. 'One of the parishioners does it for me usually, but she's not been around for a couple of days,' he said.

'Any concerns?' Tremayne said.

'She's in her eighties. I should go and check.'

'We're trying to resolve these murders. We thought you may be able to give us a new perspective,' Clare said. Tremayne noticed that the vicar stopped arranging the prayer books when she spoke.

'I'll help in any way I can, although I'm not sure I can help much. The influence of the church is not what it used to be. I'm afraid we're like the village pub, declining in patronage. I've tried to embrace the community, to encourage the youth to come, but I've not had a lot of success.'

'Even so, you talk to people,' Tremayne said. 'We were told that Claude Selwood interfered.'

'On more than one occasion. He was generous in helping the church, but he was a forceful man who wanted it to be done his way.'

'We were told about a sermon.'

'It was a dispute only. He was a great believer in that success belonged to those who strived and worked hard. I wanted to preach about helping thy neighbour, those less fortunate. To him, those less fortunate deserved what they got. The man believed in the value of hard work, and he felt that some in this village were bone idle, and needed to be reminded of the fact.'

'Did he upset anybody with his comments?'

'Once or twice. Sometimes Claude Selwood would get down the pub, a few pints in him, and he'd start philosophising. People around here don't like to be lectured. The history of the

Selwood family is well known. Claude Selwood's father, he was a tough man, not afraid to take a cane to those of his workers who slackened off, and lectures by the son were not appreciated, considering that some here remembered the stories from the past. One of the Selwoods even killed a villager, but that was over two hundred years ago.'

'It was a crueller world back then,' Tremayne said.

'Not to some in this village. There were a few who were pleased when Claude Selwood died, and now with Old Ted, they're blaming the Selwoods again.'

'What about the death of Cathy Selwood?'

'She carried the Selwood name, and she wasn't from around here. No one's concerned about her, although most would admit to having liked the woman. She didn't have their arrogance, and she was an improvement on the others.'

'Gordon Selwood. What can you tell us about him?'

'There was a scandal, but it goes back before my time.'

'How do you know?'

'Local gossip. Supposedly, the daughter of a doctor.'

'Fletcher, that was the name. Does it mean anything to you?'

'I've been here for nine years. There are some Fletchers in the graveyard, probably related, but Dr Fletcher has never been in here.'

'He's dead, the daughter isn't, and that's not gossip.'

'Believe me, I'll not repeat a word. You know how it is, the lonely old women come in here. They want to be nearer to God, but they like to talk as well. It's not for me to tell them to stop.'

'Understood. What do they say about the daughter?' Clare said.

'Gordon made her pregnant, that's all.'

'They left the village soon after.'

'How did they know she was pregnant? The Fletchers and the Selwoods went to great lengths to keep it hidden.'

'I don't know. I've not spoken to Gordon Selwood apart from at the funerals. He's not impressed me, although his wife did. She appeared capable, he appeared to be worthless. I suppose that's not charitable, but that's how I saw it.'

'The other sons?'

'Nicholas and William. Fine upstanding men, credit to their mother.'

'And Marge Selwood?'

'There are some who don't like her, but she's been agreeable to me. She and Cathy Selwood were very much alike. I suppose that's why they clashed.'

'You knew about the bad blood between them?'

'Everyone knew. It's a small village. These places thrive on gossip.'

'We believe Old Ted died because he knew something.'

'No point in killing him because of that. The man would give you an answer to a question if you asked him. Apart from that, he'd say nothing.'

'If the right question was asked?'

'He'd not lie.'

'Everyone lies,' Tremayne said.

'Not Old Ted. He wasn't a complex man. He was honest and loyal, every Sunday to church, and he didn't lie. It's a difficult concept to understand, but that was Old Ted.'

'Are you saying that he would keep a secret forever, but if someone asked the correct question, he'd reveal what it was.'

'Yes, precisely.'

Tremayne and Clare left the vicar in his church and walked around the village. 'Not much to see, is there?' Tremayne said.

'It's very quiet. We didn't gain much from the vicar.'

'Apart from the fact that Old Ted never lied.'

'Which means someone was concerned that he would speak.'

'Someone who knew what the secret was, and the fact that it could be revealed.'

'None of this makes sense. We've spoken to everyone. They've all got alibis that will stand up. Is there another person?'

'But who? We've exhausted all the possibilities.'

Chapter 13

It was not often that Marge Selwood went into Salisbury, but being back in the cottage upset her. She knew she was not thinking straight. She walked around the supermarket picking up this and that. She was not focussing, her mind going over what had happened, what needed to be done. She knew that Gordon could not continue, and now there was his son to consider. If she could prove that Gordon was not Claude's son, then all was fine. However, she had two other sons who believed in the purity of their mother. For them to hear that their mother had a past that had not included her husband and that Gordon may well be a step-brother, concerned her.

'It was you, wasn't it?' a woman alongside her said.

'Pardon. What did you say?'

'Don't pretend all innocent with me, Mrs Selwood. It was you who tried to kill my son.'

'Rose Fletcher, how dare you?'

'Dare what? You tried to kill Crispin, your own grandson.'

'The child of a promiscuous woman; I don't think so.'

'I was not promiscuous. We were both young, that's all.'

'You were paid off. Why are you here?'

'I want nothing from you. I only care for my son.'

'I know how you live, hand to mouth.'

'Your life is not much better, is it? Gordon's exercising his power. You're back in Old Ted's cottage.'

'How do you know that?'

'Does it matter? It's true, isn't it?'

'Rose, don't pretend that I want to see you, but we need to talk.'

'Very well. My house, you can follow me there.'

'I know the address.'

'Foolish of me to think that you didn't. You know everything that happens with your family.'

Marge Selwood left her trolley in the aisle and walked out of the store with the mother of her grandson. She opened the door of her Land Rover and followed Rose up to her house.

Inside the house, small and utilitarian, she could see that Rose looked after the place well. 'Crispin?'

'He won't be home for another three hours.'

'I did not try to kill him.'

'You'll do anything for the good name of Selwoods. I remember the treatment I received when I became pregnant; how you forced my parents out of the village. It destroyed them. I wasn't blameless, neither was your son, but what happened to him? A slap on the wrist, a pat on the back.'

'That's what men do. They seduce willing virgins. It's up to the woman to resist, and from what I was told, there wasn't much resisting.'

'Who told you that?'

'Is it important?'

'It is to me. You knew about us, our friendship even as children.'

'I encouraged it. I thought you were a suitable mate for him, but you were both too young.'

'And then he went and married that other woman.'

'You were better than her. Maybe I was wrong.'

'Crispin is a Selwood. He's not like Gordon, he's responsible. I've kept him away from you and your family for all his life, but now he knows the truth. Why do you insist on laying the blame on me for your life? I have done nothing to you.'

'If you two had waited.'

'But we couldn't. We were young, that's all.'

'You were only fifteen, under the age of consent.'

'The past doesn't matter any more, does it? If you did not attempt to kill my son, then who did?'

'Are you sure it wasn't an accident?'

'As certain as I can be.'

'Then it was someone else.'

Rose Goode looked at the woman in her house. She could see that she had aged, although she still remained attractive. Rose knew the woman could not be trusted, and she would have preferred not to contact her, but the situation was dangerous. Her son knew the truth, and he was anxious to meet his father, but people had been murdered. It could only be something to do with the house and farm. She did not want her son to be attacked again.

'I want Crispin to be acknowledged as a member of your family. You owe him that much.'

Marge Selwood could see a determined woman. She knew a reply in the negative would not be wise. 'Very well, bring him over to the village. I will take you both to see Gordon.'

Rose knew she had done what was important. Her son was not safe as long as he remained hidden. She phoned Clare after Marge Selwood had left the house. 'I've spoken to Gordon's mother,' she said.

'Was she pleased to talk to you?'

'She pretended to be ambivalent.'

'But what do you really believe?'

'Her? I don't trust her for one minute. She's agreed to introduce Crispin to his father.'

'When?'

'Tomorrow.'

'And you're comfortable with that?'

'No. I'm going out there now. I want you to be there with us.'

'Where is Crispin?'

'He's at school. We'll pick him up on the way.'

***

Marge Selwood was angry. She had been compromised by a woman from the past. The agreement had been with her parents, not with her, in that there was to be no further contact after Gordon had married their daughter, and now, the young woman, only sixteen then, had reneged on that agreement. And all because her son had been in an accident.

Marge Selwood knew that Crispin Goode, the son of the black sheep, was a capable young man and that Rose Goode was a decent woman. But it was not what she had planned. Nicholas and William, both of them, had had a life at the farm. They knew what was needed, whereas Crispin Goode and his mother, possibly well intentioned and honest, did not.

William arrived at the cottage. He sat down, poured himself a beer from a bottle in the fridge. 'What is it, mother?' he said. It had been a long day; he did not want a diatribe about Gordon again.

'What do you know of Gordon and Rose Fletcher?' Marge asked.

'Gordon's never spoken about it. I remember you and our father arguing, even shouting at Gordon.'

'You're old enough to know the truth. Gordon made the girl pregnant. She was under the age of consent.'

'That was the rumour.'

'I met her today.'

'What did she say?'

'She wants to introduce their son to Gordon.'

'Is there a problem?'

'He's a Selwood. Her parents were threatening legal action. We didn't want the publicity, so we agreed to Gordon marrying the fool girl. The son was legitimate when it was born.'

'Are there any more children?'

'None. That's it.

'Our inheritance?' William asked.

'It depends on Gordon and the child.'

'What are you going to do?'

'I'm going to pretend the son is welcome into the family. I want you and Nicholas to do so as well.'

'And then what?'

'We'll see what happens, but rest assured, the farm belongs to you and Nicholas.'

'And to you, Mother.'

***

Clare was uncertain of what the reception would be when she agreed to go with Rose Goode and her son out to Coombe Farm. Whatever happened, she knew that it would serve as a catalyst.

Tremayne had advised her to take care and to observe the reactions of the people. She had to admit that Crispin was similar in appearance to Gordon, although the young man was more studious. He had not had the luxury of a wealthy family, only the devotion of his mother, which to Clare seemed to be the better option.

As Clare's car drew close to the house, Rose in the front seat, Crispin in the back, they could see Gordon outside cleaning his Jaguar. 'Great car,' Crispin said.

Clare could see issues with Crispin. He was at the impressionable age, and a father with money was not necessarily the best example. Also, she had noticed Crispin looking her up and down, although he had not made any comments, not with his mother there.

The three left Clare's car and walked the ten yards to where Gordon Selwood was. He looked up at their approach.

'Sergeant Yarwood, what brings you here?'

'Hello Gordon,' Rose said.

The man stood frozen for a moment before coming forward and putting his arms around her. 'It's been a long time,' he said.

'This is Crispin.'

The two men shook hands, formally at first, before Gordon realising who Crispin was, put his arms around him. 'I never expected to meet you,' he said.

'I never knew you existed,' Crispin replied. Clare could see that he was overcome with emotion.

'Today's not a good day,' Gordon said.

'I'm sorry about your wife,' Rose said. 'Sergeant Yarwood told me she was a good woman.'

'She was, and, well, you know what's happened.'

'I only came because of the situation.'

'What situation?'

'Someone tried to kill Crispin. Otherwise, I would not have told him about you, and we wouldn't be here.'

'Out of despair comes joy,' Gordon said. 'Please come inside the house.'

'I've met your mother,' Rose said.

'How?'

'I saw her in the supermarket. I felt it was time to make contact. I'm worried for Crispin.'

'My mother, what did she have to say?'

'She was agreeable, offered to bring us out to meet you.'

'But you decided to come before then?

'Yes. I wanted us to meet without her.'

'She's not here. She's in Old Ted's cottage.'

'She's not changed.'

'Your parents?'

'They've passed away. It's just Crispin and me now. I was married for a while, a good man, but we separated, now divorced.'

'I'm sorry to hear about that. Cathy and I, we were close, and then someone kills her for probably the same reason they attempted to kill Crispin. Sergeant Yarwood, where are you on the investigation?'

'We've no weapon, no one outside of your family who could be responsible.'

'We're a feuding family, but I don't believe any of us would contemplate murder. The family bond is too strong. We'll cheat each other, argue like crazy, but to kill someone, that's something else.'

'That's as maybe, but someone's responsible, but until we find that person, then others could die. Mrs Goode, Crispin, you're both possible targets, even more so than before.'

'I'm not involved,' Rose said. 'I have no claim on the house and the farm, but Crispin does.'

Clare could see there was to be no drama. She left the three and moved away to the front of the house and called Tremayne.

'There's been a lead on the pellets,' Tremayne said.

'What is it?'

'They're a Crosman Premier Pointed .22 pellet.'

'We knew that before. What does it mean?'

'It means you can't buy them locally. There's a name for someone in the village who has purchased them recently. Probably not the only one there with an air rifle, but we'll question him. I'll be there in twenty-five minutes. Is it safe to leave Gordon Selwood with his new-found family?'

'As long as they stay at the house.'

'Okay, twenty-five minutes. I'm bringing some uniforms.'

***

Clare returned indoors. The three were sitting around the kitchen table. 'I've got to go,' Clare said.

'I'll make sure Rose and Crispin get home safely,' Gordon said. 'Cathy?'

'They'll release her body in a few days.'

'Can we go in the Jaguar?' Crispin asked.

'Of course.'

'We have a lead on who fired the air rifle at your father,' Clare said.

'Thanks for bringing Rose and Crispin out here.'

'It wasn't my idea. It was Rose's.'

Outside, Tremayne beeped the horn on his vehicle. Clare walked out of the house and over to Tremayne's car. 'Follow me,' he said.

A two-minute drive and Tremayne stopped outside the church.

'Why here?' Clare said.

'Your vicar has bought pellets in the last few weeks. We can't find anyone else, and it's not conclusive.'

'A man of the cloth?'

'Why not? It wouldn't be the first time a vicar has been guilty of a crime.'

Tremayne knocked on the door of the rectory; it slowly opened. 'DI Tremayne, Sergeant Yarwood, please come in.'

'We're here officially,' Tremayne said.

'What can I do to help?'

'You own an air rifle?'

'Yes, I do. I fire at targets in the field at the back.'

'It hardly seems to be something a man of the cloth would be interested in.'

'Why not? I'm not a monk. I'm allowed to do whatever I like as long as I don't break the law or offend my God.'

'Can we see the rifle?'

'It's locked up in the hall cupboard. I'll fetch it if you want. What's this all about?'

'You purchased some pellets: Crosman Premium Pointed .22.'

'That's correct. They're nothing special. You can buy them anywhere.'

'Not in Salisbury, you can't.'

I buy them online.'

The vicar opened the hall cupboard, Tremayne standing alongside. 'A few weapons in there,' he said.

'I don't use them very much, but I used to be keen once. I belonged to a club at my previous parish, but not here in Coombe.'

'Leave them there,' Tremayne said. He turned to Clare. 'Phone Jim Hughes, tell him to get a couple of his CSI's over here in the next forty minutes.'

'What is this? Are you accusing me of murder?'

'Not murder, but the pellets you bought give us concern.'

'They're on their way,' Clare said. She looked at the vicar, could see the man wasn't comfortable with the situation. She hoped Tremayne knew what he was doing.

'Can we sit down?' Tremayne said.

'In the kitchen,' a curt reply.

Once in the kitchen, Tremayne continued. 'We know you had issues with Claude Selwood and that the man was interventionist.'

'I've already told you this before. He wanted to tell me what to preach.'

'And you argued with him?'

'Argued? It was more of a discussion.'

'I put it to you that you were upset with his intervention and you decided to teach him a lesson. I'm not accusing you of murder, but of aggravated assault with a deadly weapon. They'll also be another charge for shooting the horse. Vicar, how do you plead? Are you guilty? If one of those air rifles matches up with the pellets removed from Claude Selwood and the horse, then it's a custodial sentence.'

'Okay, I did it. I knew the man's routine, and his interference was annoying me.'

Tremayne was surprised that it been so easy. It had been a hunch, and it had paid off. The vicar was led out of the rectory by two uniforms. He would be further interviewed at the police station.

'He's not the murderer,' Tremayne said.

'Rose and Crispin Goode are only going to cause complications.'

'Complications lead to mistakes, mistakes lead to convictions.'

'We better go and check out the house, see if they're still friends.'

'You're looking for a happy ending. That's not how it works,' Tremayne said.

Chapter 14

The publican in Coombe was pleased to see Tremayne and Clare. 'My first customers of the night,' he said. Clare looked at her watch; it was after seven in the evening.

'Business slow?' Tremayne said.

'About average. It got a little busier when Old Ted and Gordon's wife died, local gossip, but after that, it's quietened down. I saw you over the road with the vicar. Any news there?'

'News or gossip?'

'One and the same,' the publican said. For a man going out of business, he still remained cheerful.

'The vicar is helping us with our inquiries, that's all.'

'In the back of a police car, not likely. Is he the murderer?'

'No. What do you know about him?'

'He came here about nine or ten years ago. He's popular in the village, not one of those fire-breathing, rot in hell types. He'd come in here, have a pint, as well as coaching the local football team, not that they're any good. I reckon a one-legged man could outtackle half of them, but they're keen, so's the vicar. Is he coming back?'

'Not tonight.'

'Any night?'

'You ask too many questions,' Tremayne said. 'What are you like on answers?'

'It depends.'

'Dr Fletcher, when he lived here, what sort of man was he?'

'That's before my time. They had gone before I got here.'

'I would have thought us taking the vicar away would have brought the gossips in.'

'Maybe later when you've given me something.'

'We're not here to keep you informed. We're here as police officers investigating a murder,' Tremayne said. 'What do you reckon? Who do you think could have killed two people?'

'Anyone of the Selwoods.'

'Marge Selwood said she wasn't a good shot.'

'Telescopic sights and it doesn't matter, does it?'

'Do you think she killed Old Ted and then her daughter-in-law?'

Tremayne chose not to answer the publican's question. There was a man of the cloth at Bemerton Road; he needed to be interviewed. He and Yarwood had one drink before heading back to the police station. Outside, a group of villagers were assembled. 'You've no right to arrest the vicar,' one of them said.

'And you are?'

'Molly Dempsey.'

'And why shouldn't we have arrested him?'

'If he was taking shots at Claude Selwood, he had every right. Mr Selwood, he was a bad man, always interfering in this village, wanting to tell us how to live our lives.'

'In what way?'

'There's a plan to build low-cost housing in the village. Mr Selwood, he was all for it, but none of us wanted it.'

'This is the first we've heard of it.'

'Why? His wife knew about it.'

'And how do you know what we've arrested the vicar for?'

'This is a small village. News travels.'

And nosey people are everywhere, Clare thought. It was apparent that their conversation with the vicar had been overheard.

'There are laws in this country. Are you suggesting we should ignore it and let the vicar go free?'

'Yes. Reverend Walston was supporting us against the Selwoods.'

'Are they all the same as the father?'

'Yes.'

Assembled before Tremayne and Yarwood, five women, one man, and all of them drawing their pensions. Clare realised that the people who stood between Tremayne and herself, although not in a menacing way, were the sort of people who would resist progress at any cost. In the past, the transition from horse-drawn to motorised, candlelight to electricity, the corner store to the supermarket, yet all had come, and the world had not stopped rotating on its axis.

Tremayne and Clare sidestepped the people and left the village. 'Funny bunch,' Tremayne said as they drove away.

'Small village, frightened of change. Hardly a reason to take pot shots at Claude Selwood.'

At the police station, they grabbed a quick bite to eat. Afterwards, the interview room and the vicar, his dog collar prominently displayed.

'Reverend Walston, you've been charged with aggravated assault with a deadly weapon.'

'An air rifle hardly constitutes a deadly weapon.'

'A debatable point of law,' Tremayne said. 'Regardless, shooting Claude Selwood is a criminal offence, which resulted in the man's death.'

'I didn't intend to kill him.'

'What about the horse?' Clare said.

'I meant no harm.'

'Then why? Didn't you realise that in time we would discover you?'

'I did what was necessary.'

Clare could see that Tremayne was frustrated. The Reverend Walston was meant to be an upholder of right over wrong in the village of Coombe, not someone who committed a criminal offence. And then, there were the villagers who felt his actions were justified.

'We were waylaid by Molly Dempsey,' Tremayne said.

'She is one of my flock.'

'Another person who believes you had a right to take shots at Selwood.'

'I was doing the Lord's work.'

'And when did the Lord agree with you breaking the law?'

'Claude Selwood had no right to control our lives. He had no right to tell me what to preach. No right to buy up property in the village or to build cheap housing.'

'Why? It's a free world. If he had the money and people were willing to sell, then what's wrong.'

'The local people disagreed with the new development.'

'We had never heard about it before. Are you sure it wasn't only the group we met? And besides, any new building would require planning permission.'

'They would give it.'

'Why?'

'Money talks.'

'Are you assuming there would be corruption? Coombe is stagnating, you know that. The pub's about to go out of business. You probably get very few people in your church.'

'I appreciate the old ways,' Walston said.

'But you're a young man,' Clare said.

'I've found peace in Coombe. I want it to stay that way.'

'We'll check, so you may as well tell us. What do you mean?'

'I was six. My father was a violent man, drunk most of the time. He came home one night, angry. He had a knife. He killed my mother, as well as trying to kill me. I ran out of the house. Don't go looking for him. He died in prison.'

'And after that?'

'I was brought up by my mother's sister. She lives in a village like this.'

'As sad as it may be, it doesn't excuse the fact that you became involved in violence.'

'I wasn't angry when I fired that rifle at Selwood. I just wanted him to stop what he was doing.'

'Claude Selwood was a stubborn man. How would he know it was a warning?'

'I would have told him it was a sign from God for his wickedness.'

'Was your aunt a religious woman?' Clare asked.

'Devout, three times on a Sunday to church.'

'Would she condone what you have done?'

'Sometimes it is necessary to do wickedness to ensure goodness.'

Clare had even considered going out with the man if he had asked, and now, she realised that the man's view of the world was distorted. As violent as his childhood had been, the horror of seeing his mother killed, he was still a criminal. Whether it was the actions of a sane man or not was for a psychiatrist to determine.

'We'll need a statement,' Tremayne said.

***

'What is it with these villages?' Tremayne said. He was standing outside with Clare. He was enjoying a cigarette; she was tolerating the smell.

'How is it, that on the occasions that we've spoken to the vicar, he has acted normally. None of his extremist views has surfaced, and then, there's a group of villagers condoning his behaviour?' Clare said.

'Maybe it's all that fresh air, somehow it affects the brain.'

'You're in the land of the fanciful now, guv.'

'I know, but we've come across these sorts of people before. Normal law-abiding citizens who for some reason commit illegal acts. And how can they believe it's lawful?'

'A sign from God.'

'Rubbish. If the Reverend Walston can shoot an air rifle, he could have also killed Old Ted and Cathy Selwood.'

'No reason. Old Ted and Cathy Selwood were not involved with the new development.'

'We need to talk to Molly Dempsey again,' Tremayne said.

***

An uneasy truce between Gordon Selwood and his mother existed. After Rose and Crispin Goode had visited the main house, and after Gordon had driven them home in the Jaguar, he visited his mother, told her that he had met his son.

His mother had reacted calmly to the news, told him that she had been wrong in separating him from Rose.

Marge had to admit that, on reflection, Rose had done an excellent job in bringing up her grandson.

The cottage suited her, that's what she said to her son. 'Such unpleasantness. What about you and Rose?'

'Don't try and make something out of it. Cathy's not yet buried, and Rose and I were only young. Crispin's my son. I'll do the right thing by him, that's all.'

'There's something else,' Marge said. She knew the bombshell she was about to announce. 'Before I met your father…' a pregnant pause, 'there was another man.'

'What are you trying to tell me?'

'I need to be sure.'

'Of what? Are you telling me this other man may be my father?'

'It's possible. I've never thought about it before, not even when we were disputing the farm and the house, but now…'

'What's changed? Are you so desperate that you conjure up another man?'

'I need to know. You now have a son. I need to know the truth, we both do.'

'No, I don't. Crispin's my son, I know that. As for you and your men, then that's up to you. I've no intention of agreeing to DNA testing. And, as for the future, the main house is off limits to you, as am I. They're releasing Cathy's body in the next day. The funeral will be next week. You're not welcome. I don't want your crocodile tears flooding the place.'

'There's no vicar. They've arrested Reverend Walston.'

'Did the man know my mother is a whore?'

'How dare you,' Marge Selwood said. She came forward and slapped her son hard across the face. Gordon stood back, not sure what to do. His mother had made an admission which he was unable to process. He turned around and walked out the back door of the cottage, almost pulling it off its hinges as he slammed it hard.

Marge Selwood sat down at the kitchen table, not sure what to do. It was the first time she had cried for some time. Her husband's death had given her sadness, but no tears. Old Ted's had left her ambivalent, and Cathy's had left her overjoyed, but with Gordon, her own flesh and blood, even if not Claude's, she felt sorrow.

After a few minutes, she sat up straight, took stock of herself and phoned Nicholas, her second eldest.

***

Molly Dempsey was not hard to find, even the publican knew where she lived, and the woman was strictly teetotal. Busybody was his description of her.

Outside of the village, a five minute walk, the cottage of Molly Dempsey. At the front, a small picket fence with a gate that creaked on its hinges as Tremayne opened it. A dog barked from inside.

'That's Berty, he's harmless,' Molly Dempsey said. Around her waist, an apron. 'I'm just baking a cake.'

'You were very vocal earlier after we arrested the vicar,' Tremayne said. He noticed that the dog, a small terrier, had taken a shine to Clare and was sitting on the floor alongside her. Both of the police officers had been given the mandatory cup of tea, along with freshly-baked scones.

'The Reverend Walston is a good man, just the sort of person this village needs.'

'He's broken the law.'

'Who else was going to put a stop to this nonsense? Claude Selwood was a wicked man who'd do anything for his own benefit, even destroy this village.'

'Mrs Dempsey, it's called progress. You can't stop it.'

'It's not the kind of progress we want. Ten years ago, you could leave the door to your house open, and no one would come in, but now…'

'Have you been burgled?'

'No, but it could happen.'

It was clear the woman was narrow in her understanding of the world. She and Old Ted would have had a lot in common, Clare thought.

'Walston was new to his parish,' Tremayne said. 'Why have you and your group embraced him?'

'He understands our needs. He is willing to stand up to the Selwoods and their wicked ways.'

'Wicked ways?'

'Gordon and his woman.'

'Which woman?'

'The one that died.'

'She was murdered. Why are you against her when most of the people that we've spoken to liked her. It was her that had convinced her husband to not sell the farm.'

'We know her type.'

'What do you mean? She'd only be here for a short time.'

'Another one after the Selwood fortune.'

'Another?'

'Rose Fletcher, we saw her here the other week. We'd know that shameless woman anywhere. That's all the Selwoods get involved with, cheap women.'

'Rose Fletcher is, in our opinion, a good person. Why do you criticise her?'

'She made sure that the eldest son made her pregnant.'

'And then what?'

'Her parents disappeared, paid off more likely.'

'Mrs Dempsey, I'm afraid you've got your facts wrong. Rose Fletcher was a young woman. She made a mistake, as did Gordon Selwood. And as for her parents, they left here of their own free will, the shame of what had happened was too much for them to stay.'

'That's what you think.'

Tremayne and Clare could see a woman, who regardless of proof, would continue to hold to her views. Her testimony was suspect but would be noted.

They left the cottage and walked back to the village. In the main street, they ran into Marge Selwood. 'What is the story about a low-cost housing development?' Tremayne asked.

'Claude had an idea to bring some life into the village. There's some land not far from here, and a couple of buildings on it. And it wasn't necessarily low-cost. The locals around here, or at least some of them, are suspicious of change. I can't blame them, though. I wasn't in agreement with Claude on any new development, but he was adamant.'

'We've arrested the vicar.'

'I've heard.'

'We always thought he was harmless,' Clare said.

'He and Claude used to have the occasional disagreement.'

'Serious?'

'Not really. Reverend Walston was an ardent socialist, Claude was for capitalism. With them two, it was the English Civil War, all over again. On one side, the Roundheads, on the other, the Royalists. It wasn't violent.'

'Would the reverend be capable of murder?' Tremayne said.

'If he can shoot at Claude and the horse with pellets, who knows?' Marge said. 'If you've no more questions, I've something to do.'

'No more for now. How's Gordon?'

'We're not talking. He's got Rose back in his life, and Cathy not even buried. What kind of man does that?'

'Romantically involved?'

'Not yet, but they will be. She was always the woman for him, and now my grandson is hanging around. Your sergeant brought the two of them out to the house.'

'Not out of pleasure,' Clare said. 'There are two murders and all of a sudden, two more members of the Selwood family appear. I needed to understand how they fit into the puzzle.'

'They don't fit, not yet, and hopefully never.'

'Do you dislike Rose?'

'Not personally. A silly mistake shouldn't blight anyone's life, and she was always pleasant to me. From what I know of Crispin, she's done a good job.'

'She has.'

Chapter 15

Nicholas Selwood arrived at his mother's cottage thirty minutes after she had left the two police officers. Inside the cottage, the two, mother and son, sat down to talk.

One was unsure as to why he was there; the other was nervous on account of what she was about to say.

'Nicholas, we need to deal with Gordon. He's met with Rose Fletcher. Do you remember her?'

'A long time ago. She was Gordon's girlfriend.'

'There's a complication. She had a child.'

'I know.'

'Did you know she was married to Gordon at the time?'

'She was only fifteen.'

'She was sixteen at the time of the birth. Her father was firm in that he wasn't going to have his daughter give birth to a bastard. We agreed, and they were married. After the birth, the marriage was dissolved.'

'That means the child is his heir, and if it's male…'

'It is. He's sixteen, nearly seventeen.'

'Have you met him?'

'I've met Rose recently. Her son is a typical Selwood. He's intelligent, and I like him.'

'What is the problem?'

'You will never inherit the farm and the house, and I want them back.'

'Are they important? You're comfortable here, and I'm making plenty of money.'

'Nicholas, you're a Selwood. Stand up for yourself, assert your right. If Rose is there advising Gordon, and then his son, we are lost.'

'Cathy's not yet buried. He's hardly likely to do anything now.'

'Not now, but in the future. Six months, one year, what does it matter? We're out, and they're in. Do you want that?'

'Not really, but what can we do?'

'We can prove that Gordon is not your father's son.'

'What do you mean?'

'Nicholas, there's something I've never told any of you, not even your father. I was involved with another man when I met your father.'

'Are you saying that Gordon may not be our father's son?'

'I was in love with your father. I was sure it was his, I always have, but now with Gordon the way he is, I have my doubts.'

'Does Gordon know about this?'

'Yes. I told him I wanted to conduct a test. He reacted badly.'

'What did you expect?'

'I didn't expect anything.'

Nicholas Selwood, a man devoted to his mother, wasn't sure of what to say. He had not expected to be told that his mother had another life before his father. He phoned William, asked him to come over. His mother sat quietly in one corner. The pedestal that her two sons had placed her on had been firmly broken, and all because of necessity. For all her children's lifetime, she had hidden her previous life from them, and now in one day, the past had resurrected itself, the memories of what she had done when she was penniless and with no support mechanism from her parents. She knew that if Gordon wasn't Claude's son, she could not say who was his real father. A reputation cherished and embellished, destroyed.

She had not expected Nicholas to remain so calm. She knew that William would have difficulty accepting the reality. She hoped both her sons would see the need to expose Gordon.

Marge recognised in Rose Goode a more significant threat than Cathy. Rose was pure and chaste, and she brought up a son, a son who should have been adopted, but hadn't been, and there he was, not less than eight miles away.

William arrived within twenty-five minutes. Marge made a pot of tea, three cups. Her voice was steady, but her hands were shaking, so much so that Nicholas had to pour.

'Mother, you'd better tell William the truth and no procrastinating.'

Marge put down her cup, and, while holding her youngest son's hand, she recounted the story she had told to Nicholas. At the end of the telling, William was in tears.

'Was it worth all this?' Nicholas asked his mother.

'I told you because I love you both.'

'Are we our father's children?' William asked. His face was ashen as he spoke.

'I made a mistake once. Claude Selwood is your father. I was a good wife to him, you know that.'

'What do you want us to do? Nicholas said.

'In time you'll forget what I have just told you.'

'We won't. But for now, we will do what is necessary.'

'I need a sample of saliva from either of you and a sample from Gordon.'

'Gordon will not comply,' William said.

'Then you must secure certain items from him without him knowing.'

'Such as?'

'Nail clippings, a toothbrush, a sample of hair, but it will need the follicle.'

'How about yours?' Nicholas asked.

'I'm the mother of all three of you. I will send a sample as well.'

'Is this strictly legal?'

'No. I will want one of you to consent to be yourself, the other to be Gordon. You can use your own name, but we will know which is which.

'And if he is our father's child.'

'Then he and his son will take the farm, and there will be nothing we can do.'

***

Cathy Selwood's funeral was held in the local church, the vicar from the next village officiating. In the congregation, the Selwood family, although Marge wasn't present. Also, Tremayne and Clare, as the two of them had known the woman.

Gordon Selwood was comforted by his brothers. Cathy Selwood had none of her family present. Nicholas and William made speeches on Gordon's behalf. Apart from that, it was a short ceremony, Cathy's coffin being taken to a plot in the graveyard not far from Claude Selwood. Up at Marge's cottage, the woman trained a pair of binoculars on the churchyard. She was looking for the presence of Rose Goode, but she could not see her. Inside the cottage, she took a bottle of gin from the cupboard and poured herself a glass. If no one was coming to see her, then she did not want to remember the day.

After the ceremony, those in the church moved to the farmhouse. The caterers had prepared a meal, and there was alcohol available. Tremayne helped himself to a beer; Clare, after listening to a few more speeches in praise of the dead woman, left and went out to the stables. She found Napoleon at the far end. He was pleased to see her. 'What you could tell us,' she said to the horse. The horse, sensing kindness, but not understanding what was said, just shook its head.

Another of the farm's employees came up to her. 'He's not been ridden for a while. How are you with horses?'

'I used to ride a lot when I was younger.'

'Great. I'll saddle him up. We've got some riding gear that should fit you. I'll take another horse.'

'I should be at the wake.'

'Napoleon, he's the one who's suffering. He liked Cathy a lot, as much as he seems to like you.'

'Very well. Let's go.'

Tremayne came out of the house after a few minutes to see his sergeant heading up the track on the back of Napoleon. Gordon Selwood came out soon after. 'That's good to see. Cathy was fond of the horse.'

Inside, a beer and some food awaited Tremayne. He knew that Yarwood would not just be riding, she'd be asking questions of her riding companion.

***

Crispin Goode was elated; his mother was not. She had made the decision to make herself known to Gordon Selwood, not out of an altruistic need, but because her son had almost been killed. For her, she would have preferred to have stayed hidden and for her son to have never known the truth.

Her becoming pregnant by Gordon had destroyed her family: her father had never regained his position in society, her mother had faded away with shame. It had been two that night behind the churchyard, yet she, the female, had been the one who had been pronounced as the guilty party, not Gordon.

Rose knew that it wasn't necessarily Gordon's fault. He was the result of a system that excused the wealthy, blamed the less fortunate, and she had loved him. First as a friend, then as a lover, and then briefly as a husband. She remembered back to the wedding, a ten-minute visit to a registry office; her parents and his in attendance. A brief shaking of hands across the families, and then, she and Gordon were man and wife. There was no honeymoon, no kiss on tying the knot. It had been clinical and without passion, and then the man that she loved, who loved her, was gone.

After that, a hidden location, the best of care, the endless hours waiting for her child to be born. The plan had been for it to be adopted, a family was already lined up, but then, when Crispin had been born, a beautiful little boy, she could not let him go, nor could her parents.

'Rose is mature enough. She can keep the child. If anyone asks, he's ours,' her father had said to her mother. And that was the way it was, until, at the age of nineteen, Rose had declared that she was leaving and she was taking her son with her.

It had been another five years before she saw her parents again, her father helping her financially during the difficult periods while she attempted to establish herself. The next time she saw her parents, her mother had aged dreadfully, her father was still upright. And then, while working in the administration office of a factory, in walked Derek Goode.

Her parents had attended their wedding, and for once her mother had appeared to be pleased, but behind the façade, the woman was ill, succumbing after another six months; her father was gone within two years.

It was just Rose and Crispin, and Derek Goode. It had never been her intention to return to Salisbury, but Derek had accepted the transfer, and that was that.

There had been times when she had been tempted to drive the short distance to Coombe, but she had resisted for years until she had seen Gordon that one day in a shop in Salisbury. It had been fourteen years, and he had changed.

Derek was no longer around; the marriage had reached its conclusion.

The first time that Rose had driven around Coombe, it had been a quick in and out; the second, she lingered, even walked down the main street, passed a couple of women who had been friends of her mother, and they had not recognised her. She had been unable to stay away from the funerals of Claude Selwood and Old Ted, maintaining a discreet distance.

At the time of the funeral of Cathy, Rose busied herself in the small garden at her house; her son, Crispin, busy with school work.

She was sure that the events at Coombe were not over, and Gordon wanted to spend time with his son, even if she, the mother, had some trepidation. Rose had been in the pub in Coombe on one occasion when Marge Selwood had sounded off about Cathy, her daughter-in-law. 'She was a whore, you know. One minute she's turning tricks, and the next, she's keeping me out of my house.'

Rose had smiled that day, hopeful that the upturned collar on her jacket, the blonde wig she had worn, and the years that had altered her appearance, would make her unrecognisable.

She had loved the woman's son back when Crispin had been born, but now she wasn't so sure. He had appeared worthless when they had recently met. Now, he had the money, and Crispin had been enamoured of the Jaguar, hopeful of a drive, optimistic that his father would buy him a car. Even now, Crispin had a new laptop in his backpack courtesy of Gordon. 'You two should get together again,' Crispin had said to his mother.

Even in that short encounter with his father, Rose could see that her son, always so sensible, had picked up some of the bad habits of the father.

Chapter 16

Clare could see that Napoleon wasn't an easy horse to ride. Even though the horse was friendly towards her, he still reacted when she first mounted him.

'Show him who's in charge,' Callum, the farmhand, who had chosen a smaller and calmer horse, said.

'That's the problem, he is,' Clare said.

'Napoleon needs to burn off excess energy.'

Once they were away from the stables and heading up the track, Napoleon wanted to gallop. 'He's fast,' Clare said.

'Faster than most horses around here. Mr Selwood, the older one, bought him for that reason. Now there was a man who could control a horse, not that Napoleon liked him.

'Why was that?'

'Old Ted reckoned it was because the man mistreated the horse.'

'You don't agree?'

'Mr Selwood and Napoleon, they were alike. Both strong-willed, both attempting to exert control over the other. Napoleon, he's a smart animal. Mr Selwood could control him by willpower, mind over matter. Cathy, she showed the horse love, and the horse responded. With her, he wanted to please. No doubt, he'd be like that with you, but first, he needs to show you what he's capable of, not wanting you to forget.'

'He's doing a good job.'

At the top of the track, the two riders stopped to look over the view. 'It's beautiful up here,' Clare said.

'Too much death for me,' Callum said.

'What's your story?'

'Not much to tell. I've worked here for the last few years. I'm a local, wasted my time at school. I need to be on the land, not in a stuffy office, and as for university and a career, that's for others.'

'Old Ted, what did you reckon to him?'

'He was fine. Not very sociable, but he taught me plenty. I've taken over his responsibilities.'

'He was shot up here.'

'It doesn't make any sense, not Old Ted. If he knew anything, he'd not talk.'

'Everyone seems to believe he knew something.'

'We're a good people for gossiping in Coombe. People talk to people, that's all.'

'But you're not so good at keeping quiet, are you, Callum?'

'I'll admit to it, but there's nothing I know that you don't know already. I mind my own business, the same as Old Ted.'

'It didn't stop him being murdered. How would you fancy a bullet in your head? Did you see the body? It's not a pretty sight, a man's body, its head with a bullet in it. Is that what you want?'

'Not me.'

'Then tell me the truth. What did Old Ted know that is important?'

'Mr Selwood used to meet someone up here.'

'Do you know who?'

'I saw them once. Old Ted was with me, although we were not visible, at least to Mr Selwood and the man he was talking to. It was early, he told me to tell no one.'

'Why would Old Ted do that?'

'That was the man. He didn't get involved. Whatever happened, happened for a reason as far as he was concerned. If Mr Selwood wanted to build three hundred houses up here and change the village forever, then that was his business, not Old Ted's.'

'We were always told it was to be a low-impact, low-cost housing development, down in the village.'

'That's what people believe.'

'And you've told no one.'

'I mind my own business, do my job, go home, get drunk occasionally.'

'Who did Claude Selwood meet?'

'Len Dowling.'

'The man who runs an estate agency in Salisbury, fancies himself as a property developer?'

'That's him.'

'You remember the death up at Old Sarum?'

'Sort of.'

'We met him there. We'll speak to him in due course, but why up here, and how did Dowling get here?'

'The area would have gone mad if it had known. You can walk up here from another direction if you want.'

Clare knew that if Len Dowling, a man that she and Tremayne had come across before, was involved, then it was, if not illegal, at least questionable.

***

Nicholas and William Selwood were in the main house at Cathy's wake, and, aware of their mother's revelation, walked around the house. Neither would admit as to the hurt they had felt when finding out about their mother's past life.

The deceit of their mother concerned them both, and they had debated the subject long and hard. Regardless of how the future would turn out, they had to secure the title to the farm and the house. William went upstairs into their parents' bedroom. On the bed, the undeniable evidence that Gordon and Cathy had been using it. In the wardrobe, Cathy's clothes, in the bathroom, her make-up and toiletries. William took a toothbrush, obviously recently used which could only mean it was Gordon's, and found some nail clippings in the sink. He put them into a bag, as well as some fallen hair, although, he realised, that without the follicles, they would probably be of no use. He opened the bin by the sink and discovered an old bandage from where Gordon had cut himself when he had been cleaning the inside of the Jaguar's engine bay.

Downstairs, Nicholas kept Gordon occupied. 'Rose Fletcher, you've seen her?'

'We're here to mourn Cathy,' Gordon replied. For once, he had smartened himself up, and he was wearing a suit, instead of the usual tee-shirt and a pair of jeans.

'It's a day for remembering. What about your son?'

'He looks like our father.'

Gordon, not wanting to confuse Cathy's day with talking about his first wife, even if only for a short time, walked outside of the house. He saw Tremayne, a cigarette in his mouth. 'I could do with one of those,' he said.

'I've not seen you smoking before.'

'That was Cathy. She was trying to get me fit, to give up my bad habits.'

'My sergeant liked her a lot. She seemed a good woman.'

'She was. She had a rough time when she was younger, but for some reason, she loved me.'

'According to Yarwood, Cathy said it was because you treated her well, never let the past impact on your relationship.'

'She was pregnant.'

'We know that, and now you have a son.'

'It's strange, isn't it? One door closes, another opens. Anyway, today's not the day to talk about Rose and Crispin.'

'You're right,' Tremayne said. He could see confusion beneath the man's countenance. It was understandable, Tremayne thought. Within a couple of weeks, Gordon Selwood had had to deal with his wife's death and then to be confronted by a former lover and their son.

Up above on the hill, Clare and Napoleon.

'Your sergeant knows how to ride a horse,' Gordon said.

'Yarwood, she keeps me in check. The horse doesn't stand a chance.'

'Cathy loved that horse. Your sergeant is welcome here anytime to ride him.'

'I'll let her know. It'll do her good. She's into animals.'

'And you?'

'Not even a goldfish. My wife had a dog once. I'd just about trained it to fetch my slippers when she left.'

'Nowadays?'

'The dog's long gone, and if I want my slippers, it's up to me to fetch them. My wife and I, we're still friends, and we get together every few weeks for a few days. Ideal relationship really.'

***

The name of Len Dowling had raised interest in the two police officers. They had suspected him in a previous case of a fraudulent rezoning of some land in Salisbury from industrial to residential. It had not been proven and was not the reason for a succession of murders.

However, Tremayne always remained suspicious as to the legality, knowing that Dowling was a man who pushed the envelope between right and wrong when it was to his financial benefit.

Ultimately, it had been found that Dowling had been entrepreneurial, having taken a risk, and then reaping the rewards.

Dowling's estate agency, the sign outside the door announcing that it was Salisbury's finest, had not changed since their last visit. The man was initially surprised to see Tremayne and Clare inside his office, obsequious after that.

'Have you decided to sell your house, Tremayne? How about you, Sergeant Yarwood? I've got a buyer for your place. We could do a deal today.'

Neither of them liked the man, and his unusual relationship with his wife, the social climber Fiona, was hard to understand.

Yarwood and Clare followed Dowling through the agency to his office at the back, past the receptionist, the one that Dowling's wife had accused him of an affair with once before.

'We need to establish a motive as to why someone was firing pellets at Claude Selwood and his horse,' Tremayne said.

'How would I know?'

'We've been told about a plan to build some low-cost housing in the village of Coombe.'

'Yes, that's true.'

'And then we are told that it's to be more extensive and it will no longer be low-cost, more likely upmarket residential.'

'Both are correct.'

'We've since been told that there is a plan to build three hundred houses on Coombe farm.'

'They're all true,' Dowling said. The man sat smugly, his arms folded in front of him. Clare knew why they did not like him, the fact that he could pretend to be the great man when it was his wife who was the driving force. As long as he could put on the big front, the man was content, even willing to accept his wife's affairs.

'What do you mean?' Tremayne said.

'Planning permission is difficult these days. Either the building is listed, or there's a committee opposing progress. Sometimes, it's environmental or whatever. It's a quagmire.'

'You've not explained what you mean.'

'Okay. You apply for all three or one at a time depending on the circumstances, knowing full well there are bound to be objections. As one of the objections fall away, then you bring back or submit another planning application. It's a game. A game I'm more than capable of winning, although it's costly and time-consuming.'

'What are your chances of success?'

'With Claude Selwood at Coombe Farm, it was possible. Now, I don't know.'

'Does it concern you?'

'His death or the deals?'

'Both.'

'Selwood wasn't an easy man, and as for the deals, I'm not willing to let them go, but they're not the only ones. Maybe in time I'll come back to Coombe.'

'Which deal did you prefer, or is that obvious?' Clare said.

'The three hundred houses.'

'Whereabouts in Coombe?'

'Where he died.'

'And you'd met him there?'

'On a few occasions. It was always best to avoid the eagle-eyes of the locals, and his wife was none too friendly.'

'Did anyone else know?'

'We never announced it officially. The plan was to deal with the smaller developments, break through the red tape, the restrictions, set the precedence, and then put forward what we wanted at the last moment, knowing that legally they'd not be able to refuse.'

'Devious,' Tremayne said.

'I'll dispute you on that,' Dowling said. 'It's good business practice. We're probing the weak spots, waiting for the chance to go in for the big kill. If it had gone through, Selwood would have made a fortune.'

'How's your wife?' Clare asked. They needed the man disarmed, on the backfoot. They needed him to think about something else.

'We're fine. Fiona's out with her friends, I'm in here running the business.'

'Are you still involved with the woman outside in the front office?'

'I thought you were here to discuss Selwood.'

Tremayne ignored Dowling's rebuke. 'Who else in the village would have known about your ultimate plan?'

'The application for the low-cost housing is with the council for approval. Apart from that, we've not submitted the others, although the plans are drawn up.'

'Who drew up the plans?'

'A firm we use in Salisbury.'

'So the proposal for the three hundred houses is not totally secret.'

'Selwood's wife knew, although she wasn't pleased with it. As far as she was concerned, the Selwoods are the custodians of the land, and it was sacrosanct.'

'The low-cost housing?'

'She didn't like it, but she was willing to go along with it. It was in the village, and not on her land. According to Selwood, the farm was struggling to stay afloat.'

'That's not what we've been told,' Tremayne said.

'I'm not saying they couldn't pay the bills, but farming is fickle, one good year, and then a succession of bad. Claude Selwood was more than willing to diversify, and the land up at the top of the hill was ideal for what we wanted. We had plans to expand it later on.'

'Would knowledge of this have been enough to raise the anger of the people in the community?'

'You've been there. What do you think?'

'I'd say yes, but killing someone is excessive.'

'Selwood wasn't murdered, it was an accident. I read that in the local paper.'

'His death was accidental, and we have someone in custody for taking shots at Selwood.'

'The local vicar, Walston. What a fool,' Dowling said.

'You knew him?'

'Selwood felt that the vicar should be told. I don't know why, as the men did not appear to like each other.'

'If the vicar knew, then so did some of the locals. Walston was a talker, no doubt he would have informed others.'

'Regardless, we meet, all three of us. I make a speech, so does Selwood.'

'What did the Reverend Walston do?'

'He sat there and listened to us.'

'When you'd finished?'

'Walston was upset, more than you'd think.'

'Walston would have told the church committee.'

'Molly Dempsey, the local busybody.'

'She's hardly likely to be a murderer,' Tremayne said. 'It's Old Ted that concerns us. What else are you not telling us, Mr Dowling?'

'Not a lot. There are always further development plans. Land rezoned for housing is at a premium in the area, and we could have kept the price reasonable. There would have been no difficulties in selling the plots of land, and then, there's the deal with the building companies. Some people have lived in Coombe for generations, and change comes slowly to them.'

***

Marge Selwood, still embittered by her eldest son's treatment, took all that her two youngest sons had collected, along with her DNA samples, and that of Nicholas and placed them in the bag supplied by the laboratory. She then got William to falsify his name on Gordon's samples. Once done, she closed the bag and posted it. There was a degree of illegality with what she was doing, the reason she posted it to an address overseas.

If the result came back in the affirmative in that Gordon wasn't Claude's son, then she would apply for a court order to force Gordon to allow another check to be conducted with an English laboratory.

Marge wasn't sure of the outcome, only hopeful. It was unfortunate that both Nicholas and William were barely talking to her, but, in time, they would understand; she knew they would.

Life was not about regrets, only opportunities. She had made mistakes when she had been younger, so had Cathy. No doubt Nicholas and William would.

Chapter 17

'It's the best motive we've got,' Clare said, as she and Tremayne sat in the office at Bemerton Road. Outside the weather had taken a turn for the worse, torrential rain instead of the usual drizzle, and Tremayne was standing near to a heater.

'What do you reckon, Yarwood?'

'There are the developments in the village and up at the farm. That opens the possible murderer up to being anyone in the village, even the wider community. If the development at the top of the track is as big as Dowling says, then it would need some big investors.'

'Failing any additional information, let's focus on who we know.'

'Financially, whoever owns Coombe farm would benefit from the larger development. It's hard to see a reason to kill people just to lose money.'

'Villagers?'

'They may well be opposed, but those we've met don't seem to be capable of murder. It's one thing to sound off in the village, even to make a representation at a council meeting, but killing requires a different mindset, and both deaths had been premeditated.'

'Old Ted's would have been, as someone would have had to go up the track well in advance.' Tremayne said. 'I can't see Dowling as the murderer. We know this man from before. His wife was having an affair, and he did nothing. He sounds tough, but he's ineffectual. Discount him for the moment.'

'Agreed. If it were his wife, she'd be capable.'

'The lovely Fiona. You're right, she could do it, and if Old Ted had seen her husband and Selwood up the top of the hill, knew something, she'd do anything to prevent the deal being scuppered.'

'The other farmhand that I went horse riding with. He knew about the men meeting.'

'Which makes him a possible victim.'

'Or a possible murderer.'

'What about the Selwoods? Who in that family would not want the deal to go forward?'

'Marge probably.'

'We need to talk to your farmhand,' Tremayne said. 'I hope you've got an umbrella.'

***

Molly Dempsey held court in her cottage on the outskirts of the village. She was a small woman, not up to the shoulder of most of the people in the living room. In front of the six assembled, a spread of sandwiches, cake, and tea – a knitting circle it was not.

'I'm afraid I've not handled the police as well as I should have,' Molly said.

'Why?' another of the group asked.

'They've been here, asking all sorts of questions. We should not have defended the vicar the way we did.'

'But he was only doing good. Freeing us from the enslaver.'

'Claude Selwood was an evil man. He deserved to die. We couldn't let him destroy our village.'

'It was only meant to scare the man.'

'How were we to know that the horse would kill the man.'

'I prayed for it.'

'So did I.'

'The vicar, he's not mentioned our part in this.'

'He's a good man. A man to be trusted,' Molly said.

The Coombe Action Committee was in session. The item for discussion: the Selwood family and their attempts to destroy the tranquillity, the harmony, the peace of the village. The death of Claude Selwood, accidental as it had been, had been opportune. The languishing in jail of the Reverend Walston was unfortunate.

'But why Old Ted?' a man in his late-seventies said. He was the only male in the room, a situation that did not concern him.

'It wasn't us,' Molly said.

It was a group of people who should be retired, enjoying their time without the demands of a nine to five job, not a group of people discussing anarchy, breaking the law if needed to protect the life they had always known. Molly Dempsey had been born in the village, remembered a time before television, the internet. She even remembered the first time a telephone, black and plastic, had come into her home. It had seemed like fun then, the ability to phone her friends, even though they were no more than a bike ride away. Back then, she would ride into Salisbury at the weekend, but now the road to Salisbury was full of trucks and cars moving at speeds unknown before. Her father had had an old Austin Seven. The family had loved the car, even though it could barely make it up a steep hill.

Now everyone had a powerful car, and she had seen Gordon Selwood with his Jaguar in the village. Molly remembered the young Gordon, slim and attractive, but now he was verging on fat and slovenly. He had been a polite young man, and his mother, a decent woman, even if she could be overbearing. As for the father, Claude; he rarely deemed it appropriate to talk to the proletariat. 'Up himself, that one,' Molly's father had said, although she had not understood at the time, other than to know it was derogatory.

She had married in the local church, given birth to two children, one, a son, the other, a daughter, but they were both married and elsewhere.

The Action Committee had come about when Claude Selwood and Len Dowling had started buying up old properties in the village. The initial rejection of their planning application had caused the two of them to make a presentation in the church hall, outlining the benefits to the community, downplaying the negatives.

There had been some who had been swayed by the elegance of the two men's arguments, especially that of the young Dowling. She remembered that he had a smooth tongue, but he preached progress and change and new people into the community. And one thing Molly Dempsey did not want was change. The Action Committee had formed that night; a collection of locals who agreed with her.

Every time another of Selwood and Dowling's applications for Coombe was up for discussion with the Salisbury City Council, the committee would make representations opposing it. Not that it had achieved much, Molly knew that. The development in the village had been approved, but Claude Selwood was dead, although Len Dowling was not.

'What are we going to do?' Molly said to her committee.

'We wait and see. If Dowling approaches Gordon Selwood, then we will reconsider.'

Molly Dempsey knew she would be prepared.

***

After Cathy Selwood's funeral, there was a lull in the village of Coombe. It was as if everyone was taking a breather for the main event. Clare thought that Tremayne was cynical in his belief that something was stirring; not that it stopped her taking the first Sunday off in weeks. It was a chance to catch up on some reading, some sleep, and to clean her cottage. Her mother was coming down, and she was always critical. Not that she didn't love her mother, but sometimes they did not see eye-to-eye. The last visit to the cottage had resulted in her mother leaving in a hurry. Clare did not want a repeat.

Tremayne had Jean, his former wife, down for the weekend; his wife regretting the years apart, but Tremayne knew that back then she had wanted him at home more often, and he had wanted her to be more understanding. It was easy to reflect back when they had both mellowed, but Jean had had a tendency to go off on a tangent occasionally; he had a tendency to slam the door on his way out. 'I'm never coming back,' he would say.

But now, they were just happy to sit together and watch the television or even go down the pub. Jean even attempted to be interested in his attempts to pick the winning horse, although it irked Tremayne that she'd pick the prettiest, not the racing history of the assembled horses.

It irked him more when she won more races than he did. They were a good pair, he knew that, and although she had married another, and had since been widowed, he had not found anyone else to equal her.

The next get-together with Jean, he was going to stay with her eldest son and his family. He had met them already, got on well. He knew it would be fine. He and Jean had discussed remarrying, and the idea appealed. They thought in the next couple of months when the weather was better, a honeymoon in Cornwall, maybe the hotel they went to after their first wedding.

In another part of Salisbury, Len Dowling was giving Gordon Selwood an update on his plans for Coombe. 'Your father, he was all for it. We build some houses down in the village, good quality, make us plenty of money. After that, we'd use those as the precedence for the other development on your land.'

'My father kept quiet about it.'

'Your mother knew.'

'She keeps a lot to herself. Have you taken her into your confidence?'

'Your father said to be careful. It was your mother who was the stronger. Are you?'

'I can be,' Gordon said.

Len Dowling looked across at the man. He did not see the strength that he had seen in the father, and nowhere as near that of the mother's. 'Great. Then we go ahead with the one development, demolish the first building in one week's time.'

'How long to complete?'

'You've seen the plans. I'm pushing for the first building to be erected within four months. We'll make that an exhibition home. After that, we can sell the other as a house and land package.'

'And the villagers?'

'What do we care about them. We've got planning permission. It's up to us.'

'Very well. I'll sign the documents.'

Len Dowling pushed the papers across the table that would transfer the name from Claude to Gordon. Dowling sat back, knowing that Claude's death had only been a minor encumbrance.

The two men concluded the arrangement with a bottle of champagne.

'Dowling, you're a rogue, I know that.'

'Maybe, but fortune favours the brave, and tonight, you've been brave.'

'I hope so. My father probably died because of this, Old Ted as well. Did you kill my father?'

'Your father's death was an accident.'

'An accident because Walston was trying to scare him from dealing with you.'

'That's possible.'

'And Old Ted, he knew what was going on, didn't he?'

'He had overheard us once.'

'Did my father know?'

'He did. Old Ted didn't say much, but he was still smart enough to know what we were up to.'

'What are we up to, really? Are we doing this for the benefit of Coombe?'

'Don't be naïve. It's all to do with money, lots of it. Doesn't that excite you, Selwood? The chance to make your mark, out of the shadow of your father, away from your mother's apron strings.'

'You've a foul mouth, Dowling.'

'That's why we'll make a good team. I know you for what you are, the spoilt son of a wealthy family. Me, the son of a nobody.'

Chapter 18

The first time a bulldozer started the demolition work at Len Dowling and Gordon Selwood's development project in Coombe, there was a sit-down demonstration by the Coombe Action Committee.

Tremayne and Clare were not informed as it was a local matter. In the end, a team of uniforms came and lifted the protesters from their seated positions and moved them to one side.

Len Dowling and Gordon Selwood could see a halt to the day's operation; Gordon keeping his distance, Len down at the site.

After the situation had calmed, Dowling drove up to see Selwood. On the way, he saw Marge Selwood walking up the street. He stopped his car and wound down the window. 'Can I give you a lift?'

'I see you've started. There'll be trouble.'

'We have permission. If they want to protest, that's their right, but the police will intervene.'

'They'll be a nuisance.'

'For a few days. It's factored into the development's cost.'

'And Gordon? Is he with you on this?'

'Yes. How about you?'

'It's nothing to do with me now.'

'I wouldn't know. Gordon's the signatory for the Selwood family, the same as Claude was. If you're not involved, then there's not much I can do for you.'

'And if I was?'

'We'd make a deal. Claude wanted to diversify.'

'We would have come to an arrangement.'

Dowling had to admit the mother was smarter than the son and she would drive a harder bargain. If she regained authority – he knew she would try – then he would convince her of the worth of the housing development at the top of the hill. The costing showed that a fifty-fifty division would nett each party ten million pounds.

'Don't mention our conversation to Gordon,' Marge said as she walked away.

***

The Coombe Action Committee met again. The bulldozing of the first of the houses had been completed, the second was in progress. Molly Dempsey, the stalwart of the committee, a woman who remained passionate for the village of Coombe, even though her advancing years meant she would not see it for much longer, knew that passive resistance would not work. A visit into Salisbury, a last-minute attempt at an injunction to halt the degradation of the village, had come to nought.

'We need to continue to resist,' Molly said to the committee. It surprised her that she had the energy and the drive. Until Dowling had shown up in the village and had convinced Claude Selwood to go in with him, she had spent her days baking or tending to her garden. She enjoyed the thrill of what she was doing; she knew the others on the committee did as well, but none as much as she did. She opened the window of her cottage. In the not so far distance, the sound of demolition. 'Listen to that. There was a time when the only sound was a bird. This is our present and our future, and what will happen when they build on Coombe Farm? I want to spend my remaining days in peace and serenity, not bombarded by noise.'

***

Gordon Selwood walked around the two houses being built in the village. He could see others at work, as well as the curious onlookers.

'You're meant to wear a hard hat,' one of the construction team shouted. Gordon had studied the plans, seen the costs for the project, understood there was an element of risk. Dowling had schooled him well in the benefits to them both, benefits that he was willing to accept. Cathy had been the person who would have taken control of the farm; he was confident that she would approve of what he was doing. He knew that he missed her, and whereas Rose was back in his life, the bond between the two of them was no longer there. Cathy was fun, even if her past had been turbulent; Rose was dependable, but she was a woman who looked and acted as if she were a lot older.

'You'll not get away with this,' Molly Dempsey shouted from the other side of the barrier.

'Mrs Dempsey, it's progress,' Gordon said.

'It's vandalisation. You're only interested in money, the same as your father.'

'I'm sorry you feel that way, but we have the necessary permissions.'

'And who did you pay?'

'Nobody. The village is dying, you know that. What we are doing is to revitalise it.'

'Rubbish. Dowling and your father used that one on us before, in that somehow you're doing it for the community, not to line your pockets.'

'There is no denial. We intend to make money. We benefit, the village benefits.'

'And after this, Coombe Farm?'

'We have further plans for the village. My father had agreed; I'm just carrying out his wishes.'

'Rubbish. Your father was a grub of a man. You, at least, were a good child, even used to help me carry my shopping home sometimes.'

'The child grows up.'

'And what about Rose Fletcher? I've seen her around here. The young man with her, is he yours?'

'It was a long time ago.'

'I know that. Two silly people who couldn't wait till they were married and look what it got you, got her.'

'Rose has turned out fine, so has her son.'

'She's had it tough, the daughter of a doctor. Her parents were good people, destroyed by the Selwoods. How does it feel to know that you've become what your father was, your mother is, and I've heard she's living in Old Ted's cottage?'

'Mrs Dempsey, you appear to know too much about my family. I suggest you mind your own business.'

'The village is my business, so is your farm if you intend to destroy this village.'

'The law is on our side. I'll wish you goodbye, Mrs Dempsey,' Selwood said as he moved away and over to his car.

***

Tremayne and Clare were, not for the first time, uncertain on how to progress. The weapon that had been used to fire the shots that had killed Old Ted and Cathy Selwood had not been found. Forensics had not been able to offer any more ideas, other than the bullets were fired from the same rifle. Len Dowling's appearance in the affairs of the village brought in an uncertain element, both police officers knew that, but he wasn't a murderer.

'Dowling might know something,' Tremayne said.

'Clutching at straws, guv?'

'We've plenty of motives now, plenty of suspects. What are your thoughts, Yarwood?'

The two were sitting in Tremayne's office. For two days, they had not left the police station, an unusual occurrence in itself.

'Dowling's not involved in the Selwood family dispute.'

'We know that Reverend Walston took a shot at the father due to the man's interference in church matters, although it was probably to do with the developments planned.'

'Why is the mother so desperate to remove her son from the house?'

'She's a resolute woman. She kept Claude Selwood in check; no doubt she sees it as her duty to do the same to her son.'

'Cathy Selwood was in the way.'

'And she died for it. We've always regarded the mother as the most dangerous. Why is that?'

'Why is what?' Tremayne said.

'Why would a mother act in such a way with her son? What about motherly love?'

'She may see that she is showing love. To her, he's infirm, not physically, but emotionally, and Cathy was the disease, as is Rose now.'

'Is there a romance there?'

'It's premature, but they have a shared history. Maybe in time,' Clare said.

The two walked outside of the station. Tremayne to smoke a cigarette, Clare to maintain the conversation. 'Rose Goode always comes across as a good person. Is she?' Tremayne asked.

'I believe so.'

'But her son will inherit the farm and the house if Gordon dies. It must be a temptation.'

'She's never shown interest in it.'

'Her parents' lives were affected by the Selwoods. Resentment may run deep. She could have contacted Gordon at any time in the last few years, even before he met Cathy, even before she married Derek Goode, but she didn't.'

'Maybe we should ask her, but it doesn't help with the case, does it?'

'Why not? She reappeared after Claude Selwood died. Why not before?'

'She only contacted him after her son had been hit by that car.'

'No one's reported a hit and run, no one's seen the car.'

'But he was hit by a car.'

'Agreed, but what if it was just an accident, and Rose used it as an excuse to worm her way back into Selwood's life?'

***

Nicholas Selwood did not like Tremayne and Clare in his office in Salisbury. He wanted to tell them he was too busy, and they should make an appointment. He did not, realising that the two police officers would have considered his rebuff as obstructionist. 'What can I do for you,' he said.

He had to admit that he found the police sergeant very attractive. If it weren't for his current girlfriend, he would have asked her out, not sure if she would have accepted, even though she was the same age as him.

'We've always seen you out at the farm. We thought it was about time we came to your office in Salisbury,' Tremayne said.

'What can I do for you? I believe I've told you all I know.'

'That's true, but certain facts still concern us.'

'Such as?'

'The appearance of Rose and Crispin Goode. How much did you know about their history?'

'I was twelve when Gordon got into trouble with Rose. I can remember my parents being upset, but as to what Gordon had done, I didn't really understand.'

'You were twelve, approaching puberty,' Clare said.

'And interested in girls, although naïve.'

'It would be normal for boys of ten and twelve, your younger brother's age and yours, to be titillated.'

'We were. Gordon and Rose Fletcher. She was an attractive young woman, still is by all accounts.'

'She's only four years older than you, four years older than me.'

'I've not seen her yet. I've heard from my mother, though.'

'Gordon?'

'He's treated our mother abysmally.'

'Family loyalties aside, did she deserve it?'

'Mother? She should not have been so difficult with Cathy.'

'You liked Cathy?'

'Gordon was always a loser, but she was shaping him up. She had a lot of energy.'

'Your mother said some wicked things about her.'

'Even if it was true, she was married to Gordon. Cathy was a Selwood, the same as us.'

'It was true,' Tremayne said.

'I'm not judging someone by their past,' Nicholas said.

'It was important to your mother.'

'It's invariably those who marry into the family who become the most zealous to protect it. I don't know why. It never meant much to me.'

'And your mother wants it all back, and not with Gordon.'

'She was the driving force behind my father. Cathy was the driving force behind Gordon, and now she's gone, and there's Rose.'

'Any thoughts about that?'

'Coincidental, nothing more.'

Nicholas Selwood pretended to be busy, but Clare could see he wasn't, only tapping the keys on the laptop, pretending to look at the screen.

'Do you wish to speculate as to why Rose Fletcher would reappear now?'

'Not me. I'm not wedded to Coombe Farm, although Gordon inheriting instead of my mother makes no sense.'

'It's normal for the wife to inherit, in preference to the son.'

'The eldest son has always inherited. It's a family tradition, and my mother is all for tradition. But with Gordon, and then with Cathy, my mother was determined to make another decision.'

'Because of Cathy?'

'My mother recognised in Cathy a capable person, saw her as a threat.'

'Even after she defamed her in the village.'

'That's our mother. Cathy was a recent arrival in the Selwood family, we were not. The bloodline is all important to our mother. Gordon is tainted by the bad blood of some of our ancestors. William and I are not. Whatever happened, Gordon would have been well rewarded, and if he stayed with Cathy or did not, he'd not have to worry about somewhere to live.'

'Money?'

'Money enough for most people. There's no way the farm can support his extravagant lifestyle indefinitely.'

'So eventually he will be forced to sell the farm.'

'Not with Cathy alive, but now, who knows?'

'Gordon's there now, he's got a son. Where does that place you? What will your mother do?'

'She'll challenge the will in the courts.'

'But why? If there's a will with Gordon as the inheritor, there's not much she can do about it, and what if Gordon dies? What then?'

'It will go to me.'

'Not if Gordon has a son. That's how it works, isn't it?'

'It depends if Gordon has a will.'

'And if he doesn't, then by default it's Gordon and Rose's son.'

'It would be disputed.'

'Cathy stood in the way of your mother; Crispin Goode stands in the way of you.'

'When you heard about the son, what did you think?'

'Not a lot. I've no need of the farm. All I want is what's owing to me.'

Chapter 19

Coombe Farm had remained virtually unchanged for centuries, and now there was a planning application with the council in Salisbury. Len Dowling was prepared for trouble.

The first that Tremayne and Clare heard of it was when they received a phone call from Rose Goode. Not that it was anything to do with her, as her renewed romance with Gordon Selwood had not occurred, not likely to either, she had confided to Clare.

For one thing, it was premature, and secondly, Rose wasn't sure that she wanted to become involved again, although Crispin did.

Clare met Rose in a restaurant in Salisbury. 'You've heard about Molly Dempsey?' Rose said.

'Her action committee?'

'That's it. They caused trouble when Gordon started knocking those houses down in the village.'

'That's Len Dowling, not Gordon. Do you know the man?'

'I've heard of him.'

'He's sharp, always looking for an angle. He's behind the application, and he doesn't care who's hurt or inconvenienced.'

'Gordon was harmless when he was younger, full of ambition, wanting to get away from the farm.'

'And now?'

'He's changed and not for the better. He moves slowly unless he's driving his car. And he's dulled. The young girl who fell in love with him is no longer the same, I suppose, but then I've had Crispin. He's kept me going, gave me focus. Gordon only had a farm and a family that he did not like, but now he seems committed to Coombe.'

'Would you go back and live there?'

'It's not what I wanted, but I probably will. The memories, even after so many years, are still raw. Each time I go into Gordon's house, I can see my parents, my mother in tears, my father attempting to stay strong, and there were Gordon's parents, the mother angry, and the father, almost wanting to pat the son on the back. And then, it's us who left the next morning.'

'Is the family house still in your name?'

'I've not been inside it for a long time, but yes. It's rented out.'

'You could always move back in,' Clare said. 'Is it a better house than where you're living?'

'Much better.'

'It seems better to swallow your pride and live back in Coombe, doesn't it?'

'I've given notice to the tenants, not sure why.'

'Maybe subconsciously you want to go back.'

'I don't think so, but who knows? I thought about it before Gordon reappeared with Cathy, and then it became too difficult. I'd seen him a few times at a distance over the years, and the memories always came flooding back. When we were children growing up together, and then as teenagers, there seemed to be a bond between us.'

'Is it still there?'

'I don't like what Gordon's become, but when I'm with him… It's hard to explain. Maybe it's fate, karma, I don't know.'

'You'll not find out by staying in Salisbury while you have a house in Coombe.'

'Crispin will like it. I only hope he's old enough to avoid picking up too many of Gordon's bad habits.'

'You've brought him up well. He should be okay.'

'I hope you're right.'

'While we're here,' Clare said. 'DI Tremayne and I don't believe the situation has resolved itself in the village. The deaths of Old Ted and Cathy are still unsolved.'

'Will you find whoever did it?'

'In time we will. Whoever is guilty will make a mistake, commit another murder.'

'Could it be Marge?'

'She certainly has the intelligence, the ruthlessness to do it, but Old Ted makes no sense, especially now the plan to convert part of the farm to residential is known.'

'Cathy?'

'She confused the situation.'

'It always comes back to Gordon's mother, doesn't it?' Rose said. Both of the women had finished their lunch and were preparing to leave.

'Logically, yes.'

'Which means it's probably not her.'

'What do you reckon, Rose? You're an independent observer, someone who knows the people and the village.'

'Marge would not have wanted Cathy to be there, and if she's in Old Ted's cottage, she's there under duress. She sees herself as the lady of the Manor, not as the dowager.'

'That's what she was with Cathy.'

'But not any more. Although, if I moved in with Gordon, she would be again.'

'Would you move in with him?'

'I'll do what's best for Crispin, but nothing's been said. For me, I'll need at least a few months.'

'The two younger brothers, capable of murder?'

'They were only young when I left. I wouldn't know.'

'Molly Dempsey?'

'Nothing to say really. I can remember she was always friendly, a gossip according to my mother.'

'She was critical of you and Gordon when you left.'

'A lot of people were. Do you suspect her of murder?'

'Not in itself. She knew about the vicar shooting at Gordon's father and his horse with a pellet gun. She saw it as necessary, carrying out God's work.'

'Some of them can be religious, but she's an old woman. What would be the point of her killing someone?'

'She's set up an action committee to oppose Gordon and Len Dowling.'

'To do what? Drink copious cups of tea and to complain.'

'They've had a sit-in at the new development.'

'I heard about it from Gordon. Supposedly, it never amounted to much.'

'Not in itself, and maybe that'll be the end of it. Now, they have a bigger threat to the village. Do you want it to change?'

'Why ask me? I left there seventeen years ago, and from what I know, a lot of the village sees me as the scarlet woman. No one showed much kindness back then for a young woman on the cusp of being an adult.'

'Different values in the past,' Clare said.

'It wasn't that long ago. No doubt they'll be polite to my face, and then remind everyone behind my back that I was the shameless woman who committed sacrilege on church land.'

'I thought it was behind the wall.'

'It was, but they'll embellish the story. And then those who have said some wicked things about me in the past will be aiming to suck up to me, hoping I can sway Gordon's mind.'

'Would you?'

'If Gordon wants to breathe life into the village, I'll support him.'

'It's Crispin's one day.'

'That's not the primary consideration.'

'It's a good reason to want Gordon dead.'

'Good enough, but he's important to Crispin, although I'm surprised he is. I'll not take my son away from his father.'

'And if their relationship sours?'

'We'll cross that bridge when we come to it.'

***

Tremayne kept his focus on Len Dowling. He still remembered the brash man's attitude from a previous case. If there were a significant land development planned for Coombe, the approval from the council for the rezoning of the land, and the subsequent construction of the houses, complete with their services, would not be readily granted. Apart from the usual requirement, such as the form submitted with payment, there'd be environmental impact studies, approval of the neighbours, possibly the village in total.

Tremayne met Councillor Freestone, an old friend, at the Pheasant Inn on Salt Lane in Salisbury.

'The building of three hundred houses at Coombe Farm could be a motive for murder,' Tremayne said. The two men, similar in many ways: one a police inspector, the other, an accountant.

'You're determined to pin something on Dowling.'

'I'm more interested in solving two murders, preventing any more.'

'Are there likely to be any?'

'Why not? Claude Selwood dies, as well as his farmhand and Selwood's daughter-in-law. And we didn't have any knowledge of what Selwood and Dowling were up to, but now, it's apparent that their plans are extensive. It's bound to cause more friction in Coombe. There's a local woman, Molly Dempsey. She's not likely to let any further development in Coombe continue unabated without putting up a fight.'

'She's an old woman.'

'You know her?'

'Whenever there are any applications before the council for Coombe: extension to a house, new garage, whatever, she'll be in front of us putting forward a case for it to be rejected.'

'Are her arguments substantive?'

'She's more rhetoric than substance. And anyway, she's an old woman, no more than a few more years left in her.'

'She's still capable of causing trouble.'

'Tremayne, you're barking up the wrong tree with her. The council's not likely to be favourable to a change in zoning just to accommodate Len Dowling. The man's still suspect after the hornet's nest you stirred up last time, accusing my fellow councillors and me of corruption.'

'Just doing my job.'

'I've seen the application for Coombe Farm,' Freestone said. 'I'll leave it up to others more skilled than me to decide on its merits, but it looks possible. It's a risk on their part though. Rural land is at a premium, residential is currently going through a downturn. The margins will be tight, although that'll not stop Dowling.'

'What do you mean?'

'The man pushes the envelope, takes the risk, minimises the financial damage.'

'Which means if it doesn't work out, it would be Gordon Selwood who'd take the loss.'

'Chris Dowling, Len's brother, is a solicitor. He'll be working the percentages, ensuring he and his brother are isolated through a trust, limited company, whatever is necessary.'

'And Gordon Selwood?'

'It's his land. If it doesn't work out, he's still got to deal with it.'

'Would it be easy to fool Selwood?' Tremayne said.

'The proposed development is expensive. People tend to get confused when big numbers, big profits are mentioned.'

'When does the application come up before the council for deliberation?'

'In two weeks' time. It will be the time for the public and those with a vested interest to put forward their cases for and against.'

'An opportunity for Molly Dempsey to say her piece?'

'She'll monopolise the proceedings if she can. She was so vocal the last time when the house demolitions in the village were approved that she had to be escorted off the council premises.'

'Anyone else gets so emotional?'

'Only her. Mind you, she's got a point. The developers would bulldoze everything down purely for profit.'

'But you allow them.'

'We're careful. You can't halt progress totally. Sometimes decisions need to be made, and as long as the strict guidelines are followed, then we have to approve.'

'Your personal view of the Coombe Farm application?' Tremayne asked.

'I don't have a problem with it, only with Dowling.'

'Why's that?'

'The man's a slimy toad. He doesn't care about anything other than himself and his wife.'

'Fiona. Any updates on her?'

'You're the police inspector. Why are you asking me?'

'You knew her better than me.'

'She's everywhere in the city ingratiating herself. She's a councillor now.'

'Will she be involved in approving her husband's application?'

'Not this one. She's probably going to be the mayor of Salisbury next year.'

'Not bad for a cheating wife, is it?'

'And possible murderer?'

'That's a closed case. The death was recorded as an accident.'

'Fiona and Len Dowling, two of the most unscrupulous people, yet they always come up smelling of roses. Why is that, Tremayne?'

'They've no conscience, and even after we had found out about her cheating on her husband, Fiona's out there giving speeches about the need of a loving marriage, advice to the forlorn from a woman who had erred. Not once did she consider that she'd done anything wrong, nor did her husband.'

Chapter 20

Rose Goode's return to the village of Coombe breathed life into the pub for a couple of nights, much to the delight of the publican. Even Molly Dempsey had entered the premises and ordered a small sherry.

The first anyone knew of Rose's impending return was when the lease wasn't renewed on the Goode's house. The family had been there for over five years and were well integrated into the community, and had not wanted to leave. They secured another place not far away from the previous one.

The second indication was when a removal van arrived at the house. The third was when Rose walked into the corner store and said hello. One or two of the villagers had seen her up at Coombe Farm, one or two could swear they had seen her in the village wearing a coat with a hat and scarf, but none had been given official notification from the woman herself.

'Mrs Golding, it's good to see you. You remember me, don't you?' Rose said to the lady behind the counter.

'Rose Fletcher, of course. You've not changed.'

'I've decided to come home.'

'Welcome back. You disappeared all of a sudden, the last time. We all wondered why.'

'I don't think it's a secret, do you? Not then, not now.'

'They said there was trouble.'

'I was pregnant, everyone knows that. And besides, my son is a great joy. Crispin's his name. You'll see him around the village soon enough.'

'Where is he now?'

'He's at the house helping us to move in.'

'And his father?' the woman asked. Rose knew her to be another gossip. She wasn't going to allow her the satisfaction of making up stories about her to bandy about.

'Gordon Selwood is his father, you know that. And just for the record, Gordon married me before the birth, divorced me after. Crispin is legitimate, I just wanted everyone to know.'

'Where were you all these years?'

'The last few in Salisbury.'

'I never saw you, and I go there regularly.'

'I know you do. I've seen you, and besides, I don't look the same as when I was fifteen. Nobody ever recognised me, not even Gordon.'

'His wife died tragically.'

'I never met her, but I'm told she was a good person. Popular in the village?'

'We all liked her, but Mrs Selwood, she used to say some wicked things about her.'

'I've not come to say anything derogatory about anyone. I just wanted to say hello, and to ensure that Crispin is welcomed into the community.'

'He will be,' the woman said. Rose looked at the woman, knew she had not changed. The woman had a loose tongue, and any innuendo, salacious or otherwise, she would be recounting it over the counter to whoever came in. Now, she had one fact that she could not use to her advantage: Crispin was legitimate.

Rose walked out of the little shop after purchasing a few items and walked back to the house. She had thought she would never re-enter the house again, but she had entered the main house at Coombe Farm, she would have no trouble with her parents' house.

Back at the house, Crispin was excited, although a little dismayed that his mother had kept the house a secret from him. He had always believed that his mother had been entirely open with him; that they were a team, and then, as a result of the car accident, he has a father, wealthy as well, and a family home, much better than the one in Salisbury. He was confused.

'We'll talk later,' Rose said. She knew her son had changed in the last few weeks, but then he was sixteen, a susceptible age, an age where a person needs stability, and their lives had not had that since the car accident and the deaths at Coombe Farm.

Rose hoped that Gordon would be able to help with Crispin and his transition into village life, but she did not have high hopes.

It was apparent in the village that Coombe Farm wasn't performing as well as it had in the past, and Gordon Selwood seemed to be more interested in frivolous pursuits, mainly cars. The Jaguar had gone, replaced by a Mercedes, and he could often be seen either cleaning it or standing back to admire. Those in the village knew that Claude Selwood would not have been worrying about a car; he'd have been out on Napoleon or in a Land Rover, checking on the farmhands and the livestock.

But with Gordon, there was no checking, other than the minimal. And the farm had an air of impending decay, not that it would have concerned Gordon, a man who definitely did not have his eye on the ball. Although Len Dowling did, and he was in his ear, even out at the farm and in the village now. No more sneaking around, no more meetings at the top of the hill, walking across cold and wet fields of an early morning.

'Where do you want this?' Crispin said as he held a vase that his mother liked.

'In the kitchen for now. We'll tidy the place up afterwards.'

Crispin had checked out his bedroom, better than the one he had had in Salisbury. Before anything else, he had made sure to put up a few posters of cars he liked. He'd checked out the internet connection; it was adequate.

Downstairs, the removal men completed their work and left.

'We'll need more furniture,' Crispin said as he came downstairs.

'It's certainly bigger than the other place,' Rose said. She missed the old house, small and homely, but assumed she would adjust, and Crispin was pleased to be in Coombe. He had seen Gordon's new Mercedes on the way into the village; she knew he'd be up there later in the day, although it was clear that Crispin's mannerisms were being affected by Gordon's influence.

Rose preferred that they weren't, but he was his father and a decent man.

Rose knew she did not love Gordon, probably would never again, but she was lonely, and he was available. In time, at least long enough to allow the memory of Cathy to fade, she thought she may see if the three of them could form a partnership, a father and a mother married, but it wasn't for now.

A knock on the door. 'Mrs Selwood, please come in,' Rose said.

'Hello, Mrs Selwood, or is it Granny?' Crispin said as he embraced the woman.

Rose had not felt the need for an overt display of affection, having remembered back to when she had been fifteen and pregnant.

'Granny, yes, I'd like that,' Marge Selwood said. 'I've brought you some flowers, a housewarming present.'

'Thank you,' Rose said. She wanted to tell the woman to get out of her parents' house, but could not. 'Please stay and have a cup of tea,' she said instead.

A lively conversation ensued between grandmother and grandson. It was genuine on Crispin's part, Rose knew that. The grandmother, Rose could never be sure about. She had known the woman since she had been a child, yet the woman remained an enigma. On the one hand, she could be obsequious, on the other, devilish and cruel.

Rose remembered the words she had used against her in the kitchen of the Selwoods house. Even her husband, Gordon's father, had tried to shut her up, to no avail.

As Marge Selwood sat there discussing Crispin's schooling, his interest in cars, his future, Rose could see a woman who had sworn profusely, called her a hussy, a tart, no more than a common street-walker, only fit for seducing.

Rose left the room and went outside on the pretence of checking that all was in order. Apart from a tile on the footpath the removal men had broken when they had dropped the metal leg of a chair on it, everything was fine. She was finding the situation awkward. For so long, it had been her and Crispin against the world, and even when Derek Goode had been in their lives, it had not changed. Probably the reason he left, she thought. She regretted the ending of that marriage. Derek Goode, an uncomplicated man, had not come with any baggage, and definitely not with a mother-in-law who could not be trusted. His mother had been pleasant and had never interfered, and even after the divorce, the two women had kept in contact.

Rose returned inside the house. 'Crispin's going to enjoy Coombe,' Marge Selwood said. 'You will as well.'

'It's been a long time. I'm not sure how I feel.'

'It'll be fine, Mum,' Crispin said. He came over and gave her a reassuring hug.

Marge Selwood left soon after. Outside of the house, Rose watched her walk down the street. She knew that Granny Selwood was not finished and she would yet cause more trouble.

***

With the end of the demolition work at the development site in the village, a hush came over Coombe. The heavy vehicles had ceased to belch out their toxic fumes, the noise of their engines was no longer heard.

Tremayne had noticed the ambience in the village as he stood with Clare outside the pub. 'I don't like it,' he said.

'What's not to like? The serenity is beautiful,' Clare said. She had grown to like the village, just the sort of place that appealed to her.

'Did you ever watch any of those horror movies, the village just like this, and then all of a sudden, a great evil comes over it?' Tremayne said.

'Sometimes when I was young. The movie where you're sitting calmly, the next where you jump up with a start.'

'That's what this feels like. Idyllic for the moment, deathly the next.'

'A fervent imagination, that's what you've got, guv,' Clare said. She understood what he meant, though. The projected development at Coombe Farm was still planned, three people had died, and Rose and Crispin Goode were back in the village. All the characters were in their place.

'Something's brewing, I can feel it.'

'You're right. What are we doing here?'

'Someone's ready to make a move. That farmhand you went riding up the hill with?'

'Callum.'

'What's he up to?'

'He's still up at Coombe Farm.'

'Okay, let's go. This place is giving me the creeps,' Tremayne said.

'Why? Can't you hear the birds chirping, the cows mooing in the distance.'

'That's the problem, I can. Give me noise and people arguing anytime. This place has the feel of death. It's hard to explain.'

'I can feel it too,' Clare admitted.

Up at the farm, Callum was cleaning out the stables, Napoleon in one corner. Clare took a carrot she had purchased in the village and gave it to him. 'He doesn't forget kind people,' Callum said.

'You've met Detective Inspector Tremayne?' Clare said.

'Not formally. What can I do for you?'

Tremayne could see a young man unaffected by the outside world. His demeanour was of a country yokel, his haircut severe and unfashionable. It was clear that Coombe was his part of the world.

'Just a chat,' Tremayne said. 'The village is quiet, as though everything is as it should be.'

'It is,' Callum replied.

'Has everyone forgotten about Old Ted?'

'Not forgotten, moved on. In Coombe, everything moves slowly, and Old Ted, he was an easy man to forget.'

'What do you mean?' Clare said.

'He was that sort of person. Born and bred in Coombe, but when you think back to him, what do you remember?'

'A man in his seventies, unable to retire, kept to himself, never spoke unless spoken to.'

'That's it. There's nothing left to remind us of him, and even his cottage doesn't look the same since Mrs Selwood moved in and fixed it up.'

'There was something,' Tremayne said. 'And whatever it was, he was murdered.'

Clare picked up a brush and started to brush Napoleon. Tremayne looked over at her, realised that she wanted him to go away. He took the hint and went outside of the stables, taking a cigarette from a packet at the same time.

Clare stopped giving attention to the horse and turned to the farmhand. 'Callum, you're not levelling with us. What's the truth about Old Ted?'

'I don't know what you mean. Old Ted minded his business, the same as I do.'

'And he was murdered for knowing nothing. Maybe you'll be shot for minding your own business as well. Have you considered that?'

'Old Mr Selwood, sometimes he used to play up.'

'What does that mean?'

'When he was younger, he used to mess around with another woman.'

'Who?'

'Old Ted, he didn't like to talk.'

'Then why was he telling you?'

'I caught him in here once talking to Napoleon. It was as if he wanted to tell someone, but couldn't bring himself to confront the people responsible.'

'What happened?'

'I was standing outside the stable, at the other end, and the door was slightly ajar. Old Ted's inside talking to the horse. The horse is not saying much, only standing there.'

'How long were you standing there for?'

'Five, maybe ten minutes.'

'And what did you hear?'

'Mr Selwood and Old Ted's wife. No one knew, not anyone in the village, and it was a long time ago.'

'How long?'

'When they were younger. Mrs Selwood, she was expecting Gordon, and Mr Selwood and Old Ted's wife, well, they sort of got together.'

'And Old Ted told you this?'

'Not really. I just overheard.'

'Did you mention it to Old Ted?'

'Not me. I was only new at the farm, and I knew I wouldn't be here for long if I said anything.'

'Did you know Old Ted's wife?'

'Oh, yes. She was a lovely woman, not like Old Ted. She liked to talk.'

'And never a hint from Old Ted and his wife as to what had gone on?'

'No. They always seemed a happy couple.'

'Why are you telling me?'

'I don't know. Maybe you're right in that he'd been killed for something he knew, something I know.'

'Does Mrs Selwood know about this?'

'I've no idea, and that's the honest truth. There's a lot that goes on in this village, but that's the only thing that seems important.'

'What else?'

'A few affairs, that sort of thing.'

'And Old Ted continued to work here for all those years.'

'That was Old Ted. He didn't like change, nor did he like unpleasantness. He's the same as me really. I don't want the houses at the top of the hill, no more than he did. But then, we're simple countrymen. I come to work, do my bit, and go home, the same as Old Ted. Maybe Mr Selwood had to sell the land up the top, I wouldn't know. I only know that Old Ted was against it.'

Clare attempted to take in what she had just been told. If Old Ted's wife had been having an affair while Marge was pregnant with Gordon, then the child would be younger, and not legitimate either, so there was no claim on the farm. And it was known that Old Ted and his wife had been childless. It had come as a shock to Clare, as the village spoke highly of the wife.

It was clear Old Ted had a reason to be angry with Claude Selwood, but had continued to work with the man for another thirty-three years, and after the death of Claude Selwood, there was no reason to kill Old Ted. The man had nothing new to add that would have changed Gordon inheriting the farm. Clare had to admit she was perplexed. She left Callum and walked over to the main house.

The back door was open, and inside Tremayne was sitting with Gordon Selwood, as well as Rose and Crispin.

'No school today?' Clare said.

'School holidays,' Crispin said.

'You should take Napoleon for a ride,' Gordon said. 'Your DI's fine here.'

'If you want,' Tremayne said.

'Not now. Tomorrow, maybe.'

Clare took a seat at the kitchen table. On one side, Gordon, on the other, Rose and Crispin. Tremayne was standing near to the kitchen sink. He sensed that Clare had something to tell him, but, for now, he was willing to stay in the kitchen and to observe the interaction between the parents and their son.

'Dad's taking me for a ride in the Mercedes,' Crispin said.

'DI Tremayne, do you want to come?' Gordon said.

'Fine, don't mind if I do,' Tremayne said. Clare could see the chance to talk to Rose.

After the three men left, Clare, knowing that Tremayne would not be interested in the car, sat down close to Rose. 'I'm surprised to see you here,' she said.

'So am I, but Crispin was anxious.'

'He could have come on his own.'

'I know, but I'm reluctant to let Crispin go. Gordon's trying, but he's not the best influence.'

'If Crispin had not been in that accident?'

'I'm not sure. I've wanted to come back several times over the years, but I've always resisted.'

'It's still difficult?'

'For me it is. I confronted the woman in the local shop, told her I was back with the legitimate son of Gordon Selwood.'

'A harsh move.'

'Pre-emptive. The gossips around here will have a field day as it is, and I didn't want their prejudices showing towards Crispin.'

'You'd do anything for him, wouldn't you?'

'You know I would.'

'Even kill?'

'What are you saying?'

'Generalising, that's all.'

'I've not killed anyone yet, but if Crispin were threatened, I would. The same as any mother, the same as anyone would do for the person they loved. You would, as well.'

'My fiancé gave his life for me. You've heard the story?'

'I know some of it.'

'It was my life or his, the choice was black and white. In the end, he did what was right, even condemned himself. That's love.'

'You must miss him.'

'I do, but if he had lived, I would have arrested him, and he'd be in jail for murder. Sometimes the choices in life are hard to make. And now, you're being forced to make some difficult ones. Will you make the right ones?'

'For Crispin, all choices are right.'

'Don't become too closely involved,' Clare said. 'The Selwood family have a history of inviting people in, only to throw them out when they are no longer wanted.'

'Is that a warning?'

Clare realised that she had probably overstepped the mark, but then, she had fallen for a man who had ultimately been proven to be bad, and now, Rose Goode was possibly heading down the same path.

'It's just advice. Someone in the Selwood family is a murderer. So far, Gordon appears to be the least likely, but situations change, more evidence is discovered, and the puzzle becomes clearer. I don't want you to be hurt, and I don't want you to be murdered or to be a murderer.'

'Do you think I could kill someone?'

'Yes. You've led a difficult life, a life that is as a result of this family. And Gordon's mother, she remembers. There's no turning the other cheek with her.' Clare realised then, that if Claude Selwood had been involved with Old Ted's wife, there was no way a person as devious as Marge Selwood would not have known.

'She's friendly at the present moment. Because of Crispin, I suppose.'

'She may not harm Crispin, but she'll harm you. If she gets a chance to isolate you from your son, she'll take it.'

'The bond between us is too strong.'

'She can still try.'

'I'll not let her.'

Tremayne returned with Gordon and Crispin. 'It was great,' Crispin said.

'How about you, guv?' Clare asked, knowing his thoughts.

'Great.'

Outside the house, Tremayne questioned Clare. 'What did you find out from the farmhand?'

'We'll talk on the drive back to Salisbury.'

'Significant?'

'Dynamite.'

Chapter 21

As Clare recounted the story that had been told to her by Callum, she could see the look of disbelief on Tremayne's face. The man who, after a lifetime of policing thought he had seen and heard it all, was unsure as to what to make of the revelation. So much so, that halfway back to Salisbury, he asked Clare to turn the car around and head back to Coombe.

'DI, Tremayne, what can I do for you?' Marge Selwood said as she opened the front door to her cottage. Clare looked at the woman, unsure of what she was seeing. Was the woman the devil incarnate, or was she the wronged mother of an ungrateful son? She wanted to believe the latter, although everything that had occurred so far in Coombe indicated the former.

'A few questions, if you don't mind,' Tremayne said.

The two police inspectors were ushered into the living room of the small cottage. Clare was impressed. It was the first time she had had a chance to admire the work that the tradesmen had done to transform the place. Her cottage had not had the benefit of skilled tradesmen, only herself and a paintbrush, as well as a local handyman on the occasions when he was needed. Clare could see the difference between amateur and professional in Marge Selwood's cottage.

'What do you want to know?'

Clare thought the woman to be in a genuinely good mood, realising that a cheerful Marge Selwood only meant that someone else was bound to suffer.

'The development planned at Coombe Farm?' Tremayne said. Clare could see her DI aiming to break down the woman's guard before bringing up the subject of Old Ted's wife.

'What about it?'

'You knew about it?'

'Claude was keen for it. He could only see the money.'

'And you?'

'I wasn't keen, but I would have gone along with it. We had sufficient land, and farming is fickle. A couple of years with a lower than average rainfall, and we'd be at the bank looking for assistance.'

'I thought the farm was viable,' Tremayne said.

'It is under normal circumstances. The situation has changed, not only for Coombe Farm but for everyone. It might be global warning, it might not. The only thing I know is that for the last nine to ten years, the weather has changed for the worse.'

'It's been warmer,' Clare said.

'That's the problem. Great for us, not so great for the crops.'

'Are you in approval of the current application for Coombe Farm?'

'I've not been consulted.'

'But if you had?'

'I would have considered it with Claude, not with Gordon.'

'Is there any reason?'

'Claude would have listened to me. I'd have made sure that Dowling did not get the upper hand.'

'And with Gordon?'

'Gordon is putty in the hands of an unscrupulous rogue. He may be my son, but he is a foolish man.'

'A foolish man who controls your destiny, as well as this village.'

'As you say.'

'And what are you going to do about this, Mrs Selwood?'

'I'm going to fight back.'

'If you do, your son could remove you from this cottage.'

'Let him try.'

'I thought the relationship between the two of you was stable.'

'It is, but I'm a fighter, Gordon's not. I want what is rightfully mine.'

'Even if you use illegal means to gain it?'

'There will be nothing illegal. And besides, you're making small talk. What are you here for, really?'

Clare felt she should broach the subject, as it had been told to her in the first place. 'Mrs Selwood, we have reason to believe that your husband had an affair around the time Gordon was born.'

'Scurrilous rumours, that's all.'

'You've heard the rumour before?'

'Not for a long time, but the gossips in the village, they make up anything.'

'Are you a gossip?' Tremayne said. 'You were bad-mouthing Cathy Selwood to anyone who could listen.'

'I only told the truth.'

'You embellish the truth. You continued to bring up the fact she had sold herself, a crime you've been guilty of.'

'Maybe I was a little harsh.'

'You recognised a threat in the woman, worldly-wise and smart, the same as you, not the same as Gordon. You defamed her to the village, and then you killed her.'

'I did not kill the woman. Okay, she was capable, but she reminded me of myself. A strong woman, a weak man. Claude accepted my past; Gordon accepted hers.'

'And her hold was getting stronger. Would she have approved of the development of Coombe Farm?'

'I doubt it.'

'Why?'

'Cathy had led a more troubled life than me. She wanted what the farm and the village offered. She would not have agreed to anything.'

'Nothing would have changed with her, and Dowling would not be around.'

'So, either she was killed because she would have objected to the developments, or because she stood between you and your control of Gordon.'

'Are you accusing me of murder?'

'Every time we evaluate the murder of Cathy, it comes back to you, and the development would have netted you and Claude a lot of money.'

'I wouldn't have had control with Gordon.'

'But now, there is no Cathy, and you don't have control over him. What about Rose and her son?'

'Rose is not a Cathy.'

'But Crispin is a Selwood,' Clare said.

'He has all the attributes of a Selwood. Gordon does not.'

'Yet again, Mrs Selwood, you back yourself into a corner. If Gordon's dead, then the property goes to Crispin.'

'Crispin will need guidance.'

'But it is Rose who controls the youth,' Tremayne said.

'I'm well aware of that.'

'Whatever you do, you must realise that your chances of being back at the main house and in control are slim.'

'I'm what Coombe Farm needs.'

'You're avoiding my question regarding your husband and another woman,' Clare said.

'I've always known. Do you want me to elaborate? It was a long time ago.'

'Yes. It's important,' Tremayne said.

'Very well. Claude was sleeping with Old Ted's wife. It wasn't a big deal to me.'

'You accepted this?'

'Claude had accepted me for what I'd been. I forgave his occasional indiscretions.'

'But she was the wife of an employee,' Clare said.

'She was a woman, he was a man. What's that got to do with it?'

'But why?'

'She was married to Old Ted. Even as a young man, he was slow. No doubt, not the world's greatest lover, and Old Ted's wife was an attractive woman back then. Anyway, the affair didn't last long.'

'And Old Ted?'

'You knew Old Ted. Not a man to make waves, was he? If he didn't like it, he never mentioned it.'

'We were always under the belief that the man was strange, but that takes the biscuit.'

'And Old Ted's wife?'

'The romance ended, and in time, she put on weight, and spent her days fussing around the village.'

'Gossiping?'

'Not her.'

'And your relationship with her afterwards?'

'She knew her place, I knew mine.'

'Did Claude have other affairs?'

'Not in Coombe.'

'And you?'

'Never. You'll find no more rumours in Coombe about us. There were only four people who knew about Old Ted's wife and Claude.'

'And three of them are dead.'

'Obviously, someone else knew. I would prefer if this is not discussed again. It's not part of your murder investigation, is it?' Marge Selwood said.

The woman confused the two police officers. At times, she could be magnanimous, agreeable, and above all, logical. Her explanation of her husband's affair had all the attributes of a forgiving woman, yet her treatment of Cathy Selwood had been venomous.

***

The construction of the two houses in the centre of the village continued unabated. Apart from Molly Dempsey being a nuisance, no one else was concerned. The villagers' day-to-day lives took precedence over the houses that attempted to look as though they belonged but did not.

After meeting with Marge Selwood, the two officers visited the pub.

'I've not seen you for a while,' the publican said as they entered.

Clare recognised the clichéd patter. They had been in twice in the last week, and this would be their third.

'A pint of beer, a glass of wine for Yarwood.'

'Coming up. How about a pork pie? My wife's speciality.'

'I'll take one,' Clare said.

'Make that two,' Tremayne said.

Tremayne and Clare settled themselves at a table in the corner of the bar.

'What do you reckon, Yarwood?'

'Old Ted wasn't ambitious, and, by all accounts, neither was his wife. Why, if from what we know of her, would she have an affair?'

'And why Claude Selwood? Old Ted never gained from it. He was the same person up until the day he died, and the cottage before Marge moved in was nothing special.'

'It is now.'

'It puts my place to shame.'

The publican came over with the pork pies. 'Take a seat,' Tremayne said.

'Five minutes, that's all I can give you?' the publican said.

'You've got your finger on the pulse in this village?'

'I suppose I do. What do you want to know?'

'Rumours, any current that is of interest?'

'I'm not into local gossip, just a bit of humour here and there.'

'You're a man who observes and keeps his ear pricked.'

'I'll not deny it. That's the function of a publican, apart from selling drinks and pork pies.'

'What's the reason for Old Ted's death? There are several possible motives for Cathy Selwood's death, none for his.'

'Why is hers easier?'

'Frayed family relationships, her taking over Coombe Farm.'

'Gordon Selwood controlled the farm.'

'You've met Gordon. What do you think?'

'Not a lot. The man goes with the flow.'

'As I said, Cathy took over Coombe Farm. She was going to make a decent job of it as well.'

'Marge Selwood was very vocal about her.'

'We know, but apart from her, anyone else talking about Cathy?'

'Dowling, he seemed to know something.'

'When, how?'

'He was in here a few days before she died. He wasn't talking to me, but, as you say, I hear things.'

'Who was he talking to?'

'A woman, same height as him, attractive, drove a Range Rover.'

'Did you get a name?'

'I assumed it was his wife.'

'Fiona?'

'I never heard a name mentioned. They were sitting at the bar talking. I didn't pay them much heed, but I've learnt to pick up conversations.'

'What did they say?' Clare said.

'Sorry, customer needs a pint. I'll be right back.'

Tremayne emptied his drink of beer and shouted over to the publican. 'Another one, and bring one for yourself.'

'Generous?' Clare said. She was keeping to one glass of wine.

The publican returned carrying two pints. 'Fiona, that was probably it. I'm surprised she's Dowling's wife. He's not much to look at.'

'They're a matched pair,' Tremayne said.

'What was said?' Clare asked.

'I only caught snippets.'

'What were they?'

'The woman said Cathy was standing in the way.'

'Is that all that was said?'

'Maybe not the whole conversation. I had customers to serve.'

'Any more?'

'No, that's about it. They had the one drink and left. I've not thought any more about it until you asked. Is it important?'

'Probably not,' Tremayne said. 'What you've just told us is confidential. I would appreciate if you don't mention it to anyone else.'

'Not me, and besides, it makes no sense to me.'

It did, however, to Tremayne and Clare.

Chapter 22

Tremayne and Clare, for once, were glad to be back at Bemerton Road Police Station. It wasn't often that either would have said that, but there was normality in that august building that the village of Coombe did not have.

The police station had rules and regulations, decent people, as well as a superintendent who was always after Tremayne's retirement. Out in Coombe, there had been three deaths: a vicar who regarded shooting at another man and his horse as acceptable behaviour, one of the landed gentry who saw that sleeping with his farmhand's wife wasn't inappropriate, and a woman who had forgiven her husband's indiscretion. And she had a history of selling herself in her youth, the same as her eldest son's wife.

Tremayne and Clare wondered what was coming next.

'If Cathy Selwood had objected to the farm being carved up, then the Dowlings are thrust to the forefront,' Tremayne said.

'Len Dowling was always a weak character.'

'His wife is not.'

'Is the money that the Dowlings would make, Gordon would make, sufficient to warrant murder?'

'We need to check, and what is it with these people? Don't they understand we will solve this?'

'It's their arrogance that allows them to believe we never will.'

'Fiona was acquitted for the accidental death of another person once before. Do you think…?'

'It's past history, guv. We need to focus on the present.'

'True, but Len, not much backbone in him, certainly not enough to commit murder.'

'It depends on the reward. Any ideas on how to find out?'

'Peter Freestone, he'll be able to advise.'

'You place a lot of faith in that man,' Clare said.

'He's an accountant, as well as a Salisbury City Councillor.'

It took less than ten minutes to drive to Freestone's office in Guildhall Square. Inside Freestone's office: the smell of his pipe, the windows open, an attempt with an air freshener. Clare appreciated that he had made an effort, knowing full well her aversion to smoking. Tremayne always liked coming on his own as he could smoke a cigarette, Freestone could smoke his pipe.

Peter Freestone, probably the closest there was to a friend of Tremayne, sat behind his desk. For once, he had cleared it of paperwork. 'What can I do for you Tremayne, Clare?'

'Len Dowling.'

'What do you want to know that you don't already?'

'The developments out at Coombe.'

'Dowling's involved with all of them,' Freestone said. 'But that's how the man operates. You have to give him ten out of ten for tenacity.'

'Fiona?'

'She's the driving force, but Len, he works hard.'

'That sounds like admiration for the man,' Tremayne said.

'Why not? You may not like him. I can't say I do either, but he never gives in.'

'The approvals for the development work at Coombe Farm. We need to know more about it.'

'What's to tell. We'll need to approve rezoning the land from rural to residential.'

'Difficult?'

'Not in itself, but that's a long way from allowing any building work on the site. We'll need full evaluations of the environment, traffic flow, impact on the local area, infrastructure. No doubt the village of Coombe doesn't have the electrical capacity to take on another three hundred houses. There'll need to be an upgrading of the power transmission into the area, as well as a consideration of the number of additional vehicles, some heavy, passing through the village.'

'Insurmountable?'

'The planning approval or the development?'

'Both.'

'A hefty capital outlay on Dowling's part initially for the planning approval. He'll need to use independent experts to prepare the necessary reports, then there are the feasibility studies, and if they find any endangered wildlife, that'll present another complication.'

'Endangered wildlife?' Clare said.

'A pair of nesting birds not seen in the United Kingdom for over a hundred years, and the application is shelved. It's happened before, no reason it couldn't happen again, although it's unlikely that will occur out at Coombe.'

'Why do you say that?'

'Statistically, the odds are against it. Similar to your horse betting, Tremayne.'

Clare suppressed a laugh at Freestone's ribbing of Tremayne.

'Last pint I'll buy you, Freestone,' Tremayne replied.

'Sorry, couldn't resist. Anyway, the amount that Dowling will need to put forward to be even considered for approval will be costly.'

'If he does?'

'Then there's the locals' right to offer comment.'

'Against?'

'They can submit their willingness for it as well, I suppose. But inevitably, it's against. Molly Dempsey will be in the thick of it, not that she holds much sway.'

'Why's that?' Clare asked.

'As I've told Tremayne before, not sure if you were there, but Mrs Dempsey is more rhetoric than substance.'

'And rhetoric holds no validity.'

'Not with us, it doesn't. If hard facts are presented, then we'll listen and respond accordingly. Statements such as 'it will destroy the village', 'it'll never be the same again' will achieve very little.'

'It will destroy the ambience of the place,' Clare said.

'Change is inevitable. Our responsibility at the Salisbury City Council is to ensure the change is for the better, and its progressive. Men like Dowling don't care about anything other than profit. It's up to us to temper their ardour with reason.'

'Dowling must be frustrated by the process,' Tremayne said.

'Not really. Men like him get enjoyment from pushing. He'll be in the thick of the battle.'

'Where does Gordon Selwood come into this?'

'That's up to him,' Freestone said. 'If he sells part of Coombe Farm to Dowling, then he's not involved. If he doesn't, and he intends to sell to the developers after the approvals are granted, then he'll need to be a signatory on the applications.'

'Is there a difference?'

'He'd be crazy to sell it before. If the application fails, he's sold part of the farm. If the application succeeds, the value of the land will go up significantly.'

'We'll assume he doesn't sell the land, but who'd advise him?'

'Dowling, but the man would only give advice that benefited him. Selwood needs independent advice.'

'Profit on the development?' Clare asked.

'Let's assume the approval is given, then the development costs will run into the millions. Even before they've sold the one plot of land, they'll need to bring in the sewerage, the electricity, build the roads.'

'Who'll finance that?'

'Dowling should be able to secure bank financing, maybe bring in an additional investor.'

'And Gordon Selwood?'

'That depends on the man. Is he financially smart?'

'Unlikely. His father would have been, his mother, definitely.'

'Then men like Dowling spit out the weak at the first opportunity. Selwood could find himself losing on the deal.'

'Cathy would have known this,' Clare said.

'No doubt that was why she objected. She could see the potential problems.'

'Cathy?' Freestone asked.

'Gordon Selwood's wife. She was murdered.'

'Because of what we're discussing?'

'It's possible, although not proven.'

'And Dowling may be involved?'

'There's no evidence against Len Dowling.'

'Fiona?'

'None against her, but she's smarter than her husband.'

'Fiona is ruthless. I knew her as a schoolgirl, but then you knew that.'

'A friend of your daughter's.'

'It was some years ago. She was attractive back then, still is, but there was something about her. She always seemed to be calculating the odds. Once my daughter ceased to have any value, she dumped her. They've not spoken for years.'

'Your daughter now?'

'Married with two children and living in London.'

***

Rose left her house in the village of Coombe and walked to the local store. It was a trip she made most days, only a two-minute walk, and she had to admit she had warmed to the village. After her speech in the store on the day she had arrived back, in that Crispin was indeed the son of Gordon Selwood and he was legitimate, there had been no more scurrilous rumours. Not that there weren't some people, Rose knew, who still revelled in the gossip of what went on behind the church wall all those years before. Rose realised she had developed a thick skin anyway. She thought it was remarkable as to how little the village had changed, even the people, apart from their looking older. She walked past the two houses under construction, a sign at the front indicating that they were for sale.

Rounding the corner at the end of the street, Marge Selwood.

'How's Crispin?' Marge asked.

'Fine,' Rose replied, which was true. She realised he had adjusted to Coombe even better than she had, although he was spending too much time with his father, neglecting his school work, but, on balance, the father's bad habits had not impacted as much as she feared they would.

'I see that Gordon's bought him a car.'

'It's not new. I was firm on that, and I objected to anything too fast.'

'You've heard about the plans for the farm?'

'I have.'

'What do you reckon?'

'I've not given it much thought. I'm just pleased to be back in the old house.'

'You must have some sway with Gordon,' Marge said.

'Not really. Crispin and Gordon get on well, that's all I know.'

'Rekindling the romance?'

'I've changed, Gordon hasn't.'

'That's true. But then you were always the more sensible. Even when there was that trouble, you handled it better than Gordon. He was all for you moving into the main house and living as man and wife.'

'Why didn't you let us?'

'You were children. How could you make such decisions about your future at that age?'

'And now?'

'That's up to you. I'm still not speaking to Gordon, and I'm not sure he's making the right decisions. You would be good for him.'

Rose looked at Marge, not sure of what she could see. Was it the concerned grandmother, or was it something more sinister? She knew that Gordon's mother had been right in that Gordon was only a child back when she had become pregnant, but she was not, at least not mentally. She had just been fifteen, but she had understood who had been the driving force in removing the Selwood family from scandal; it had been Marge Selwood. The woman's attempts at pretending to care did not work with her. Rose knew that behind every word that Marge Selwood said, there was an ulterior motive.

The two women parted. Rose entered the store; Crispin was bringing a friend from school to spend the night. She realised her son was at the age when Gordon had made her pregnant. She hoped he would not make the same mistake. The last that Rose saw of Gordon's mother, she was walking out of the village.

Chapter 23

Fiona Dowling, the driving force behind her husband, Len, and his burgeoning property empire, had not expected to see Clare. They had met in a café in Salisbury, away from the police station, away from Len Dowling, but more importantly, away from the Salisbury City Council Chambers.

'Neutral ground, is that it?' Fiona said. Clare had to admit the woman still looked as attractive as when they had suspected her of manslaughter in a previous case.

'We need to talk, that's all. I don't think you, as a city councillor would appreciate us calling you into Bemerton Road Police Station.'

'What for? I've done nothing wrong.'

'I was told that you're to become the mayor of Salisbury soon,' Clare said.

'I'm hopeful. Why are we here? You didn't come to talk about me.'

'The village of Coombe.'

'What about it?'

'You've been there?'

'Once or twice. It's pleasant enough, but I prefer to be in Salisbury.'

'Your husband is involved in some property transactions in the village of Coombe and at Coombe Farm.'

'You should ask my husband, not me.'

'Mrs Dowling, we know each other well enough. If your husband is involved with the development at Coombe Farm, you'll be there advising, expressing caution.'

'I'll admit to that, but what's so important in Coombe?'

'Murder, that's what's important.'

'I know that Gordon Selwood's wife was murdered, but I never met her.'

'But you knew her name.'

'Cathy Selwood. I read it in the newspaper. You're not accusing Len and me of murder, are you? We've been down that road once before, and you and Tremayne made us look like fools. I've not forgotten the humiliation.'

'You were both cleared. Len can talk plenty, but he's not an action man, hardly likely to be capable of killing anyone,' Clare said.

'But I am, is that what you're saying?'

'I'm not saying anything, but you're the stronger in your marriage. Not only have you risen from adversity after your affair became public knowledge, but you've changed it into a virtue. And now you're a councillor in the city.'

'I'm proud of my achievements, as I am of my husband. We're a good team.'

'So were Gordon and Cathy Selwood. He was a weak man bolstered by a strong woman. You would have liked her.'

'This is all very interesting, but what's it got to do with me?'

'Your husband and Gordon Selwood have agreed to develop a part of Coombe Farm. The plan is for three hundred houses.'

'It makes good business sense.'

'Gordon Selwood is not the most astute man. He's basically harmless, but he's not a businessman, just someone who's inherited wealth.'

'So?'

'Claude Selwood, his father, was astute, but failing due to dementia. However, he had a strong woman behind him. Any deals that would have been concluded with your husband would have needed her approval.'

'It's amazing how many successful men have a strong-willed woman behind them.'

'With Claude dead, it was up to Len to set up another deal with the son. We believe that Gordon's wife, Cathy, had objected to the deal.' Clare realised that was hearsay, but she thought to add it in as a possibility.

'And you're accusing Len of striking a less than favourable deal with Gordon Selwood?'

'It's a possibility.'

'Len would have tried for the best deal possible, and Gordon Selwood is over the age of eighteen. No one was forcing him to sign.'

'Cathy may have told him not to, but now she's dead.'

'Len took advantage of an opportunity. We can all be sorry for the dead, but it's for us remaining to carry on.'

'In conversation, it's been recorded you mentioned to your husband that Cathy was in the way.'

'Assuming I did, what does it mean? It's only a figure of speech, not a declaration the woman had to die.'

'What it means is you knew about the deal with Gordon Selwood.'

'I asked Len's brother to ensure it was watertight, and that it was legally binding.'

'Advantageous to Selwood?'

'That's not our concern.'

'And Cathy was objecting?'

'Yes, but we didn't know if it was a negotiating tactic or whether it was an outright no.'

'What did you finally decide?'

'The woman wasn't going to agree.'

'That's when you said she was in the way.'

'Maybe I did. We were willing to walk away from the deal, but then the woman was killed. Sad for her and her husband, good for us.'

'Were you upset when it happened?'

'Her death? Should I be?'

'Did Len take advantage of Gordon's situation?'

'You should ask Len, ask Gordon Selwood.'

'I wanted your take on the situation.'

'It wasn't us. If Coombe hadn't come off, we would have looked elsewhere. We're opportunists, not killers.'

***

'Marge Selwood, this is the first time that you have been in my cottage,' Molly Dempsey said. Both of the women were sitting in the living room, a pot of tea in front of them, some homemade cakes.

Neither of the two women pretended to like the other.

'We have a united cause,' Marge said. 'I don't want this village to change for the worse.'

'Are you opposed to what they intend to do at Coombe Farm?' Molly asked. She had been shocked when she had answered the door to find Marge Selwood standing there. In the past, their interaction had been limited. The cursory acknowledgement in the street, the nodding at each other in the church, but in all the years, the two women had never sat down for a conversation.

'I like Coombe Farm the way it is.'

'Your daughter-in-law?'

'Cathy did not want it either. She was killed because of her objection, I'm sure of it.'

'And now it will be you or me.'

'What is more important? Coombe Farm and the village, or our lives?' Marge said.

'I would give my life for this village,' Molly said.

'Then we are united.'

'What can you do?'

'Mrs Dempsey, let me be blunt. You're well-intentioned, but you've no expertise in dealing with building and development applications, nor with unscrupulous property developers.'

'Whereas, you're fully aware of what to do.'

'Are we in agreement? Can we work together on this?'

'What will you do?'

'I'll assist you when you attend the city council hearings into the application.'

'You'll stand beside me, your son on the other side?'

'I will. Together, we will save this village and Coombe Farm.'

***

Tremayne and Clare met William Selwood at his university. Clare had phoned ahead to let him know they were coming. He would have preferred just Clare, but their visit was not social.

'Mr Selwood, I'll be honest,' Tremayne said. 'We're no closer to solving who killed Old Ted and your sister-in-law.'

Clare realised that the admission of honesty by Tremayne was the prelude to some tough questioning.

'What do you want me to do? I wasn't in Coombe, and besides, I don't make a habit of shooting people.'

'That's as maybe, but you have a vested interest in the farm, and you wouldn't have been happy with Cathy usurping your mother.'

'Not totally.'

'What does that mean? You are, or you aren't?'

'Mother can be a bitch.'

'It's not a word we would expect to hear from her son,' Clare said.

'She's changed since our father died.'

'Since your father died or when she moved out of the main house?'

'The latter.'

'At least you're honest,' Tremayne said. 'We never saw much in the way of sadness when your father died. In fact, not much from any of you.'

'There wasn't.'

'Why?'

'We're cold people, not easy for us to show our emotions.'

'It's more than that,' Clare said. 'You were not interested in how your father died, only in a game you were playing on your phone, or maybe you were letting your friends know about the good news. What is it? Did you care for your father?'

'Not a lot. We were always close to our mother, but now…'

'But now, what? What are you trying to tell us? What has your mother done?'

'Nothing. She's changed, that's all.'

Clare looked over at Tremayne. 'Go and get us three coffees, will you?' she said. Tremayne understood the ploy. She wanted to question Selwood on her own, to get under his guard, to use her feminine guile.

Tremayne left and walked over to the cafeteria. It was only a short distance away, but he'd not be back until he received a message on his phone.

'William, you appear to be a decent person,' Clare said.

'I like to think I am.'

'What is it? And please, the truth. Your mother is a strong woman, and strong people sometimes do things that are not good or decent. We know more about your mother than you probably do.'

'Such as?'

'It's not relevant at this time. What is, though, is that Gordon is in the main house, Rose Goode is in the village, and her son is Gordon's legitimate son. How desperate were you for the farm?'

'It's not so much the money, more the life. Of the three sons, I'm the only true farmer. Gordon's not interested, Nicholas prefers accountancy, but I'm a farmer. It's in the blood.'

'Would Gordon let you run the farm?'

'He would, but he'll make wrong decisions to finance his frivolous pursuits.'

'Such as?'

'Cars, women, and whatever else takes his fancy.'

'And you?'

'I only want the farm. I've no need of travel or fast cars.'

'Women?'

'A good homely woman, that's what I want. There's one or two close to Coombe.'

'Level with me, William. Do you suspect your mother of killing Old Ted and Cathy? And please, don't try to protect her. We'll find out eventually.'

'I don't think so. She wanted Cathy out of the way, that's for sure.'

'Did she dislike her?'

'I think my mother liked her. She never said that to us, or to her, but sometimes our mother would let her guard slip. She's tough, our mother, but her interest has only ever been in the family.'

'And Cathy was not family?'

'My mother never trusted her motives. You know Gordon, you knew Cathy, what do you think?'

'Agreed, the two of them didn't seem a matched pair, but in fact, they were. You knew of Cathy's past?'

'I heard from my mother. Was it true?'

'Fundamentally it was.'

'And Gordon knew?'

'Cathy loved Gordon because he forgave her past, and he treated her well. She would never have left him, never strayed, and she loved the farm as much as your mother, even the family history. I liked her very much,' Clare said.

'So did I,' William said. 'I can understand my mother wanting to take control of the farm, but I can't accept her method. It came as a shock to Nicholas and me.'

'What do you mean?'

'It's not something I want to think about.'

'Either you tell me, or we'll find out through other means. Our discretion is assured, you know that. Is it something that you don't want to become general gossip?'

'If it does, my mother will not be able to deal with the shame.'

'Your mother, when did she care what other people thought of her?'

'Not when she was in the main house, and besides Nicholas and I care as well.'

'What is it? What is your mother up to? If she didn't kill Old Ted and Cathy, we need to know why?'

'She's going to disinherit Gordon from the farm and the house.'

'But how?'

'By proving that Gordon is not our true brother, that he is another man's child.'

Clare sat back in her chair. She messaged Tremayne to return.

With Tremayne back with the other two, Clare repeated what William had just said.

'Is it possible?' Tremayne asked.

'Our mother is getting his DNA checked.'

'Did he give his permission?'

'No. Mother falsified the documentation, obtained a toothbrush, some dried blood.'

'Illegally?'

'Yes.'

'What part did you have in this?'

'I helped Nicholas to pick up certain items in the main house.'

'Why are you telling us this?'

'If the results are in the negative, she'll obtain a court order to force Gordon to allow testing of his DNA by a laboratory in England.'

'Your reaction when she told you of this possibility?'

'What do you think? We'd always worshipped our mother, and then to find out that she had been with other men.'

'Parents have history, the same as their children,' Clare said.

'Is it possible that Gordon is not our father's son?' William said. 'You've checked into my mother's history, the same as all of us.'

'It's possible.'

'That's not what I wanted to hear.'

'Maybe it's not, but what is more important? Clearing your mother of murder or learning the truth?'

'Is she clear?'

'Nobody's clear, not even you. You were right to tell us the truth. Whatever the outcome of our investigation, it's been assisted by your openness.'

'It's a mess, isn't it,' William said.

'It's always those left behind who suffer the most. Murder always exposes the raw emotions, the unpleasant truths, the skeletons in the cupboard.'

Chapter 24

Molly Dempsey, a woman who had been born in Coombe, and rarely left it, had loved the village. Her actions to protect the village were criticised by some, admired by others, but she had never expected to die for it, but that was apparently what had happened.

In the back garden of her house was a small pond with a few fish swimming around, the woman's head immersed in it.

Tremayne and Clare were at the house within fifty minutes of receiving a phone call. They had just left William Selwood and were heading back to Salisbury. Tremayne put on the car's flashing lights; Clare, as usual, driving. 'Put your foot down,' Tremayne said.

For once, Jim Hughes and his crime scene team were at the cottage before the two police officers arrived. Outside, a crowd of onlookers, amongst them Marge Selwood.

'Mrs Selwood, I never expected to see you,' Tremayne said.

'I was here earlier. I may have been the last person to see her alive, apart from the murderer.'

'You'd better come in the house. We'll take a statement from you first.'

Marge Selwood waited in the house with a uniform while Tremayne and Clare checked out the crime scene. 'I'd say three to four hours,' Jim Hughes said, pre-empting the question that Tremayne always asked first.

'How?' Clare asked.

'She was held under the water till she drowned. There doesn't appear to be any signs of a struggle.'

'Which indicates?'

'Nothing at this moment. We've still got a few more hours of work yet. I'll let you know what we find.'

Tremayne knew Jim Hughes well enough to ask no more. The man knew what he was doing, and he knew what Tremayne wanted: evidence of another person near to the crime scene.

Inside the house, Clare looked up at a clock on the mantlepiece. It was showing 5.36 p.m., the same as her watch. Elsewhere in the house, some of the CSIs were conducting a check.

'Mrs Selwood, when was the last time you saw Molly Dempsey?'

'I left here at around 11.30 a.m., just in time for lunch at home.'

'Around?'

'I never took much notice. I left my house in the morning at 9 a.m. I remember the time, as I didn't want to knock on Mrs Dempsey's door too early.'

'Can this be proved?'

'I met Rose in the village. She'll be my witness.'

'Were you friends with Mrs Dempsey?'

'Not really. We had a common cause, that's all. I offered my support.'

'For what?'

'The opposition to the development of Coombe Farm. She had the enthusiasm but not the ability to stop it.'

'But you did?'

'I could put forward a cogent argument, present the necessary facts.'

'Are there some facts?'

'There are always facts. Whether they're good enough to stop it, I can't be sure.'

'You're willing to go against your son?'

'It's not against my son. It's for the farm and this village. Mrs Dempsey needed help, so did I.'

'What help could she have given you?'

'Moral support, not much more.'

'You don't seem upset by her death.'

'I barely knew the woman.'

'Why?'

'We had nothing in common before. She was a busybody. I was with Claude at Coombe Farm. We'd be civil to each other, but until I came in here earlier today, we had never had a conversation.'

'That sounds unusual,' Clare said.

'Maybe it does to you, but the people in this village know their place.'

Outside in the garden, Tremayne could see Hughes beckoning.

'What is it?'

'We've found some footprints on the path. They're not good,' Hughes said.

'What can you tell us?'

'Size 8 boot, probably male.'

'You can't be sure? Whoever it was, they would have been seen in the village, or their car would have.'

'There's an open field at the end of the garden. It looks as if the person came from there, and the hedgerow around it would have given sufficient coverage. It's probable that you'll not find anyone,' Hughes said.

'The woman inside?' Tremayne said.

'Is it likely?'

'I don't think so, not for this murder.'

'The others?'

'No proof.'

'Any sign that the woman was dragged from the house?'

'There's no sign of other footprints near the back door. I'd suggest the woman knew her murderer.'

'That doesn't help much. Molly Dempsey knew everyone in the village.'

'I can't help you much more. I'll file my report, Pathology will conduct an autopsy, although they'll confirm what I'm telling you. The woman was held under the water until she drowned. There's no sign of force, although with a woman her age, she wouldn't have been able to resist anyway.'

Tremayne returned indoors. Clare was still talking to Marge Selwood.

'Anything?' Clare said.

'Only that she would have known the person,' Tremayne said.

'Mrs Selwood, why was she killed?'

'Why ask me? I didn't do it.'

'My question was not accusatory.'

'You know why.'

'Len Dowling and your son.'

'Gordon wouldn't kill anyone.'

'Why not?'

'He's my son. I know the man, all his strengths, all his weaknesses.'

'You don't appear to have a lot of affection for your son,' Clare said.

'Have either of you ever had children?'

'No.'

'I thought so. I carried him for nine months, wiped his bottom, and then fed and cared for him until he was an adult. And now, he kicks me out of my house. He's my son, that's a biological fact, but as someone to love? I don't think so, not at this time anyway.'

'And your objection to Gordon developing Coombe Farm?'

'I'll fight it with every breath in my body.'

***

It was 8 p.m. by the time Tremayne and Clare left Molly Dempsey's cottage; time for a meal at the pub and a drink. Clare phoned her neighbours, more out of courtesy than anything else, knowing that if she weren't home by six in the evening, which was most days, they'd feed her cat for her.

Inside the pub in Coombe, the inevitable grilling by the publican; the non-committal answers.

'I can't say I knew Molly Dempsey,' the publican said.

'She was against any more development in the village.'

'A lot of people are, although, give her due, she was the only one who was willing to stand up and be counted.'

'You weren't?'

'A few more people in the village wouldn't do me any harm. I'm only paying bills at the present time, although your murders buck up trade for a couple of days.'

'Why Molly Dempsey? Any ideas? Agreed she could stick her nose in where it wasn't wanted, but it's hardly grounds for murder. It's the same with Old Ted. The man was inoffensive, said little, and he dies.'

'Maybe it's someone who's not right,' the publican said.

'What do you mean?'

'Someone mental.'

'Not in Coombe. Whoever's committing these murders is as sane as you and I,' Clare said.

'Don't include me. Staying here with this pub is hardly the act of a sane man.'

'Why do you?'

'I like it, that's the trouble. I could go and work with my brother in his engineering firm. Plenty of money, but it'd bore me to tears.'

'It's hardly a reason to stay.'

'It's like policing to you. It gets in your blood, the same as running a pub does for me. And anyway, another year of Gordon Selwood and Len Dowling, and this place could be viable.'

Tremayne thought the man to be optimistic but did not comment.

'What do we have?' Tremayne said after the publican had left. Clare could see that Tremayne was onto his second pint and he would not be stopping until they left the pub.

'It always comes back to Marge Selwood.'

'That's the problem, too easy. And as we know Marge Selwood only visited Molly Dempsey today.'

'Rose Goode confirmed that Marge Selwood was in the village just after nine this morning and she was heading in the direction of Molly Dempsey's cottage.'

'So why kill Mrs Dempsey? If Marge Selwood was going to assist the woman, then she's the target.'

'She's family. If it's one of her children, no matter what they may think of her, they're hardly likely to kill her.'

'Killing Molly Dempsey is one way to deter the mother.'

'No one in the Selwood family or in Coombe doubts the mother's resilience. Only a fool would believe that Marge Selwood could be deterred by someone else's death.'

'Or someone young.'

'Crispin?'

'We're here. We should confront him now,' Tremayne said.

'You'll need a walk around the village first and some strong mints. You can't go questioning people with stale beer on your breath.'

'You're in charge, Yarwood.'

'I hope it's not the son.'

'What you hope is not important. If someone has committed a crime, then it's up to us to arrest the person, as simple as that.'

'I understand, guv, but…'

'There are no buts. We do our job impartially.'

***

At Rose and Crispin's house, the lights were ablaze, loud music blasting. Tremayne knocked hard on the front door. After three minutes, Clare phoned Rose.

'I'm up at Gordon's. Crispin's got some friends staying the night. I left them to it.'

'What time did Crispin get home?'

'Six in the afternoon with two of his friends.'

'And before that?'

'He was at school. Any reason?'

No, that's fine. Are you free?'

'If you can stand a couple of people after a bottle of wine, I am.'

'We'll be right up.'

Clare ended the call and spoke to Tremayne. 'I'll check tomorrow, but Crispin was at school when Molly Dempsey died. It can't be him unless he could somehow get from Salisbury to here and back within two to three hours.'

'It seems improbable, but check it out anyway. What now?'

'Rose and Gordon are into the wine at the main house. We'll go up there.'

It wasn't far, no more than a six-minute walk, but Clare drove the short distance. In the kitchen, Rose and Gordon. On the table, two bottles of wine.

'Help yourself to a drink,' Gordon said.

'We're on duty,' Tremayne said.

'You're not in the army, and we're not going to tell.'

Tremayne and Clare accepted the offer. Tremayne would have preferred a beer, but he'd put up with wine on this one occasion.

'Why the celebration?' Clare asked.

'No reason. Crispin's got friends over. We just thought he'd enjoy the place to himself.'

'As long as he doesn't sneak in a couple of girls,' Gordon joked.

'Like father, like son.'

'Not me, I only had eyes for you.'

Clare could see a romance developing, or maybe it was just the alcohol, but it was more than two people sharing a son. Clare could see the ruffled hair of Rose, the unbuttoned shirt of Gordon. She knew they had made love in that house. She smiled at the thought of it. Rose, who had not had a man for a long time, had solved that problem. She, the police sergeant, who had remained chaste for too many years, had not. She envied Rose her good fortune, although not her choice of man.

'You've heard about Molly Dempsey?' Tremayne said. Clare realised he had not seen the tell-tale signs of two lovers.

'Tragic,' Rose said. 'She said some wicked things about us in the past, but it's still sad. Do you know who did it?'

'Not yet. The woman was a busybody, everyone agrees on that, but she was regarded as harmless. She was against your plans for Coombe Farm,' Tremayne said directing his comments at Gordon.

'So's my mother, but the application procedure is straightforward. Our paperwork will be meticulous.'

'Your mother could delay it.'

'It's unfortunate, but that's how it is. I'd like to make friends, but it's not going to happen as long as I control the farm.'

'How is the farm?'

'It's not going as well as it should be. I've advertised for a farm manager, but no takers yet.'

'William?'

'It's his if he wants it, but with our mother, it's uncertain.'

'A standard question. Where were you between the hours of 1 p.m. and 2 p.m. today,' Clare asked.

'I was at home preparing food for Crispin and his friends.'

'I was outside working on the car.'

'I thought it was new,' Tremayne said.

'I've bought another, a vintage Aston Martin. I intend to fix it up. Crispin's going to help me with it.'

'Show me,' Tremayne said.

'Okay, bring your glass with you.'

Chapter 25

'Rose, what's the truth? Are you back with Gordon?' Clare asked once the two men had left the house.

'You know?'

'I'm a woman. Of course, I know. You and Gordon are lovers.'

'It's easy with him. It's not love if that's what you're thinking. He still misses Cathy, still loves her, and I needed a man.'

'Your involvement with Gordon throws you into conflict with his mother.'

'I know. I don't know how it's going to resolve itself, do you?'

'It will, once we arrest the murderer or murderers.'

'More than one?'

'It's possible. Molly Dempsey wasn't shot, her head had been held under water. Do you know she had been with Marge?'

'I told you she was heading in the direction of Molly Dempsey's cottage.'

'She was going to work with Gordon's mother on opposing the rezoning and development of Coombe Farm.'

'I'm against it as well. I've told Gordon that I don't approve.'

'Why's that?'

'Before I came back here, I couldn't care either way, but now I don't want it to change. I want Gordon to make this farm work.'

'Can he?'

'He can't, but others can.'

'Such as?'

'His brothers, Marge, even me with time.'

'And what will Gordon do?'

'He's torn between being dynamic and forward-thinking, and pulling out of the deal with Dowling.'

'Can he?'

'He needs legal advice. Dowling's incurred costs. He'll want them covered, and Gordon doesn't have that sort of money.'

'He's just bought a vintage car.'

'It'll cost more than the value of the car. He could always borrow from the bank, but the last few years, the weather's been against Coombe Farm.'

'Are you taking an active involvement in the farm now?'

'If Gordon asks my advice, I'm willing to give it. The car's pure folly, but that's the man. He means well, but he doesn't have the discipline for this farm. Marge would have done a better job, Cathy as well.'

***

At the garage, not more than thirty yards from the stables, Tremayne looked over the Aston Martin. All he could see was something old and probably unreliable.

'It's worth a fortune once it's fixed up. I've offered Crispin half the profit if he helps.'

'Does he know much about cars?'

'Nothing at all. I'm a competent mechanic, and besides, with cars of this vintage, it's not for the amateur. We'll need to bring in professionals to fix it up.'

'Expensive?'

'So is life. This is what I enjoy, not farming. I remember the early starts as a child, tramping across frozen fields to feed the cattle, and my father there, excited, oblivious to the discomfort. The man loved farming, the same as William, but Nicholas and I, we're not so keen.'

'What's it with you and Rose?' Tremayne asked.'

'We're just friends. I'm not sure I want anyone after Cathy.' The man stood to one side, tears welling up in his eyes.

He took stock of himself and stood up straight. 'Sorry about that. Cathy was special, Rose is a good friend.'

'Will she spend the night?'

'Probably.'

'What did you reckon of Molly Dempsey and your mother?'

'My mother phoned me to tell me that she was going to lodge a formal objection to the development of the farm.'

'What did you say?'

'I didn't get much of a chance. She just gave me the facts and hung up.'

'Are you prepared for her?'

'Dowling will be.'

'I hope you're careful with him.'

'I know of his reputation, and Rose, she thinks that Cathy was right in objecting to it.'

'A bit late now?'

'Not too late, although Dowling won't like it if I pull out.'

'He'll get his brother, Chris, on to you. Have you met him?'

'What do you reckon to him?'

'He's smarter than Len, tougher too.'

Tremayne walked away from the car, opened a packet of cigarettes and took one for himself. 'How about you?' he said, offering a cigarette to Gordon.

'Sorry, Cathy, I know they're not good for me.' Selwood looked skywards as he took one of the cigarettes.

The two men stood outside looking at the front garden of the house, the lights of the village down below. 'Cathy loved this place,' Selwood said.

'And you?'

'As a young man, I couldn't wait to get away, but now, I'm happy to stay. It's just this damn farm that concerns me. As much as I want to be enthusiastic, I can't.'

'Your mother telling the neighbourhood about Cathy?'

'I told Cathy to ignore it.'

'Was she upset by it?'

'Not that she'd show it, but yes. A tough woman, but she still had a soft side. Why else would she have chosen me, a lame dog.'

'You're not lame.'

'Immature then. Here I am, with a farm and a beautiful house and responsibilities, and I'd rather spend hours in a garage fixing up an old car. That's for adolescent teenagers.'

'It's a big job looking after this place. I wouldn't want to do it,' Tremayne said.

'You're right. You're a policeman, that's what you want to be. I want to spend time buying and selling luxury motor cars, vintage mainly. I could run the business here, fix up one of the barns as a place to keep them. Other men are doing it, making plenty of money. Enjoying themselves, doing what they're best at.'

'How do you resolve this place? William is hardly likely to come back here as a farm manager, a man on a salary.'

'He'll come, so will Nicholas in time. They're Selwoods, they'll do their duty. My mother always wants to portray me as the black sheep of the family, but I'm not. That's how families like mine gloss over those who don't fit in.'

'Why such emphasis on your family history?'

'The class structure, it was much stronger in the past. Some of the old men in the village, when I was a child, would doff their cap to my mother. Nowadays, the younger generation won't do it, although my mother would like them to.'

'What do you know about your mother?' Tremayne asked.

'What do you mean?'

'Why does she like the doffing of the cap?'

'Her father was an army officer, so I suppose she was used to men saluting him.'

'That was military regulations. In Coombe, it's a subtle line between who is superior to the other.'

'Our mother loved the family history, the pure bloodline. She'd do anything to preserve it, even…'

'Kill? Is that what you were about to say?'

'I'm not accusing my mother of murder. Have you seen the family tree?' Selwood said.

'No. A few rogues and villains in there?'

'A few, and not all were black sheep. One was a bishop, kept a mistress in Salisbury. That's a few hundred years back. Another, when fighting the French, had his troops burn down a church where the villagers had protected some enemy soldiers. A war crime if it happened today.'

'Back then it would not have been.'

'Bad form killing civilians, but the man was one of the most illustrious in the Selwood dynasty. It was he who started buying up some of the smaller farms around Coombe. Coombe Farm was a lot smaller then. At one stage, the family virtually owned the village.'

'And now?'

'It's been progressively sold off over the years. Apart from the development in Coombe, the Selwoods own nothing else.'

'What are you going to do about your mother? Does she stand a chance with Salisbury City Council?'

'She can slow it down.'

'And if she does, you'll be taking on additional cost.'

'I know. Len Dowling says it's costed in.'

'Do you trust him?' Tremayne said.

'Do you?'

'I wouldn't let him sell a garden shed for me.'

'That bad?'

'Selwood, you'll lose this farm and this house if you let Dowling and his brother control you. It's not my job as a police officer to tell you this.'

'Why are you?'

'Out of respect for Cathy. My sergeant, she's a soft touch. She liked the woman.'

'You're a soft touch, as well,' Selwood said.

'I'd appreciate it if you'd keep that to yourself. And Rose, she's a good person, as is your son.'

'And me?'

'I'll reserve judgement on you.'

'I would never have harmed Cathy.'

'How about Molly Dempsey? She was causing trouble.'

'What trouble? She had no real clout.'

'Your mother was going to work with her, to give her the assistance she needed.'

'Then why didn't they kill her.'

'They?'

'He, she, I don't know who. My mother is a force to be reckoned with, not Molly Dempsey, not Old Ted.'

'Why kill Old Ted? Did he know something about your inheritance?'

'It's not open to dispute. My father gave it all to me.'

'He gave it to his son. Are you, Gordon Selwood, the legitimate son of Claude Selwood?'

Tremayne noticed Selwood take two steps back. The man did not speak for at least two minutes as he walked around the car he had just bought.

'My mother is desperate,' Selwood said once he could no longer avoid answering the question.

'Is this how your family acts?'

'Too often, I'm afraid.'

'How far would you go to maintain control?'

'Are you suggesting murder?'

'I'm not suggesting. I'm putting forward the hypothesis.'

'You're wide of the mark. It's my mother who is the bane of my life, not anyone else.'

'Could your mother have killed Cathy?'

'Yes.'

'Could you have killed Old Ted, even Molly Dempsey, to protect your lifestyle?'

'Yes, but I didn't. I'm innocent of all charges, apart from falling in love with a decent and now-dead woman.'

'Thank you for your honesty. Will your mother be able to prove your illegitimacy?'

'I don't know. I wasn't there, was I? Does my mother have a past that makes this possible?'

'Unfortunately, she does. I'll need to ask you for a sample of your DNA for analysis.'

'Do you have a court order?'

'No, but I could get one.'

'Don't bother. I'll comply. When do you want to conduct the test?'

'I have everything in the car.'

'You're a bastard, you know that, Tremayne.'

'I'm a police officer doing my duty. If you're the legitimate son, then you're a target, and then, it will be Crispin.'

'And if I'm not?'

'Then you will no longer have any influence. Your importance will be significantly reduced.'

'And the deal with Dowling will no longer be valid?'

'You should have checked what you were signing. Whatever happens, you, Gordon Selwood, have single-handedly placed the Selwood family in serious trouble. I only hope your mother can get you out of it.'

'If she's free.'

'She's still our prime suspect.'

***

After Tremayne's interrogation of Gordon Selwood, the two police officers left Coombe Farm, complete with a swab of Selwood's saliva. There were questions from Rose as to what was going on, questions which Gordon Selwood could answer.

Clare could see from the faces of the two remaining in the house that there would be very little romance that night.

'How did he take it, your accusation?' Clare asked once they had left the house.

'In some ways, he seemed relieved. He's not cut out to run Coombe Farm, he knows that. He's probably the only true innocent in this whole sorry saga. A child in a man's world, that's how I'd describe him, how he'd describe himself. If he's got his expensive toys, he doesn't want for much more.'

'And Rose?'

'What did you reckon? From a woman's perspective, that is.'

'They're lovers.'

'Is it love?'

'Not from Rose. She's matured, Gordon hasn't. She doesn't come with Cathy's baggage, and she's got a comfortable existence in the village. She may move in with Gordon at some stage, or she may not.'

'The mother,' Tremayne said.

'It's late to go knocking on doors.'

'She's the one who wants to know if Gordon is her son. We'll do it for her legitimately, not through a third-rate laboratory overseas. Whatever the outcome, the Selwood family will have to deal with the facts.'

Marge Selwood did not appreciate being woken. The pieces were fallen together, Tremayne knew it, and nobody, not even the formidable Marge Selwood, was going to stop him.

Thirty-five minutes later, a sample of the woman's DNA was in Tremayne's possession. In Salisbury, Forensics had a record of Claude Selwood's DNA on file.

It was three in the morning before Clare made it home, and Tremayne wanted her in the office by seven. Her cat was occupying her side of the pillow as she pushed it gently to one side.

Chapter 26

Fiona Dowling was not pleased. Molly Dempsey, a known opponent of her husband's property developments, had been murdered. Not that the woman's death concerned her, only the impact it would have on her becoming the next mayor of Salisbury. Guilt by association as she saw it.

Her husband disappointed her. He had let one old woman jeopardise his business plans, and for what? There had been no substance in the Dempsey woman's arguments, and she had been largely ignored in her community and at the Salisbury City Council meetings, but now, she had been murdered.

Fiona Dowling knew what it would mean. The dead woman would become a martyr for the cause of restraint, for leaving sleepy villages such as Coombe as they were. There'd be an investigation into who could have killed her, who had a reason to want her to be dead, who would have been delighted.

Fiona knew the answer to the last two: her husband, Len. But he was a weak man. That was why she had picked him as her mate when they had been in their teens. He had been the most likely candidate to mould to her satisfaction. The man, never as intelligent as her, had the drive, the ability to charm, to convince, and above all, the ability to follow her directives.

She had warned him about impinging on her run to become mayor, and what had he said. 'Don't worry. Coombe will cause us no trouble. I've got Gordon Selwood under control, and, as for that interfering old woman, she's just the laughing stock of the village.'

And now that laughing stock was dead, and people would realise she was only interested in her community, and those who had persecuted her with their unreasonable greed were responsible for her death, even if they had not thrust her head into the fish pond.

Fiona drove down to her husband's office in town. She parked in Guildhall Square as she always did, and walked across to her husband's office. Inside, the receptionist. 'Mrs Dowling, how are you?'

'Don't give me any of your sweet words. I want that bastard who's going to destroy us.'

The receptionist said no more. She had not seen the woman in such a mood before. Len Dowling came out from his office. 'Fiona, come in.'

Inside Len's office, his wife took a seat. 'Are you still screwing that bitch outside?'

'Please, Fiona, you know I'm not.'

'What do I care? You've really done it this time.'

'What?'

'The old woman out at Coombe. The one they found dead.'

'Molly Dempsey.'

'Did you kill her? No, you couldn't have. You don't have the backbone.'

'Fiona, you've got to stop with this paranoia. I've done nothing wrong. I've certainly not slept around, that's more for you than me, and as for killing people, I'm innocent.'

'Gordon Selwood's wife was against your developing of Coombe Farm, so was the Dempsey woman, and they're both dead.'

'Are you concerned about them, or becoming the next mayor?'

'I'm concerned about us. I've guided you over the years, carefully weighed up the pros and cons, and as for my affairs, I've always been careful.'

'You've made a career out of them. The prodigal daughter returned from sin and back to the path of righteousness, that's you. And you've got all those social-climbing friends of yours kissing your feet. Fiona, you're pure evil. You don't care for anyone, not even me, only yourself.'

'You were meant to do what you were told. If you could have resolved Coombe without killing people, then fine, but not you. You kept pushing, riling the natives, hoping they would back off, and they haven't. And now, they're dying, and I'm going to have to take the flak for you.'

'Fiona, think about what you're saying,' Len Dowling said. 'You blame me now, but we've been through worse than this.'

'Len, you're a fool,' Fiona said, her frustration exhausted. 'It's up to me again to get you out of this mess.'

'It is a mess, I'll agree, but I did not kill Molly Dempsey. Her death makes no sense. She had only just made an agreement with Marge Selwood to oppose what we wanted to do on Coombe Farm.'

'Marge Selwood!'

'Yes, Marge Selwood. You know what that means.'

'She'll hold it up forever.'

'Not forever, but certainly for long enough to make it not feasible.'

'Are we in for much money?'

'Gordon Selwood can take the cost.'

'Has he agreed?'

'He signed the documents.'

'How do we isolate you from Coombe?' Fiona said.

'And ensure you become the mayor.'

'I'll take care of that. You can deal with Selwood.'

'We shelve our plans?'

'Get real, Len. Just put them on hold until I'm the mayor. Once it's in the bag, then you can go back to Coombe.'

'With you as the mayor, it should be easier.'

'It may be, it may not. I suggest you go and tell Gordon Selwood the good news, and the village if they'll listen to you. Something along the lines of "in consideration of the sad and unexpected death of Molly Dempsey, we'll be holding back on the development of Coombe Farm to allow a full and consultative approach with all the good people in the village of Coombe".'

'How long are we delaying?'

'Six months, no more.'

'And the consultative approach?'

'That's what you tell the country yokels.'

'We'll make you mayor first, take Selwood for the costs incurred so far, and then we'll come back with a more obliging council.'

'Don't mess up, Len. I'm tired of getting you out of your disasters.'

'Disaster, I don't think so. We're going to clean up here.'

'You do your part, I'll do mine.'

***

Rose Goode had incurred the criticism of the village of Coombe once before, but then she had only been fifteen, and she had left the village that same night.

What she encountered now was far worse. She had seen it the first time she had entered the village store. The scathing attitude of the shopkeeper muted when she had announced that Crispin was legitimate, and where she had become a regular since. On each occasion, the lady behind the counter had been friendly, although always prying for any gossip.

Inside the store this time, the other patrons giving Rose a wide berth; not so easy, as the shop was only small. 'What do you want, Rose?' the lady from behind the counter said.

Rose had sensed the curtness, the unwillingness to indulge in the usual harmless banter. 'I'll look around, see what I need.'

'As you wish,' the shopkeeper said. Rose knew that in the past, the woman would have been telling her what was on special-offer. 'You've heard about Molly Dempsey?'

Rose realised it was a dumb question. It was a small village where news travelled fast.

'She harmed no one. She only cared for this village, and now, that bastard developer and your boyfriend have murdered her.'

Rose did not intend such a slur to go without a response.

'Mrs Golding, you have a foul mouth. Gordon Selwood, who's not my boyfriend, did not murder Mrs Dempsey, and I doubt very much if Len Dowling did, either.'

'It's suspicious, that's what everyone is saying.'

'And who's everyone? You and the other frustrated women in this village. Is this how you get your kicks, sticking your nose in where it's not wanted, accusing people of crimes without proof? It's slander, you know. You could be charged with a criminal offence.'

'Your threats don't hold sway with us.'

The other patrons in the shop left, although not without offering whispered comments as they brushed past Rose.

'Gordon would not kill anyone,' Rose said. She had not expected such hostility in the village that she had come to appreciate. However, as she stood there, she realised that nothing had changed since she had left the village seventeen years previously.

At that moment, standing in front of that shopkeeper, she realised that she hated them all: Gordon, his mother, the shopkeeper, the women who had brushed past her. She regretted returning to the village; she regretted sleeping with Gordon on the night of Crispin's friends visiting. She left the store without purchasing anything and drove up to see Gordon.

Gordon opened the door to her at Coombe Farm. 'Rose, it's all gone wrong,' he said.

Rose, angry with him before, calm now on seeing the downcast expression on his face. 'What is it?'

'Dowling's pulling out.'

'Why?'

'He says that with Molly Dempsey's death, public sentiment would be against the development of Coombe Farm.'

'The village is blaming you for her death. I've just had an altercation with the woman down at the store. The mood on the street is ugly, and they're making every effort to shun me, and all because of you.'

'Dowling, he wants me to pay my share of the costs.'

'Can he?'

'He says it's legally binding. I don't have that sort of money, and he's stopping work on the two houses in the village.'

'What for? They're half-complete.'

'That's Dowling. Tremayne told me to be careful.'

'We need to get you out of this.'

'You'll help?'

'You're Crispin's father. What else would you expect?'

'You were always a better person than me,' Gordon said.

'What sort of costs are you up for?'

'I don't know yet.'

'Then you'd better find out. Your brother's an accountant. Phone him up.'

As Gordon sat on a chair phoning Nicholas, his brother, Rose realised that he needed someone to look after him. She saw it as her duty, not out of love, but for Crispin. He could not have the ignominy of reconnecting with his father, only to find out the man was a fool, and that if life had not given him a privileged upbringing, he would have struggled to find his way in the world.

'Nicholas will be here within the hour,' Gordon said.

'How much, more or less?'

'One to two hundred thousand pounds.'

'You don't know with any more accuracy?'

'Dowling was keeping the account. I just needed to know that it was in safe hands.'

'Gordon, argue with your mother, shun your brothers, but never forget, they're Selwoods. Whatever happens, they're your family, Dowling is not.'

'Tremayne warned me the other day when we were looking at the Aston Martin. He also said to be careful of his wife; she's running for mayor in Salisbury.'

'She'd not want any dirt sticking to her. That's why Dowling's pulling out.'

Rose picked up her phone and made a call. 'We need you at the main house,' she said.

'Who did you call?' Gordon asked.

'Your mother. She's the best person to deal with this, not you.'

'If it hadn't been for my arrogance.'

'Don't go soft on me and pretend you're the little boy lost. You're a man. Stand up to your mother, take her advice when it's given.'

'You'll be here?'

'I will, on Crispin's behalf. You'll need someone to handle the family discussion for you. If your mother wants me out, you resist. Is that clear?'

'It's clear. Thank you.'

'Don't thank me. I'm doing this for Crispin, not for you.'

Chapter 27

'You've got your murders in Coombe now,' Superintendent Moulton said as he walked into Tremayne's office.

'More than I expected.'

'Anything tying them together?'

'Coombe Farm's the key.'

'It's always you and Yarwood, isn't it?'

'We work best that way. We had a young constable once, but he was killed in the line of duty.'

'Yes, I remember. We never found a murderer.'

'It wasn't murder. It was an unfortunate chain of events that killed him and the woman in the passenger's seat.'

'Sergeant Yarwood always thought it was more than that.'

'That's not why you're here, is it? You're not into reminiscing.'

Clare came into the office and gave both men a cup of coffee. She left straight afterwards.

'You've done a great job with her.'

'She's a fine police officer,' Tremayne said.

'Praise indeed from you. You were never keen on a partner before.'

'Maybe I wasn't, but I'm fine with Yarwood.'

'Run the motives past me, Tremayne.'

'Coombe Farm, as I said, is the crux. Claude Selwood, the patriarch of the Selwood family, was the first to die.'

'Patriarch?'

'You've read the reports.'

'Humour me.'

'Okay. The Selwood family goes back several hundred years. The land was originally bequeathed by a grateful king for services rendered by an ancestor. A murdering bastard if the stories about him are true.'

'More violent times back then.'

'I only deal with the present. Anyway, Claude Selwood is killed in a riding accident, the horse trod on his throat. His death is accidental, although he'd probably still be alive if the Reverend Walston hadn't started shooting pellets from an air rifle at the man and his horse.

'Why not murder?'

'The pellets wouldn't have killed Selwood.'

'So why does a man of the cloth shoot at someone?'

'He said it was a warning to leave him and his church alone.'

'Do you believe him?'

'Not totally. We should interview him again in light of Molly Dempsey's death.'

'After Claude Selwood?'

'Old Ted, the farmhand.'

'He was shot?'

'A .22. The motive for his death still remains unclear. The man knew all of the Selwood family's secrets, but the man was the soul of discretion.'

'Soul of discretion?'

'Old Ted minded his own business, never spoke unless spoken to. He had the dirt on everyone, but, even to us, he wouldn't talk. And then we find out that Claude Selwood had an affair with Old Ted's wife around the time of the birth of the eldest son, Gordon.'

'Good God, Tremayne. Where do you find these people?'

'They may be a little extreme, but most families have plenty of secrets. It's just that we're paid to find them. It's a good job I'm able to go home at night and switch off.'

'Yarwood?'

'She's not learnt to detach totally, not yet. She'll get there.'

'And become old and cynical like you,' Moulton said with a smile.

'I'd prefer mature and realistic.'

'I'll accept that. Old Ted's wife and Claude Selwood, what happened?'

'The affair ended, and nothing is said by Old Ted, not even to Claude Selwood.'

'This Old Ted appears to be an odd character.'

'Out of time, I'd say. But he killed no one. He was the first murder victim. After that, there is Cathy Selwood, the wife of the current owner of Coombe Farm. Here's where it becomes more complicated. There's a battle royal between Gordon Selwood and his mother, Marge, the widow of Claude. Gordon, he's a decent man, not as smart as the others in the family, and definitely not a farmer. Claude Selwood was showing the early stages of dementia. The tradition in the family was that the eldest son would inherit. The will, however, been drawn up some years earlier when Gordon was younger. Marge Selwood realised that with her husband's health ailing, she needed to go against tradition and to draw up another will, making her the beneficiary.'

'And she did?'

'It was drawn up, but Claude died before he could sign it. After that, Gordon attempts to take control, the law's in his favour. Marge, his mother, a tough woman, attempts to as well. And then, you've got Cathy Selwood, Gordon's wife, and she's as strong-willed as Marge. She would have made a go of the farm with Gordon's blessing. All he wants to do is to mess around with old cars.'

'Old cars?'

'Vintage. They don't do much for me, but supposedly they're worth a fortune to those who are interested.'

'They are. Carry on.'

'Cathy's shot, a bullet to the head. The motives start to become obscured. On the one hand, Cathy's taken over Marge Selwood's position as the lady of the house and of the farm, and also, unknown at the time, she's attempting to talk Gordon out of progressing with a residential development on the farm.'

'The last murder?'

'Molly Dempsey. The woman was nearly eighty. She had lived in the village all her life, and she was a gossip, but basically harmless. She's vocal about any changes to the village of Coombe, good or bad. She likes it the way it is, and every time there's a building application before the Salisbury City Council, she's there registering a complaint. Not successfully most times, as she strong on enthusiasm, short on facts.'

'Why was Molly Dempsey killed?'

'We're drawing a blank on that at the present time. We know that Marge Selwood and Molly Dempsey were going to join forces and oppose the development at Coombe Farm. They had met the morning of the woman's death.'

'What would Marge Selwood gain from forging an alliance with Molly Dempsey, and why would she go against her son?'

'Marge Selwood is a resilient woman. She will never accept Gordon as the owner of Coombe Farm and the house. The house, a listed building, is over two hundred years old. She's against the development of the land regardless of how much money it could make for the Selwoods.'

'Was Marge Selwood financially secure?'

'She had sufficient money for her needs. With her, it's not money, but family and prestige. If it were up to her, she'd go back to the past where the locals knew their place.'

'Her background?'

'The same as Cathy Selwood. Both women had sold themselves in the past, but now Marge Selwood is the pillar of respectability.'

'But you know of her past?'

'We're police officers.'

'Any more?'

'Marge Selwood was attempting to prove Gordon was not the child of Claude.'

'Possible?'

'Yes. She was attempting to check his DNA against one of her sons. What she was doing was illegal, as Gordon had not given his permission. We're now conducting an independent test in the UK.'

'And if he isn't?'

'The house and the farm belong to the eldest son of Claude and Marge Selwood. That would be Nicholas, the second born.'

'People could die to prevent that happening.'

'In the past, but not now. Everyone is well aware of our independent testing. The results will be indisputable.'

***

'I'm not comfortable with Rose being here,' Marge Selwood said on entering the main house, realising that her objection to the woman was not the same as it had been with Cathy.

'I've asked her to be here,' Gordon said. 'And besides, her son is a Selwood. She's here on his behalf.'

'Let her stay, Mother,' Nicholas said. He had arrived late at the meeting. William, the youngest son, was still not there.

'Very well,' Marge said. She looked over at Rose, a woman who had brought up her grandson better than she had her eldest.

Marge had to begrudgingly admit she liked Rose. She wasn't as tough as Cathy, but tough enough to keep Gordon under control whether he ran the farm or not.

The call to the house had come as a shock, but life in the sleepy village and in the Selwoods home always seemed to be long periods of nothingness, and then intense drama.

William arrived. 'Sorry, I was in an exam, the final one for the year.'

On the dining room table, a pot of tea and some sandwiches which Rose had prepared. 'You'd better help yourself before we start,' Gordon said.

'Level with us,' Nicholas said.

'Very well. An event has been precipitated by the death of Molly Dempsey, although it could have occurred at any time due to our mother's interference.'

'Don't you go laying the blame on me, Gordon. Just because you can't handle yourself, there's nothing to be gained by blaming others.'

Rose stood up. 'I believe that I, as an independent member of the family, should outline the situation.'

'Good idea,' William said. The others in the room nodded their heads in acknowledgement.

'The rezoning of part of Coombe Farm to residential was due to be discussed by the Salisbury City Council in the next two weeks. Molly Dempsey would have put in an impassioned plea for permission not to be granted. Approval would have allowed the area to be subdivided into three hundred residential blocks of land.'

'We know this,' Marge said.

'Molly Dempsey would have been disregarded with little credence. However, Mrs Selwood offered to help Molly in her objection. This, as we all know, would have changed the situation dramatically. Your mother is a competent woman, and there's no way the council would have been able to ignore her. At the very least, there would be significant delays, cost overruns.'

'I did what was right. Coombe Farm belongs to the Selwoods, always has, always will,' Marge Selwood said.

'It was my decision,' Gordon said.

'It was a bad decision.'

'Can we forget this for the moment and let me continue,' Rose said. 'The matter is more serious than petty squabbling. Molly Dempsey was killed, not less than two hours after Mrs Selwood left her cottage.'

'It was nothing to do with me,' Marge said.

'That's understood, but the police think your visit and her death are related.'

'This is all interesting, but why are we here?' Nicholas asked.

'Len Dowling is pulling out of the deal.'

'Isn't that what we wanted?' William said.

'There's a complication,' Gordon said. 'Dowling wants me to pay for the costs incurred so far.'

'You've done nothing. What costs are there?' William said.

'There's the two houses in the village, as well as the costs incurred for the various reports, the experts, the soil analysis, even a check of the local fauna. Believe me, the costs are extensive.'

'How much?' Nicholas said.

'The final figure's not in yet, but it will be somewhere in the vicinity of two hundred thousand pounds.'

'Which you don't have,' Marge said.

'Nor does the farm.'

'You can refuse to pay.'

'In the short term, but the agreement with Dowling is legally binding.'

'Why are we here?' Nicholas said.

'If Dowling takes the matter to court and wins, I will be liable for the outstanding money, plus costs. I will have only one recourse but to sell the farm.'

'Over my dead body,' Marge said. 'No son of mine would allow such a thing to happen.'

'I'm your son, Mother. The question is, who is my father?' Gordon said. 'What did you do before you married him? Do you even know the name of this man?'

'Please,' Rose said, 'this is getting us nowhere. Dowling's wife is running for mayor in Salisbury. She doesn't want any dirt sticking to her. We think Dowling's pulling out now to give his wife a clear run.'

'And once she's elected, then he'll be back with a tighter deal, and we'll be forced to comply,' Marge said.

'It's probable. We've not thought it through fully, as yet.'

'Okay, Gordon, you need me whether you like it or not,' Marge said.

'What do you suggest?'

'We fight as the Selwoods have always fought. If Dowling's wife wants to be mayor, she'll need to deal with us. Gordon, do you have Dowling's phone number?'

'Yes.'

'Okay, phone him up and tell him to be here within the hour, and to bring his bitch wife with him.'

'Bitch?'

'I know all about her, the sanctimonious tart. That woman's been around.'

***

Jim Hughes, the crime scene examiner, was in Tremayne's office. The two men were sitting, Clare outside at her desk.

'Yarwood, in here, please,' Tremayne shouted through the open door.

'It's about time you called her Clare,' Hughes said.

'Not possible, and besides, she's used to it. She'd think I'd gone soft in the head if I start calling her by her first name. You'll have me buying her birthday presents next.'

'And what's wrong with that?'

'I'm not into birthdays.'

'Starting to feel your age?'

'Don't tell Moulton, but the joints are starting to creak.'

'You'll not give in, Tremayne. They'll have to carry you out of here.'

Clare entered Tremayne's office and sat down. 'What is it, guv?'

'I thought we'd go over with Hughes what we have so far,' Tremayne said.

'Can we focus on Molly Dempsey. That's more recent, fresher in our minds.'

'Very well. Hughes, what can you tell us that we don't already know?'

'It's all in the report, and Pathology confirmed that she drowned.'

'Could it have been an accident? After all, the woman was old.'

'We've been through this before. The angles were all wrong. If she had slipped, banged her head on the edge of the pond, then maybe. But that's not the case here. She was held under and there's no sign of bruising.'

'There was violence?'

'Mild. The woman was frail. What more do you want me to tell you? I can't make this up,' Hughes said.

'The field at the back, anything there?'

'Not really. It was in the afternoon, the grass in the paddock was short, and it was dry. Also, some of the local kids get in there to kick a football around.'

'Could one of them have come in through the gate at the bottom of the woman's garden and killed her?'

'The ones we saw were only children. I'd rule that out.'

'How do they get into the field?'

'There's a gate on the far end. It leads into a lane at the back of the village. You're asking me to say how someone could have got in unseen, but I can't. It's the afternoon, the village is quiet, and anyone could have ambled down the lane, up through the field and into the woman's garden.'

'But why? Did someone know of Marge Selwood visit earlier in the day, and if they did, why Molly? Marge Selwood is the one person who could cause trouble.

'Unless Molly Dempsey knew something about the Selwood family history. Something she revealed to Marge, and that it was Marge who returned through the field and killed her.'

'But what? We know about Gordon Selwood's uncertain parentage, but that's about to be resolved once the results come back. Is there anything else we don't know?'

'The reason Old Ted died,' Clare said.

'The man's a mystery. He accepts his wife's affair with Marge Selwood's husband, he says nothing unless asked, and he could keep secrets.'

'But how do you find out the reason?'

'We question Marge again. If she's the murderer, then she knows the secret. If she's not, then she tells someone who makes a decision to kill the old woman.'

'Am I driving?' Clare said.

Tremayne did not answer Clare. Instead, he looked over at Jim Hughes. 'Thanks, you've solved this case.'

'Have I?'

'You've clarified the investigation into Molly Dempsey's death. Yarwood and me, we'll take it from here.'

'I'm glad to have been of assistance.'

'Yarwood, I hope the neighbours will feed your cat. We're not coming back from Coombe without a murderer. And make sure there are some uniforms at Coombe Farm.'

'What if some of the family is not there?'

'We'll deal with it in Coombe.'

Chapter 28

Fiona Dowling did not appreciate being summoned to Coombe Farm. There was a function that night at the council chambers, a chance to further cement her hold on the mayoral robes.

'It's Gordon Selwood,' Len, Fiona's husband, said.

'Tell him you'll talk to him tomorrow, through our solicitor if necessary.'

'He says his mother's willing to sully your name throughout Salisbury.'

'My past is not a secret.'

'It is to most, and it's not fresh in the mind of the others. Have you met Marge Selwood?'

'On several occasions. She's a vexatious woman.'

'She could reopen old wounds, denounce you.'

'Okay, we'll go, but don't expect me to be agreeable.'

'Nor me,' Len said.

Fiona did not enjoy the drive out to Coombe Farm. She liked even less knocking on the back door of the main house, only for it to be opened by Marge Selwood.

'Please come in,' Marge said.

'We only came because of scurrilous comments you intend to spread about me,' Fiona said. The two women had met before, that was clear to those assembled.

'Your mother attended one of my motivational talks,' Fiona said to the Selwood family. 'Where I opened up about my imperfect life, my husband and his forgiving nature, and that with time, a loving relationship can be regained.'

'No wonder they're making you the mayor,' Marge said. 'If you can come up smelling of roses as well as that down at the council meetings, they'll have no option but to give you the job.'

'My elevation to the position of mayor is an acknowledgement of my good service to Salisbury and the area.'

'We'll bypass your saintly aspirations for now. We've got to resolve this hold you have on my dim-witted son.'

Gordon rose to comment, but Rose placed her hand on his knee to stop him from replying.

'There is no discussion. Your son signed of his own free will. The terms of the agreement were clear. Three months after commencement of the two houses in the village, Gordon would take responsibility for all costs incurred. It further stated he would then ensure completion of the project while I focussed on marketing,' Len said.

'They can't be sold the way they are,' Gordon said.

'The contract is clear in that you would take responsibility for all costs.'

'That wasn't the agreement. The plan was for the houses to be finished and on the market.'

'Verbally we may have discussed such a possibility. Unfortunately, your lack of attention to the contract is not my concern.'

'Len, we're wasting our time here,' Fiona said. 'We can still make it in time to the council chambers if we leave now.'

'Fiona, dear Fiona,' Marge said. Rose remembered such words said to her parents in that room all those years before. Back then, they had been directed at her parents, now they were focussed on Fiona Dowling.

'Please don't pretend to be my friend,' Fiona said. 'You've nothing on me, and we've got better things to do than listen to your lies.'

'Fiona Dowling, you're a nasty piece of work who can fool others with your heartfelt confessionals, somehow pretending to be pious and contrite, but you don't fool me.'

'And you Marge Selwood, I've seen through you. I did the first time we met.'

'Then we know where we stand.'

'Your reputation is still important to you, mine is shattered,' Marge said. 'If you want to be the mayor of Salisbury, then I suggest you sit down with your pathetic excuse of a husband and discuss the situation sensibly.'

Len Dowling looked over at his wife. He could see that she had met her match. He had to admit he enjoyed the spectacle.

'We need a resolution,' Gordon said, not because he had anything to add to the discussion, just the need to exert his influence as the man of the house.

Rose nudged him in the ribs. 'Be quiet. Let your mother deal with this for now,' she whispered.

Nicholas and Williams Selwood, the younger sons, sat quietly, not sure how the night was going to unfold.

'My position on the Salisbury City Council is secure. My past indiscretions are well known,' Fiona said.

'They'll not be so keen when they find out that you've been complicit in cheating my son out of this farm.'

'On the contrary, they will applaud both mine and Len's business acumen. The fact that your son has no clue is not our concern.'

'You bitch. You've no right to talk about my son in that manner.'

'Why not, you do?'

'He is a Selwood. We do not allow you or anyone outside of this family to cheat or badmouth us.'

'A Selwood? What makes you say that? From what I heard you were trying to prove that he wasn't.'

'Scurrilous lies. Who told you that?' Marge said.

'Gordon, sounding off about you to Len.'

'Is this true?' Marge said turning to Gordon.

'I may have.'

'You're a disgrace.'

'Maybe I am, but I don't go murdering people.'

Len Dowling turned to his wife. 'It looks as if this house is about to sink into the ground. They'll not address the deal I have with Gordon tonight.'

'Don't you think of leaving,' Marge said. 'We're not finished yet. My late husband negotiated a deal with you against my better judgement. However, it was legally sound. After his death, you negotiated another one with Gordon. Apart from his ability to marry whores, he doesn't understand much else. You, Len Dowling, took advantage of him. And you, Fiona Dowling, made sure that he did.'

Gordon wanted to climb across the table and hit his mother. Rose held him back. 'Let it go. We've got to deal with the Dowlings first.'

'He signed of his own free will,' Fiona said.

'He signed as a Selwood.'

'Are you willing to disown him to get out of the agreement. My husband staked a lot of money in Coombe. We didn't, however, count on all the murders.'

'I've enough dirt on you, Fiona Dowling, to cause those who will elect you mayor to waiver.'

'You've nothing on me.'

'How about innuendo, unfavourable reports in the local newspaper and on social media. A reawakening of your tawdry love affairs, the attempt by the police to charge you with murder. What do you reckon your chances will be after that?'

'They're all lies. I'll sue you for slander, libel.'

'None of it will be attributable to me, or any of my family.'

Fiona Dowling sat back, not sure what to say. The woman opposite was using scare tactics, tactics which could work. Fiona knew that Marge Selwood would be able to destroy her. The need for a man other than her husband still continued, and she had slept with his brother on more than one occasion, and there was that man in Southampton. She shuddered at the thought.

'Very well,' Fiona said. 'What do you want?'

'Gordon, say something,' Marge said. 'You're the person who got us into this sorry mess.'

'Be a man, stand up and say your piece,' Rose said. She could see the father of her child was a hopeless case. He needed her, as much as she needed him.

Standing up, clearing his throat first. 'The two houses in the village. They are to be completed and sold, the profits to be divided between Len and me,' Gordon said.

'I'm still guilty by association with the murder of Molly Dempsey,' Fiona said.

'Let me finish,' Gordon said, feeling emboldened by Rose's encouragement. 'We will discuss how to resolve that, but first, let's deal with the business side. There are to be no demands on me and the Selwood family for their completion.'

'I'm carrying a lot of debt,' Len said.

'Shut up and let the man finish,' Fiona said.

'Are we agreed on the first point?' Gordon asked.

Len stood to talk, only to be pulled down by his wife. 'We agree,' Fiona said.

'Very well. Certain costs have been incurred with the housing development at Coombe Farm.'

'I can't cover them,' Len said. 'And besides, some of them go back to Claude.'

'Nicholas has checked through the figures for us. What are they?'

'So far, they amount to forty-six thousand pounds. A long way short of the original demand.'

'That was a negotiating point,' Len said.

'Rubbish. You were trying to take advantage of Gordon's gullibility,' Marge said. 'And where are we going to get the money?'

'Gordon will sell the Aston Martin,' Rose said.

'But…' Gordon mumbled.

'Don't worry. You can get another one. We need to save the family first.'

'If we go along with this, what guarantees do we have?' Fiona said.

'The word of a Selwood is your guarantee. Although, that cannot be said of the Dowlings. We will want this in writing and checked with our accountant, Nicholas in this case, and a solicitor.'

'And what about Molly Dempsey?

'What about her? The houses in the village are almost completed. There are no further plans for Coombe Farm. She will be forgotten within a couple of weeks,' Marge said.

'If there is no adverse publicity against Len and me,' Fiona said.

'There will not be, you have my word on that.'

Rose could see that Marge had saved the family, as she had so many times in the past. In a patriarchal family, it was, as is so often the case, the women who save the day.

Chapter 29

Tremayne and Clare arrived at Coombe Farm just as the Dowlings were leaving. Both cars wound down their driver side windows. 'You've been visiting the Selwoods?' Tremayne said.

'We had a business meeting,' Len said.

'As you're here, I'd appreciate you back at the main house.'

'We've got another appointment.'

'I wasn't requesting,' Tremayne said.

The Dowlings turned their vehicle and parked next to Clare's. A marked police car parked twenty feet away.

'Do you want the Dowling's here?' Clare said as they walked to the house.

'They know the routine.'

'But you don't think them to be guilty.'

'Not this time, but they'll supply leverage.'

Tremayne knocked on the door, a reluctant opening. 'Tremayne, what brings you here?' Gordon Selwood said. In his hand, a glass of champagne.

'A celebration?'

'We're working out our differences.'

'I'm back here with the Dowlings. I need to solve these murders.'

'Tonight?'

'Someone in your family is a murderer. We're not leaving here without that person.'

None of those in the house was pleased to see the two police officers.

'I've asked Len and Fiona Dowling to be here,' Tremayne said. 'We are going to solve this case. Where's Crispin?'

'He's down at our house,' Rose said.

'Yarwood, ask one of the uniforms to go and pick him up,' Tremayne said.

'He's studying for an exam tomorrow.'

'His presence is important.'

By the time Crispin arrived, the champagne had been put back in the fridge, the boisterous mood replaced by a sense of impending doom.

Tremayne stood to one side of the room. 'Let me make one thing clear. Molly Dempsey did not die as a result of her interference into Len Dowling and Gordon Selwood's developments. The facts don't stack up. The woman was an irritant, no more, and she was regarded as harmless. She died because of something she knew, the same as with Old Ted.

'We know about Claude Selwood and Old Ted's wife. This happened around the time of Gordon's birth. Claude Selwood is an accidental death, although the vicar will be convicted for shooting at him and the horse. Reverend Walston had been a soldier before he became a vicar. His history is complex, but it is not relevant to outline here. The subsequent deaths have been as a result of that one accident.'

'Why are we here?' Fiona Dowling asked.

'You and Len were outside, that's all. Neither of you is guilty of murder.'

'Then can we go?'

'No. Let me ask Len a question,' Tremayne said. 'You met Claude Selwood at the top of the hill on several occasions, is that correct?'

'It is.'

'Why?'

'Why not? That was where we planned the development.'

'But why the secrecy? Why did you walk across the fields to avoid being seen in Coombe?'

'Marge, she wasn't so keen on the idea. Claude wanted to strike out on his own, make a decision. With Marge, he'd always get the third-degree every time I was around.'

'He needed me to make sure he wasn't about to destroy the farm,' Marge said. 'God knows, I had enough with him, and now, I've got his lame-brained son to worry about.'

'You don't need to worry about him,' Rose said.

'You're going to marry my father?' Crispin said.

'I'm not sure. I was married to him once. That didn't work out so good.'

'Apart from Crispin,' Marge said.

Tremayne did not want the gathering to digress. 'Old Ted is killed for a reason. We all know the man did not say much, and whatever he knew, he was unlikely to tell anyone. Let me ask Marge a question. You were aware of the affair between your husband and Old Ted's wife?'

'I was. Not at the time, but several months afterwards.'

'And what did you do?'

'Claude said he was sorry, and that was that.'

'As simple as that?'

'No, it wasn't that simple, but what do you want me to say? I struck him, he hit me back. I wasn't going to walk out of this house if that's what you think I should have done. Claude had an affair. He's not the first person guilty of the offence. Fiona Dowling's had plenty, and she's planning to be Salisbury's next mayor.'

'We're discussing your family, not mine,' Fiona said. 'If Claude wanted to screw the farmhand's wife, so what?'

'You're a right one to talk,' Marge said. Clare moved between the two women before it got out of hand.

'We're not here to discuss right and wrong. We're here to arrest a murderer,' Tremayne said. He could feel the tension in the room. It was only a matter of time before someone would say something that he or she would regret.

'Then get on with it,' Len Dowling said.

'I would suggest you keep quiet, Mr Dowling. No doubt, as a result of events in Coombe, there will be another investigation into whether any fraudulent activities have occurred, and, as to whether your wife's influence as a councillor in Salisbury has been misused.'

'That's slander,' Fiona Dowling said.

'It's a police investigation. Just be thankful that we're here to apprehend a murderer, not a pair of rogues,' Tremayne said. 'Let us come back to Old Ted. We originally thought he had heard something confidential. And even if he had, he wouldn't have mentioned it to anyone. Everyone in the village and at Coombe Farm knew that. The reason as to what he had heard is unknown. If it's someone from outside the village, it's either Len or Fiona Dowling.'

'Don't go accusing us,' Fiona said.

'I'm only putting ideas forward. I'm not accusing anyone. I can tell everyone in this room, that we discount Len Dowling. The man is not capable.'

'Not capable?' William said.

'We know the Dowlings from before. Len is a good talker, but he's not an action man. He's the boy who would have run away from the school bully, rather than stand up to him.'

'How dare you!' Len Dowling shouted.

'Shut up and sit down, Len,' Fiona said.

'Fiona, however, is capable,' Tremayne said.

'Are you determined to arrest one of us?'

'I said you were capable, but you're smart. You wouldn't have killed Old Ted, not because you could not, but even if you had contemplated it, you would have realised we would solve the crime. Old Ted's death was committed by someone with the arrogance to believe they would get away with it.'

'But who?' Rose said.

'Cathy killed Old Ted,' Tremayne said.

Clare looked over at Tremayne, not sure of what she had just heard.

'How dare you accuse Cathy of such a thing. She was good friends with the man,' Gordon said.

'Maybe she was, but she knew something that others only realised afterwards.'

'And what was that?' Crispin said.

'That Gordon is not the legitimate child of Claude Selwood.'

'I don't understand.'

'Crispin, both your grandmother and Cathy Selwood have an unsavoury past.'

'Prostitutes?'

'I was an escort, not a whore,' Marge said. 'Life was tough, and I was attractive. It was only for a short time, maybe two months, and then I met Claude. I did love the man, even if I had chosen him initially to better my life. Cathy was the same. She loved Gordon, and she was a decent woman. Crispin, maybe you don't understand, but life is not always ideal. Sometimes, we have to do unpleasant things to survive.'

'He understands. Our life wasn't that good either,' Rose said, 'not that I sold myself, but sometimes, we barely had enough to eat.'

'How would Cathy have known that Gordon is not legitimate?' Marge said.

'How did you?' Tremayne said.

'You gave me the idea. You mentioned that Gordon is unlike Nicholas and William. I realised it was a possibility, and if he were not Claude's son, then Nicholas would take over the farm.

'Cathy must have seen it. She was an outsider, and she wasn't clouded by a lifetime of memories of the family. She knew that if anyone knew, it would be Old Ted. She confronted him one time when she's out riding. We know that Old Ted would not reveal a secret, but he would always answer truthfully to a direct question. Cathy asked the man, he told her the answer.'

'It's pure conjecture,' Gordon said. 'And how do you explain the same rifle being used to kill Cathy?'

'That's another question. First, we need to solve Old Ted's death.'

Clare realised Tremayne was throwing ideas into the room, hoping to see who would run with it, who would contradict, who would make a mistake.

'Mrs Selwood, did you get the results back from the laboratory?' Tremayne said.

'Yes, but they made a mistake.'

'What laboratory is this?' Gordon asked.

'The overseas laboratory that was conducting DNA analysis on your parentage,' Tremayne said.

'I objected when my mother asked. Has she done it anyway?'

'She took an old toothbrush, an old bandage, or at least, Nicholas and William did,' Clare said.

'You bastards,' Gordon said, standing up and moving over towards his younger brothers. It was Tremayne this time who kept them apart.

'Do you need us here for this?' Fiona Dowling said.

'Yes,' Tremayne's reply. 'You and your husband's position is not clear. Your greed would not be concerned if people died.'

'I'll not deny it, but this is murder. Neither Len nor myself is too keen on a prison sentence.'

'How much money would you have made on developing Coombe Farm?' Marge asked.

'It was a fifty-fifty deal with the Selwoods, you know that.'

'How much?'

'Depending on the property market, somewhere between three to four million pounds after costs. The same as the Selwoods.'

'Judging from your recent behaviour, you intended to cheat us there as well.'

'It's business, not personal,' Fiona said.

Clare realised her opinion of the woman had not improved over the last year. She still did not like her.

Tremayne turned to Len and Fiona Dowling. 'You can both go now. I would warn you about repeating what you've heard here tonight. This investigation has not concluded, but I am willing to accept that neither of you is the murderer.'

'Thank you,' Len said. His wife just scowled.

After they had left, Tremayne turned to the Selwood family. 'This is what I reckon. Old Ted knew that Gordon was not Claude's son. How and why, we don't know yet, but we will find out during this meeting. Cathy, aware that Old Ted knew and he could reveal it, killed the man. The rifle that killed both Old Ted and Cathy is a problem. We've seen your rifles, checked that they're registered, and it's not in this house. If we have that rifle, we have the murderer.'

'Why would anyone kill Cathy?' Nicholas asked.

'Your mother wanted her out of the house. I assume that everyone knows that Cathy was pregnant when she died.'

Nodding heads in the room indicated they did.

'Cathy knew something, and remember she was friendly with Old Ted, even though she killed him. She was killed to stop her taking control of the farm. There is only one person with a sufficient motive, Marge Selwood.'

'I wouldn't do that.'

'Mrs Selwood, you'd do anything to protect this family.'

'You're right. I'd do anything, even murder, but I did not kill Cathy.'

'But you did kill Molly Dempsey.'

'No, it's not possible. We were going to work together.'

Tremayne had the breakthrough. He was not going to let up.

'What did those lab results say?'

'They were inconclusive.'

'As you've said. What did they say? I know what our report says. And Molly Dempsey, she told you something, didn't she? Something so terrible that you were forced to leave her cottage and to walk through the village and up the lane, through the field, and then you're in her garden. She sees you and out she comes to see her new friend. Molly Dempsey's a gossip, but for some reason, she has kept this secret for so long, and then, there you are, the wife of Claude Selwood pretending to be friendly, and she relents and tells you.'

'It's all lies.'

'No, it's not. There is no one else that could have killed the woman. What is it?'

'This is unacceptable,' Gordon said. 'She's our mother.'

Clare could see that the tension in the room was electric. Tremayne continued unabated. 'What was it she told you? What is the great secret? No one is leaving this room until we know.'

'I did not forgive Claude after his affair with Old Ted's wife, I couldn't. But I pretended for the family, for myself, for Gordon. And then, Claude's in hospital with a broken neck after falling off one of the motorbikes, and there's Old Ted. He was a lot younger then, rugged, masculine.'

'You had an affair with Old Ted?'

'Yes, it was a mistake. I didn't want to, but I was angry and lonely. It was only one time in the stables. After that, we rarely spoke.'

All of the sons in the room were on their feet. Crispin, sixteen and still naïve, sat glued to his seat. Rose was in tears, knowing full well the immense strain that Gordon's mother was under.

'The result from the laboratory, what did it say?' Tremayne said.

'That Gordon and Nicholas do not have the same father.'

'Who is the father of Gordon, who is the father of Nicholas.'

'I don't know.'

'But you suspect?'

'Yes.'

'Mrs Selwood, we know who is the father of Gordon Selwood. The results came through just before we came out here.'

'And who is my father?' Gordon said.

'Your father is Claude Selwood. Mrs Selwood, Nicholas' father is Old Ted. Am I correct?'

'Yes. It must be him. I never knew. I always assumed that Claude was the father of my three sons.'

'Molly Dempsey knew?'

'Yes. She was a busybody. Somehow, she knew. I don't know how. Maybe Old Ted told her, or his wife suspected. For whatever reason, she had kept the secret all these years. I was frantic. I wanted to protect my family.'

'You'll be charged with murder,' Tremayne said. 'Yarwood, ask the uniforms to come in and to wait to one side.'

Tremayne, buoyed by his success, turned to the others in the room. Crispin had his arm around his grandmother.

'I'm sorry, but I'm only carrying out my duty. Gordon, the farm and the house belong to you. The proof of your parentage will be given to you.'

'I'm not sure I want it now.'

'You will. There's Crispin to consider, as well as your brothers,' Rose said.

Gordon turned around to Nicholas. 'Nothing changes. We're still brothers.'

Nicholas smiled weakly. He had gone through life believing in the superiority of the Selwood family, and now, he had found out that he was not one of them, only the mongrel child of a farmhand. He wanted to leave the house, never come back.

'Detective Inspector, we need to wrap up the other murders,' Clare said.

'There were only two people who knew of Old Ted and Mrs Selwood. Mrs Selwood wasn't going to tell anyone, although Old Ted had. If he had told his wife or even Molly Dempsey, then he could have told Cathy. Old Ted was a very moral man who had sinned, the guilt of it haunted him. And then Cathy comes along. She treats him as a friend, something he had not had for many years. He talks to her, opens up. He may not have mentioned about sleeping with Mrs Selwood, but he mentions that Gordon is probably not a Selwood.'

'On the day of his death, Cathy was in a strange mood,' Gordon said. 'I asked her what it was, but she wouldn't tell me. She left the house early that day and went for a walk. Cathy liked to walk, and sometimes she'd be gone for an hour, sometimes two. I didn't worry that she was gone for so long, and I never thought any more about it, not until now. Cathy was a Selwood, the same as my mother. She would do anything to protect the good name of the Selwoods, to protect me.'

'Even murder?'

'Even that,' Gordon said.

'We'll never prove this,' Tremayne said.

'Then I'm pleased she's dead. I loved her, you know that. I couldn't bear the thought of her being locked up in prison.'

'Who killed Cathy?' Clare said. 'It's the same rifle. Where is it?'

'It's in the barn at the top of the hill,' Marge Selwood said.

'How do you know this?'

'It's where Old Ted kept it. He kept it hidden, just in case there were foxes in the area. I knew where it was.'

'How?'

'I was up there once when he took it out. He must have shown it to Cathy.'

'Did you kill Old Ted?'

'No, that would be Cathy.'

'And Cathy?'

She wanted to take me away from the farm, away from my son. I couldn't let her. I shot her, and I killed Molly Dempsey.'

'Mother, how could you?'

'I'm sorry, Gordon,' Tremayne said, 'but Cathy was a murderer as well. If her fingerprints are on the rifle, then we'll have our proof.'

Rose Goode, the new matriarch of the family, took control of the situation. She assisted Marge, accompanied by a uniform, into the living room and sat her down. She then returned and told the four Selwood men to sit down. 'We need to make plans for the future. Nicholas and William are your brothers, Gordon. You'll need to make provision for them. William, we want you here to run the farm. Nicholas, if you don't want to be involved, we'll understand. And as for Gordon, if he wants to run his vintage car business from here, then that's what he can do.'

'And my grandmother? Crispin said.

'We'll make sure she's treated well, whatever happens.'

The End

ALSO BY THE AUTHOR

Murder in Notting Hill– A DCI Cook Thriller

One murderer, two bodies, two locations, and the murders have been committed within an hour of each other. There's a connection, but what is it?

They're separated by a couple of miles, and neither woman has anything in common with the other.

Isaac Cook and his team at Challis Street Police Station are baffled as to why. One of the women is young and wealthy, the daughter of a famous man; the other is poor and hardworking and unknown.

Death and the Lucky Man – A DI Tremayne Thriller

Sixty-eight million pounds and dead.

Hardly the outcome expected for the luckiest man in England the day his lottery ticket was drawn out of the barrel.

But then, Alan Winters' rags-to-riches story had never been conventional, and there were those who had benefited, but others who hadn't.

Death and the Assassin's Blade – A DI Tremayne Thriller

It was meant to be high drama, not murder, but someone's switched the daggers. The man's death took place in plain view of two serving police officers.

He was not meant to die; the daggers were only theatrical props, plastic and harmless. A summer's night, a production of Julius Caesar amongst the ruins of an Anglo-Saxon fort. Detective Inspector Tremayne is there with his sergeant, Clare Yarwood. In the assassination scene, Caesar collapses to the ground. Brutus defends his actions; Mark Antony rebukes him.

They're a disparate group, the amateur actors. One's an estate agent, another an accountant. And then there is the teenage school student, the gay man, the funeral director. And what about the women? They could be involved.

They've each got a secret, but which of those on the stage wanted Gordon Mason, the actor who had portrayed Caesar, dead?

Murder is the Only Option – A DCI Cook Thriller

A man, thought to be long dead, returns to exact revenge against those who had blighted his life. His only concern is to protect his wife and daughter. He will stop at nothing to achieve his aim.

'Big Greg, I never expected to see you around here at this time of night.'

'I've told you enough times.'

'I've no idea what you're talking about,' Robertson replied. He looked up at the man, only to see a metal pole coming down at him. Robertson fell down, cracking his head against a concrete kerb.

The two vagrants, no more than twenty feet away, did not stir and did not even look in the direction of the noise. If they had, they would have seen a dead body, another man walking away.

Death Unholy – A DI Tremayne Thriller

All that remained were the man's two legs and a chair full of greasy and fetid ash. Little did DI Keith Tremayne know that it was the beginning of a journey into the murky world of paganism and its ancient rituals. And it was going to get very dangerous.

'Do you believe in spontaneous human combustion?' Detective Inspector Keith Tremayne asked.

'Not me. I've read about it. Who hasn't?' Sergeant Clare Yarwood answered.

I haven't,' Tremayne replied, which did not surprise his young sergeant. In the months they had been working together, she had come to realise that he was a man who had little interest in the world. When he had a cigarette in his mouth, a beer in his hand, and a murder to solve he was about the happiest she ever saw him. He could hardly be regarded as one of life's sociable people. And as for reading? The most he managed was an occasional police report or an early morning newspaper, turning first to the back pages for the racing results.

Murder in Little Venice – A DCI Cook Thriller

A dismembered corpse floats in the canal in Little Venice, an upmarket tourist haven in London. Its identity is unknown, but what is its significance?

DCI Isaac Cook is baffled about why it's there. Is it gang-related, or is it something more?

Whatever the reason, it's clearly a warning, and Isaac and his team are sure it's not the last body that they'll have to deal with.

Murder is only a Number – A DCI Cook Thriller

Before she left she carved a number in blood on his chest. But why the number 2, if this was her first murder?

The woman prowls the streets of London. Her targets are men who have wronged her. Or have they? And why is she keeping count?

DCI Cook and his team finally know who she is, but not before she's murdered four men. The whole team are looking for her, but the woman keeps disappearing in plain sight. The pressure's on to stop her, but she's always one step ahead.

And this time, DCS Goddard can't protect his protégé, Isaac Cook, from the wrath of the new commissioner at the Met.

Murder House – A DCI Cook Thriller

A corpse in the fireplace of an old house. It's been there for thirty years, but who is it?

It's clearly murder, but who is the victim and what connection does the body have to the previous owners of the house. What is the motive? And why is the body in a fireplace? It was bound to be discovered eventually but was that what the murderer wanted? The main suspects are all old and dying, or already dead.

Isaac Cook and his team have their work cut out trying to put the pieces together. Those who know are not talking because of an old-fashioned belief that a family's dirty laundry should not be aired in public, and certainly not to a policeman – even if that means the murderer is never brought to justice!

Murder is a Tricky Business – A DCI Cook Thriller

A television actress is missing, and DCI Isaac Cook, the Senior Investigation Officer of the Murder Investigation Team at Challis Street Police Station in London, is searching for her.

Why has he been taken away from more important crimes to search for the woman? It's not the first time she's gone missing, so why does everyone assume she's been murdered?

There's a secret, that much is certain, but who knows it? The missing woman? The executive producer? His eavesdropping assistant? Or the actor who portrayed her fictional brother in the TV soap opera?

Murder Without Reason – A DCI Cook Thriller

DCI Cook faces his greatest challenge. The Islamic State is waging war in England, and they are winning.

Not only does Isaac Cook have to contend with finding the perpetrators, but he is also being forced to commit actions contrary to his mandate as a police officer.

And then there is Anne Argento, the prime minister's deputy. The prime minister has shown himself to be a pacifist and is not up to the task. She needs to take his job if the country is to fight back against the Islamists.

Two government analysts have provided the solution. Will DCI Cook and Anne Argento be willing to follow it through? Are they able to act for the good of England, knowing that a criminal and murderous action is about to take place? Do they have any option?

The Haberman Virus

A remote and isolated village in the Hindu Kush mountain range in North Eastern Afghanistan is wiped out by a virus unlike any seen before.

A mysterious visitor clad in a space suit checks his handiwork, a female American doctor succumbs to the disease, and the woman sent to trap the person responsible falls in love with him – the man who would cause the deaths of millions.

Hostage of Islam

Three are to die at the Mission in Nigeria: the pastor and his wife in a blazing chapel; another gunned down while trying to defend them from the Islamist fighters.

Kate McDonald, an American, grieving over her boyfriend's death and Helen Campbell, whose life had been troubled by drugs and prostitution, are taken by the attackers.

Kate is sold to a slave trader who intends to sell her virginity to an Arab Prince. Helen, to ensure their survival, gives herself to the murderer of her friends.

Malika's Revenge

Malika, a drug-addicted prostitute, waits in a smugglers' village for the next Afghan tribesman or Tajik gangster to pay her price, a few scraps of heroin.

Yusup Baroyev, a drug lord, enjoys a lifestyle many would envy. An Afghan warlord sees the resurgence of the Taliban. A Russian white-collar criminal portrays himself as a good and honest citizen in Moscow.

All of them are linked in an audacious plan to increase the quantity of heroin shipped out of Afghanistan and into Russia and ultimately the West.

Some will succeed, some will die, some will be rescued from their plight and others will rue the day they became involved.

ABOUT THE AUTHOR

Phillip Strang was born in England in the late forties, during the post-war baby boom. He had a comfortable middle-class upbringing, spending his childhood years in a small town to the west of London.

An avid reader of science fiction in his teenage years: Isaac Asimov, Frank Herbert, the masters of the genre. Much of what they and others mentioned has now become a reality. Science fiction has now become science fact. Still an avid reader, the author now mainly reads thrillers.

In his early twenties, the author, with a degree in electronics engineering and a desire to see the world, left England for Sydney, Australia. Now, forty years later, he still resides in Australia, although many intervening years were spent in a myriad of countries, some calm and safe, others no more than war zones.